Circle Of Time

Recy Dunn

Black Rose Writing

www.blackrosewriting.com

ISBN: 978–1–61296–182–8

PUBLISHED BY BLACK ROSE WRITING

www.blackrosewriting.com

Printed in the United States of America

Circle of Time is printed in Georgia

In Memory of

Recy & Myrine Dunn

Circle Of Time

PART ONE

PRELUDE

The British seized the Cape of Good Hope area in 1806, forcing many of the Boers headed north to form their own republics. After the Voortrekkers – Boers had failed to negotiate with the Zulus the secession of land for settling and grazing. They endured numerous catastrophic assaults. Finally, the Boers assembled at the Ncome River for a decisive battle near Lesotho, known as The Battle of Blood River.

On December 16, 1838, 464 Boers, led by Andries Pretorius, defeated more than 10,000 Zulu warriors. The deeply religious Boers declared their military victory as a sign and message of God. Before the great battle, the Boers had prayed and made a vow that if God would grant them victory over the Zulus; they would celebrate the victory annually. Afterwards, they believed even more strongly that white predominance over blacks was God's own will. The discovery of diamonds in the year 1867 and gold by 1886 created great wealth and led to intensified subjugation of the native inhabitants.

January 11 to July 4, 1879, was the period of another bloody Zulu war in South Africa. The Zulus effective use of the Iklwa, an assegai spear used as stabbing weapons and their war cry, Ngadla, proved to be a great fighting force against the British. However, a British victory brought the end of the independent Zulu nation. The British forces continued with their quest to establish a colony in South Africa and the Boers resisted British invasions, but were defeated in the Boer War (1899–1902). This led to the formation of the Union of South Africa and in 1948 operated under a policy of apartheid – the separate development of the races. It also led to the establishment of the African National Congress.

CHAPTER ONE

They Who Dare

South Africa – 1948

"They killed my father! You don't understand," screamed Jan. "The bloody bastards detonated a bomb in their sleeping quarters. The examiner found his legs on top of a bench and the other one outside the window. For Pete sakes, I could not recognize him."

Jan Linden's belief in a possible link between the African tribes and apartheid has long provoked the ire of his myriad critics.

"Who are they, Jan?" shouted the captain.

"Please don't patronize me. You know bloody hell what I'm saying," Jan was furious. His blood–shot eyes focused on trying to convince his captain and co–workers that the leaders of the ANC were responsible for the death of his father.

"But Jan, who are the leaders? If we knew their identities, I would personally arrest them myself."

Jan tapped twice with his finger on a pack of Kools and pulled out a cigarette. He lit up, took a long drag, and slowly exhaled towards the captain. The captain arched his eyebrow and frowned at Jan. "I will not rest until I have made those people pay dearly for what they've done. I don't care how long it takes. I'll follow every lead and trail from here to kingdom come. Believe me captain, I will make them pay." Jan turned and walked away.

"Lieutenant Linden," shouted the captain. "Just make sure that it's done within the bloody parameters of the Queen's Court."

It had been six months since his father's death. As each day passed Jan became more convinced, a terrorist group from the African National Congress was responsible for his blowing up the barracks that killed his father. The group responsible had adopted a

Program of Action calling for *'freedom from white domination and the attainment of political independence.'*

He stood at his desk staring down at a picture of his father teaching him the art and technique of fly–fishing. They both were smiling after his father helped him catch a two–pound trout at the age of twelve. Now fifteen years later and six months later, Jan had hoped he and his father would still be going to their favorite lake for game fishing. He had grown to be a tall, well–built man with a full head of reddish hair.

"The key to any terrorist campaign is money, and money is power. If properly used, and carefully placed in the hands of the right people, a successful revolt could be launched," he said to himself. His Dutch dialect represented more than just his birth origins. Jan was extremely proud of his heritage and country.

———————————————————————————————

A secret society known as the Circle, whose watchword was "sacrifice, service, and suffering," had agreed that, its diverse membership would join forces against apartheid. The rebel band, unlike the others, had a different kind of leader: An old man with a vision of the future. Somewhere deep within the homeland territory of Transkei in an unknown village sat eight chieftains, each representing a tribal group: Zulu, Xhosa, Sotho, Venda, Swazi, Ndebele, Tsonga–Shangaan, and Tswana. It was an unusual cool July night. They stood by a robust fire and before a full moon, known by the natives as the Full Thunder Moon. Thunderstorms were most frequent during this time of year. Cinders floated through the air from a second sturdy campfire and the sound of burning wood were surrounded by the chieftains' lieutenants performing a ceremonial dance.

In the background to the right of the fire sat the old man, slightly gray–haired, but lean and athletic in appearance. His father fell from the side of a mountain cliff and died at the age of ninety–six; his grandfather was the victim of snakebite, when he was 102 years of age. The old man's great–grandfather died peacefully in his sleep at

105 years old.

The old man sat on a knitted and decorative blanket matching the pattern of his dashiki. A peculiar odor permeated his clothing. The leaves from the wag'n–bietjie tree in his rucksack tainted his clothes. He used the leaves for many purposes. When crushed they served as a cure–all ointment in its natural state. Properly mixed with certain other ingredients, the homely wag'n–bietjie leaf had other uses; one was a deadly poison. He stared at the natives, particularly at one man. The old man thought of a story told to him by his father. It was about Shaka, a famous warrior of the Zulu clan–chieftain that controlled an area larger than Britain. His conquests were brutal and bloody and as his victims slid off his assegai blade called "Iklwa" in imitation of the sucking sound as it was drawn from the victim. Shaka would shout, "Ngadla!" *I have eaten!* Shaka also created a force of men who acted as spies and signal watchers. He made extensive use of psychological warfare. Eventually, his half–brother Dingane, assassinated Shaka in 1828.

The old man looked at the men and motioned to one of the chieftains to begin. The first to rise and speak was Abozuthu Shaka Masekela, a Zulu warrior named after the great chieftain, Shaka. Abozuthu represented the inheritance of Shaka's legacy of ferocity. He too was a proud chieftain and carried an assegai blade. Abozuthu glanced at the rest of the chieftains seated in a large circular formation around the robust fire. They spoke neither a word but listened to the war–like sounds of the drums beat throughout the kraal. Abozuthu raised his blade above his head to quiet the natives but they continued their dancing around the fire.

"Shaka! Shaka! Shaka!" chanted the young warriors, dressed as their ancestors once did. They also had assegai blades. The ground trembled beneath the syncopation of Zulus stamping and dancing to the monotonous but insistent rhythm of the drums. The warriors chanted their deep choruses, barely moving their lips. In the background an innocent cry of infants came from the hut of Nyerere and Rhosida, the caretakers. The old man smiled at the ceremony. It reminded him of the old days.

"Mayibuye Afrika!" shouted a tall, long–legged, Zulu warrior. He stood seven feet tall. A painted yellow streak extended from the center of his forehead, down the nose, across his lips and stop at the base of his throat. He also had painted white streaks on both sides of his face. Under each eye was white paint smeared with a dab of red. "Mayibuye Afrika!" the Zulu warrior shouted again. Silence filled the small village. He picked up a torch and walked toward a dead body wrapped in ceremonial tribal garments on top of grassy stilts and set it afire. The body burst into flames and shined brilliantly in the dark.

The chieftains and the people had gathered for two reasons: To mourn the death of one of their leaders killed by South African police, and to discuss the meaning of apartheid and its effects on their people.

"Ssss – Ssss – Ssss! Ssss – Ssss – Ssss!" chanted the warriors from each tribe as they pointed the assegai towards the sky. Their pale–soled, bloodless, and hardened feet stood rooted to the earth, their muscles quivering frantically. The young Zulus used incantations to summon the spirits of the dead warrior.

"Ssss – Ssss – Ssss!" They chanted and hissed snakelike sounds that grew in intensity. Their black sweating bodies moved close and formed a circle as they hissed. "Ssss – Ssss – Ssss!" The warriors' shoulders shuddered along with a long bob of their heads. Their feet, calloused from years of toil, inched closer to the circle until their blades touched. The hissing stopped. The warriors slowly removed the blades, turned, and pointed them at the chieftains.

A jet–black petite woman with smooth skin dressed in wag'n–bietjie leaves that covered her breasts and womanly parts except for the buttocks, uncoiled herself from the center of the circle. The chieftains rose to a standing position and bowed in homage.

Abozuthu, a tall manly figure with dark black skin and a natural air of authority, thrust his spear into the center of the fire. His voice was deep and had a piercing sound. "Isikhathi sesisondele! Isikhathi sesifikile! Kufaneka sensi esikwenzayo," shouted Abozuthu. (The time is near! The time has come! We must act!) He had a ferocious expression and a three–inch scar at the tip of his left ear lobe to the center of the neck.

"Elethu!" "We!" Thambo Langeni shouted. He was chieftain of the Xhosa people. He stood and purposely spoke in English, much to Abozuthu's dismay. Thambo was lighter–skinned and smaller in stature. "Since when does the mighty Zulu chief speak of we? The Zulus did not take assistance from other tribes unless they were the victims of a Zulu bloodbath. My people, the Xhosas, were the first to make contact with the whites and use their knowledge to produce writers, lawyers, doctors and ministers."

"Isiphakanyisa sami inkosi u Thambo akawazi umahlukathi kobandlululo nenhululeko," answered Abozuthu, back in his native tongue. (My esteemed learned chieftain Thambo does not know the difference between apartheid and freedom). "Sonke asivunyelwe ukuba sibesemihlangahweni," continued Abozuthu. All of us are prohibited from meeting together in groups).

"Speak in English", demanded Thambo.

Abozuthu looked over at the old man. He adjusted himself on the blanket and said nothing. He just stared at him. Abozuthu turned and walked briskly in a forceful manner towards Thambo. He invaded Thambo's personal space and looked down at him into his eyes. "Take a look around you," Abozuthu spoke forcefully. "We were told that this was our homeland! All of South Africa is our homeland. It's time to plan! It's time to unite and it's time to act." Abozuthu facial expression revealed his frustration.

"Abozuthu!" shouted Thambo. He used his blade to help him rise. "I too am angry that our people were forced to migrate to the cities. The labor shortages for skilled workers to produce munitions and military supplies forced our people to live in squatter camps around the townships of Johannesburg, Durban, Capetown, and Pretoria. Now, the Afrikaners, faced with overcrowded villages, have coined this word apartheid, which means apart–hood, and now, tomorrow morning it will become a South African official state policy."

"Apartheid is the word created by the white people of South Africa," shouted Abozuthu, "and they will one day live to regret it."

Thambo stared at Abozuthu. "Step back," he shouted. "You don't scare me. We all know your reputation. You are a troublemaker, a self–professed agitator of the South African government."

Abozuthu smirked at Thambo's demand, and then stepped back. Thambo stared at Abozuthu, recalling three years ago when he first conceived of the idea. Only three people know his organized plan. He knew that the main participants might not live to see it to completion. However, he had finally succeeded in getting the leaders in the member tribes to believe in his cause and commit to die before jeopardizing the success of the mission. Of the conspirators, Thambo knew that he and Abozuthu indeed shared one idea. The time to act was now, but not in the manner Abozuthu wanted.

"Abozuthu, sit down!" The old man shouted. He rose slowly from his comfortable blanket. "Fellow chieftains and brothers, Abozuthu speaks from the heart; however, violence and force are not the answer. My great ancestors fought six so–called "Kaffir Wars" against the Dutch–speaking people. As we fought each war, the Boers became more sophisticated, had advanced weaponry, and a more organized army."

"Yes sir, you are right, said Thambo. This is not the time to fight! We must organize, for I, Thambo Langeni, have conceived a plan along with the old man's vision. A plan so fool–proof, it will take many years to implement. Our children will be better off, but their children will reap the benefits. I have asked each of you here tonight because of your influence with your fellow tribe members. Abozuthu is correct, the time will be near, the time will come, but the time to act is not now! Tonight, with your support, phase one goes into effect. Each of you must make a sacrifice so the children of tomorrow will live to see our accomplishments."

"(Thambo, I, Aakintola Gomba, am chieftain of the largest Sotho tribes. We are mountain people, cultivators of maize, farmers, not warriors). "Singabantu abahlala ngoku thula phansi kwenkosi yesigodi sakithi."(Our people live peacefully under the rule of the village chiefs). "Yini nje nempela engingayenza ekulweni nohulumeni omhlophe ohlome ngezikhali ezibukhali kangaka?"(What can I

14

possibly do against the well—armed white government)?

"Chief Gomba," answered Thambo, "you are the paramount chief to whom all Sotho owe their allegiance. The Sotho people and the children of tomorrow will play an important role in the years to come. That alone, your support and your willingness to sacrifice are all I require."

"Thambo, I, Macomma Le—thu, am chieftain of the Tswana people," he said from his seated position. "I too, like my fellow chieftain Gomba, have some doubts if your plan can be successfully carried out. The Tswana people also have reasons to distrust the whites. It has been passed down from our grandfathers how the Boers and then the British established military posts within the heart of Tswana territory. They treated our people as children and therefore are not capable of ruling. They limited our movement to the cities.

"Chief Le—thu," Thambo started, trying to interrupt.

"No, Thambo, listen to me," Le—thu continued. "We were once great developers of law and dispensers of justice in the tribal system. We have become conditioned to respecting the law of the Afrikaners. However, the young people grow restless each day and I am afraid if we don't return to our original values, we will lose our youth in a fierce bloody battle."

Le—thu looked at the other Chieftains, then walked towards and faced Thambo with a clenched outstretched fist. "I, Macomma Le—thu, chieftain of the Tswana people, support Thambo's plan."

Thambo looked at the old man who nodded for Thambo to speak. "Each of you was briefed earlier on what you must do. Raise your hand if you agree. The other chieftains raised their hands, but not Abozuthu. They noticed his displeasure and the large wrinkles in his forehead.

"Wait, I have something to say," shouted Abozuthu.

"Ugh, ugh." The old man coughed and cleared his throat. Abozuthu looked at the old man. He reluctantly raises his hand.

"Great. It's unanimous." Thambo felt a gleam of honor at the unanimous acceptance of his plan. It was the only way for the conspiracy to succeed.

"Good," said the old man. "We must not be seen together in or around the cities. We must not reveal the identity of the other members. Phase one will take several years to implement before we meet again."

The attractive, petite, and shapely jet–black woman, still dressed in wag'n–bietjie leaves slowly approached the chieftains. She held a naked newborn in her arms. Abozuthu turned and smiled for the first time. She carefully handed him the infant boy. Carrying the child in his strong arms, he walked out before all of the assembled people of the village and lifted up the infant.

"Abozuthu! Abozuthu! Shaka!" The warriors shouted.

Abozuthu lowered the infant, turned, and walked to the edge of the large blazing campfire where he could hear the crackling sound of fresh twigs. He stood close to the fire and again lifted the infant and held him high over the flames. He pointed the boy's head toward the stars, and shouted, "Mayibuye! Afrika!"

The old man rose from his blanket, walked towards the center of the circle, and motioned with both hands for the chieftains to come. Abozuthu handed the infant to the woman and is the first to approach the old man. Without speaking a word, the old man lifted a string of ornaments from around Abozuthu's neck. The necklace, symbolizing the Zulu chieftain's powers, was a gift from his grandfather. He placed the string around his right hand. He turned and faced Thambo and lifted the sacred necklace. The other chieftains followed and the old man repeated this procedure without uttering a word until he had all eight sacred collections of objects threaded on string around his right hand.

"Isikhahti sesifikile," (The time has come) said the old man. He turned and slowly disappeared into the darkness.

CHAPTER TWO

One That Challenges

December 1948

It had been six months since his father's death. As each day passed Jan Linden became more convinced, a terrorist group from the African National Congress was responsible for blowing up the barracks that killed his father. The group responsible had adopted a Program of Action calling for 'freedom from white domination and the attainment of political independence.'

"Good morning, Officer Linden. Did you say something?" asked one of the secretaries.

"No, no, I was just thinking to myself."

"Sure, you were. You mean chattering", answered the secretary. "Here, please have some coffee, I made it just for you, and I know you like it fresh. By the way, you know what my granny once said about talking..."

Jan smiled back. "Yeah, I know, just don't answer yourself." He smelled the coffee before taking a sip. "You certainly know the way to a man's heart."

"Just give me a week alone and I will have you eating out of my hand." A newspaper article on the corner of the duty sergeant's desk caught his attention.

JOHANNESBURG DAILY NEWS
@ PRETORIA GOVERNMENT PAPER
Thursday – August 12, 1948
*ANC rebels kills 12 Afrikaners, wound thirty
outside supermarket chain. Spokesman for British
Embassy denies his government is behind terrorist
activities. A secret document obtained from a
source links the British government to support
payments to radical groups in Israel, South Africa
and other countries.*

Jan snatched the newspaper. "So that's where the money's coming from."

"What money, sir?" asked the secretary. "Oh, I read that article. That can't be true. What dire reason could the British government have for supporting those rubbish scums behind the African National Congress?"

"I don't know. What's the little weasel's name that acts as a liaison between the Embassy and the local police when it comes to providing protective custody for some of their visiting dignitaries?"

"That scoundrel's name is Rogers," answered the duty sergeant as he drank his coffee. "Oh he thinks he's so cute and the department is supposed to jump when he calls to request officers for visiting dignitaries."

"I always had a funny feeling about him. Mr. Rogers was never very cordial about how the government treated the Arab countries," said the secretary.

"By golly, you're right. That SOB got into a heated discussion with the Inspector on the Israel crisis at the annual gala ball. They debated at length how the western allies were divided on whom to support," answered the duty sergeant.

"I'm going to pay him a little visit. Sergeant, sign me out for the British Embassy," snapped Jan. He had nothing to go on but a hunch. Jan felt some government official or someone with a lot to gain, was backing the terrorist group.

Jan knew that Rogers, the liaison officer, had an English, Islamic, and Indian background. His father had close ties with high officials within the parliament. He often bragged of his English, public school education and often compared it disparagingly to the South African school system. He lived and dressed extremely well and gave the impression his late father was from a family of wealth. Jan arrived at the Embassy to find the staff packing boxes.

"Excuse me guys, where is Mr. Rogers?"

One of the three men gave Jan a sidelong glance. "Mr. Rogers should be home packing."

"And where exactly is his home?" questioned Jan.

A second man, carrying a medium sized box, walked passed him and said, "His apartment flat is six blocks to the right on Kruger Street, number 18."

"Thanks", said Jan. He jumped in his Volkswagen and looked at his watch. It was nine o'clock in the morning by the time he arrived at the flat. He parked the car in the courtyard. Jan stared at another Volkswagen parked in front of Flat 18 with the back seat filled with suitcases. He looked around and slowly walked towards the door. He knocked on the door but a minute passed, and no one answered. Jan knocked again. Finally, a fellow appeared through the stained decorative glass door.

"Mr. Rogers, James Rogers?" Jan asked.

The door opened only as far the latch allowed. The man inside rubbed his eyes. "Who wants to know at this ungodly time of morning?"

"I'm Jan Linden, a police officer. I'd like to ask you a few questions regarding the Consulate involvement with terrorist activities." The man slammed the door.

Jan pounded on the door. "Mr. Rogers. Open this bloody door. This is official police business!" He pounded again.

Rogers quickly opened the portier which cause Jan to almost to lose his balance.

Rogers blocked the entrance. He smiled because Jan was so angry that the veins stood out on his forehead. "Look here, my dear man. I have already answered all pertinent questions relevant to the subject. Besides, you are just a lowly ranked beat–officer. You have no authority in such matters." He turned his back and walked away, leaving the door open.

Jan walked in. "I didn't come here because I've nothing else to do, Mr. Rogers, so turn around and give me your full attention. I have information that my superiors may wish to investigate."

Rogers stopped, paused for a second, and then continued to walk toward an elegant antique coffee table. He picked up his pipe, flicked a match head with his right thumbnail. He lit the pipe tobacco, took a deep draw on his pipe, and slowly exhaled the tobacco smoke.

"All right, come on in. Go ahead chap, and ask your bloody questions," scowled Rogers.

Jan snapped back. "My name is Officer Linden, not chap! I have information, which leads me to believe that the Consulate was also involved in supporting members of a terrorist group backed by the ANC. Since you are the liaison for security matters, were you aware of such activities?"

"*Was* the liaison, my dear officer, was."

"Just answer the question, Mr. Rogers."

"Officer Linden, much to my chagrin, I'm also a subject of the British government and while I'm here, a loyal one. Why is someone of your statue interested in such high important matters?"

Jan stared at Rogers. Their eyes met. "My father was killed in the barracks explosion."

"Tssh, Tssh, poor fellow. My deepest condolences."

Jan grinds his teeth. "Mr. Rogers, I find it hard to believe you were not aware of the ANC activities. Do you know a man who calls himself Abdul?"

"No, I don't personally know Mr. Abdul, however, a man in my position has from time to time had access to classified government information. Let's just say I've heard of the gent."

"You've heard of him, that's interesting. Did you hear that he had claimed responsibility for the attacks on SADF headquarters last year?"

"Officer Linden, Mr. Abdul does not keep me abreast of his activities. Besides, from the information I have read about him, the man is a political assailant, not a common run–of–the–mill killer. Mr. Abdul has class, my dear man, class; something of which you are not accustomed to. Do you know that his average hit is a half million dollars? I don't think your father or anyone in that barracks would command such an ungodly sum."

"Your humdrum responses are beginning to piss me off," said Jan. "But I will tell you one thing, when I find those persons responsible for my father's death, I will..."

"You will what? Shoot them! Oh, please spare me."

"No! But I'm sure the government authorities have questioned you thoroughly, which leaves me with no basis to put you behind bars."

"How civil of you. It's simply amazing how little regard you have for the law. I might add the laws you are sworn to uphold. Tssh, Tssh, neither you nor your superiors have the slightest authority to arrest me. Have you forgotten about diplomatic protection? I really don't know why you're here."

"I'm looking for any information leading to Mr. Abdul's whereabouts."

"My, my, you will not find him here."

Jan glanced around the room filled with antiques and an étagère with a large mirror and enclosed cabinet base.

"I see you have excellent taste in furniture," said Jan. From the corner of his eye, he noticed an elaborate stainless steel poster bed in the other room. "You did quite well for yourself working with the Embassy."

"What you see my dear man, are precious pieces of art that I purchased with my mother's inheritance."

"I must say; you do have good taste."

"Ah, a compliment," said Rogers smiling. He continued to look around the room. Suddenly, Jan stared at a bulky single envelope on the mantel. Five, 1000 dollars bills were slightly exposed. Jan walked toward the mantel and picked up the envelope.

Rogers extended his hand. "Thank you, Officer Linden, I'll take that."

Jan hesitated. He noticed a small tattoo butterfly on Rogers's index finger. "Mr. Rogers, there must be over 10,000 dollars bills here."

"Twelve to be exact," said Rogers, as he tried several times to light his pipe. "The closing of the embassy has given me the opportunity to take a well–earned vacation to London."

Jan noticed that Rogers' hand shook a bit, making it difficult to light his pipe. *"For some reason, he's extremely nervous,"* Jan thought. *"Ah, finally a dent in his armor."*

"Do you always travel with so much cash? Since you are going to London, why didn't you wire the money to a local bank?"

"Detective, may I please have my money?" Rogers took the envelope, placed it back on the mantel next to an antique vase. "Thank you."

Jan turned his back to him and looked at the entrance to the bedroom. Suddenly, he felt a sharp excruciating pain at the back of his head, followed in a few seconds by what he felt was more severe and potent than a slap when the left side of his face slammed against the cold floor. It felt as if a horse had kicked him.

Rogers looked at what was left of the bloody vase. He looked at the shattered glass on the back of Jan's shirt, head, and the floor.

"Oh Shit!" Jan felt his warm blood at the base of his chin.

"Officer Linden, dear fellow, is that the best English words you can say," Rogers chuckled. "Give me a Dutch word that describes this feeling." Rogers planted the heel of his shoe in the side of Jan's stomach.

"Neuken jou, ezel groeve," shouted Jan.

"Fuck me. Good boy, but by calling me an asshole, you are challenging my manhood." Rogers kicked him again.

Jan coughed several times. Blood ran from his mouth. He felt sharp pointed pains in his chest, each time he coughed. It felt like some of his ribs were broken. Half–dazed, he saw the fuzzy figure of someone dragging him by the ankles. Blood rushed to his head.

The rattle of papers was unnaturally loud in the silence. It took a few seconds for his vision to clear. It was Rogers. He staggered to his feet and immediately felt the blows of fists that struck repeatedly.

"Damn, I was fooled by Rogers' mannerism. The bastard's personality changed to a savage animal possessed with one thought———killing me." His thoughts centered on Rogers.

Unable to repel his attacker, Jan once again fell to the floor. He shouted out the name of his assailant. "Rogers!"

Rogers smiled boldly. He then planted a swift and powerful kick to the Jan's face. "Ah! Ah! Jan covered his nose. His swollen face hit the parquet like a lead balloon. He bled from the nose and mouth. The blow on the head caused his thoughts to be woozy. He heard Rogers opening a drawer and saw the big toe of Rogers' foot several feet from his face.

"Old chap, old boy, you will not live to see what South Africa will experience in the future." Rogers' entire face beamed with satisfaction. He cocked the gun, walked back to Jan and pointed it at his head.

"James! Please. You know how much I despise bloodshed," cried a thin but muscular fellow at the bedroom's door. "We have a good thing going here. Let's not cause any more suspicion with the death of a police officer. Oh, please put the damn gun away. He does not know anything, and there is nothing he can tell the authorities."

"Babe, I need to blow this man away. He can hurt you," said Rogers, cocking the trigger.

Roger's roommate pleaded again. "Sweetheart, please get the money and let's get the hell out of South Africa. There is no way in hell that we will ever come back. The plane should be ready. I'm looking forward to seeing London again."

"All right, babe, you may be right. So far we have not directly killed anyone." Rogers got down on his knees and elbows. He rested his chin on the floor beside Jan's face. "Oh Mr. Jan Linden, some big bad police officer you are. I think it's time for you to take your morning nap."

Jan raise his head to look at Rogers' roommate.

"Goodnight Detective Linden." Rogers hit Jan on the temple with the butt of the pistol.

It was pitch dark outside when Jan came to. He placed his hand on his head.

"Oh... my head." Jan coughed and spat blood. His vision was still blurry. He blinked several times. His eyes focused on the open entrance door, and then centered on the doorknob, a couple of feet within arm's reach. He grabbed for doorknob to regain his balance, but the door was also his enemy. Each time he tried to lift his battered body, the door moved, with his hand still on the doorknob he rested his swollen face and lips on the hardened floor for a moment.

Jan grabbed the doorknob hard and slowly lifted his body from the floor. He looked straight ahead, then to his left and right, his eyes searching the room. He was still in the apartment. Rogers and his friend were gone. Jan's body felt cold. Jan set to brace himself. He saw the bathroom mirror. He stumbled to the floor. *Get up!* Jan said to himself. *Get up. You can make it!*

He felt a sharp piercing pain as he pulled himself from the floor. "Oh damn, that hurts!" His ribs must be broken. How many, he did not know nor did he care. His growing hatred for Rogers blocked out the pain.

"Damn! Damn!" Jan shouted in disgust. He had never received such a beating. "Two tours of duty in the Philippines, forty search and destroy missions and I get my butt kicked by an ass hole."

CHAPTER THREE

Oh Where Art Thou's Head?

Five months later – deep within the territory of Transkei

Thambo was concerned. His eyebrows had a high arc and the wrinkles in his forehead, followed by beads of sweat, displayed a worried look. The trial of Chieftain Aakintola Gomba opened on a hot November day in a crowded classroom at a remote administrative outpost at Lesotho some two hundred miles north of Swaziland. Gomba was a prominent leader of the unlawful Circle, secret society. The government, hampered by a lack of direct evidence had to rely on a handful of witnesses. The main prosecution witness was a member of the Sotho tribe. His name was Nigel and Thambo knew time was of the essence.

Thambo authored the bylaws for the Circle. A member had to pass three tests in order to gain membership in the secret society, and Nigel had failed the "test of life." After passing the "test of sacrifice and servility," Nigel was cocky and boasted of his plans to replace Chief Gomba. Failing the "test of life" meant disgrace and loss of power among the tribal leaders. Nigel wanted a second chance, but there were no second chances among the Circle members.

The government's plan was to show that Gomba, because of his enormous influence, had formed a rebel group committed to treason against South Africa's government. Nigel's role was to testify that he actually saw Chieftain Gomba administer oaths of conspiracy to members of the Circle.

It was time for the seven chieftains to gather to discuss the fate of Chieftain Aakintola Gomba. It was an hour past dusk. This was to be their last meeting together. The South African government had stepped up its actions to discover their identities. Phase one of the conspiracy was completed and there was too much at stake to allow the government to interfere.

"Thambo, we cannot let Gomba go to trial, nor can we allow Nigel to harm our brother chieftain," said Chieftain Ahidjo Samora of the Swazi tribe.

"I agree," said Thambo, "however, we must be careful not to expose ourselves or do anything that will bring to light our overall plan." He paused and looked down at the large blazing flame. The crackling sound of twigs and sparks from the freshly lit fire caused both men to raise their voices. "Now that phase one is in place, Abozuthu's spies have confirmed everyone is safe and will act when the time is right."

"We must somehow stop Nigel from testifying or allow our fellow chieftain, Gomba, to die with honor," shouted Abozuthu. He stood and stared at Thambo. "There's only one thing for us to do, and I, Abozuthu, chieftain of our fighting warriors, will rob Nigel of his ability to harm the Circle and its mission. I will nail his hide to a wag–'n–bietjie tree!"

"Abozuthu!" said Thambo, "I agree that Nigel must die, but we cannot risk your capture or death. Send one of your men."

"Thambo, Thambo, Thambo," shouted Abozuthu. "You are the mastermind and our leader, but violence is not in your blood. That is why the council has chosen me to lead our armies. A Zulu warrior thrives on killing and conquering his enemies. Nigel will be taken care of it in a manner that will not cause any suspicion to be directed toward the Circle chieftains."

The other chieftains continued to argue with each other: Two sides with Thambo and three with Abozuthu.

"Silence!" shouted the old man. He rose from his blanket. The chatter ceased. The brisk fire emitted the only sound. "Let's not argue among ourselves. Nigel will die. His death will be as in the old days and will serve as a message to those who dare challenge the council. Come and draw straws to see who will take care of Nigel." After the straws were drawn, the old man turned and once again, slowly walked to the trees until his figure faded into the darkness.

Lesotho – two days later

At the Lesotho outpost, the police had placed Nigel under protective custody and doubled the guards around Chief Gomba's cell. Nigel lay naked in his umbhede with a petite jet–black woman. He boasted on his successful plot to turn Gomba over to the South African government. In the process, he would collect R$250000 about $29,000 is U.S. dollars.

"My beautiful ubumnyama, your face is so smooth," said Nigel. His hand rubbed the side of her face.

She smiled. Her hand massaged his crotch. She kissed him on each nipple and suddenly grabbed his genitals and whispered, "My ubudoda, give it all to me."

Nigel moaned, he laid his head back and grinned, he imagined himself a Sotho chieftain, with many wives. Nigel rolled over on top of his woman, entering her with such force. She gasps and uttered, "ubuningi umthondo, ubuningi umthondo."

The police were unaware that the outpost was once a meeting place for members of the Circle. It had underground tunnels that surrounded most of the buildings.

The figure of a broad shouldered man whose face was shielded by the darkness quietly entered the room. The man had an Iklwa spear. Nigel's body rested on both palms and his shoulder blades protruded outward nearly touching each other with each thrust into his woman. The intruder stared at Nigel's black, shiny body and raised the spear. He drove it with brutal force through Nigel's back causing the blade to enter the heart of the woman, and created a sucking sound when the blade withdrew from the victim's body.

"Ngadla!" shouted the intruder standing over his dead prey. The mysterious warrior pulled a sharp knife from his waist, lifted up Nigel's head and cut deeply, making a complete circular motion around his throat and back of neck. He paused, placed his right hand in the puddle of blood, and proceeded to write something on the floor. The warrior quietly escaped through the hidden tunnel.

A young police officer making his rounds heard the loud cry and ran to the hut. "Nigel. Nigel, are you and your lady friend okay in there?" He heard nothing and he was afraid. He was scared shitless. His eyes bulged. He paused.

"Nigel, is everything okay?" The guard blew his alarm whistle and waited for the other guards to arrive. He cocked the chamber on his rifle. His swift kick was no match for the weak branch door and rushed in.

"Ugh! Ugh, Mother Teresa. Oh my God!" The young guard gagged at the sight of Nigel's head resting on the assegai Iklwa blade anchored to the floor in the center of the room. He vomited when he saw the rest of Nigel's body lay in bed on top of his woman drenched in blood. The blooded words *Ngadla,* were written on the floor.

CH APTER FOUR

This Land is Whose Land?

Johannesburg – the same year

Jan was seated in the family library by his father's favorite reading lamp. He rubbed his hand on an old, black tattered, dog–eared, cardboard binder. Twelve inches long, nine inches in width, the word, *TIDINGS*, embossed in white letters on the front. The old binder with its two holes, four inches apart, was held together by a long black shoelace. The ragged binder, six inches thick, was separated by a manila cover page, marking each year's events.

A collection of old books filled the room. Jan's father was an ardent history buff; he loved world events. His father was determined to keep a diary of major news events that occurred in each year of his life: 52 years captured on the black paper inserts. His father had bequeathed the binder and everything in the library to him.

His father called Johannesburg, (Jo'burg, the city of gold). His mother preferred 'I'Goli'. Jan felt Jo'burg, the largest city in South Africa south of Cairo, had an irresistible lure. Its sole reason for existence is the reef of gold that lies under the high–veil.

Like his father, he was a well–read man. He continued the tradition and vividly recalled dates of events in 1948 and the struggle for political power, the same year his father was murdered. They both had discussed comparisons between India, Israel, and South Africa, each government trying to maintain a status quo.

His father's assignment, the South African Press Association, was a job that he loved. He would rumble through the teleprinter's clippings searching for something of historical importance. It also provided him with the source of their lengthy discussions.

Jan blew his nose, then wiped his eyes with the same

handkerchief and stared at the dated headlines. One particular newspaper clipping depressed him.

The year – 1948

January 30 – Gandhi is assassinated in New Delhi.

February 15 – The Johannesburg police barracks bomb, killing one.

April 8 – Four days of fierce fighting, over 2000 Arab soldiers attack the village of Kastel, gaining strategic control of vital highway between Jerusalem and the coastal waterway.

April 16 – The word heard throughout Palestine is Armageddon. Jewish and Arab armies in a fierce battle on the plain of Jezreel.

May 10 – A truce is declared in Jerusalem!

May 14 – Israel proclaims its independence.

United States recognizes the new nation, Israel.

May 17 – The Soviet Union recognizes the state of Israel.

May 27 – Apartheid. This Land is Whose Land.

Jan glanced at his watch. "Damned, the captain will have my neck." He was late for work. Twenty minutes later, He was in the city center, laid out on a straightforward grid dominated by huge office blocks. With the exception of the red light district around the intersection of Bee and Trope, the city was about to become a ghost town. It was five–forty in the evening, the surrounding shops will close in twenty minutes and it becomes unsafe to be in the area unless you are in a car. Jan stopped for the light where he saw several black beggars. He glances at the red light, then at the three men; two were at his drivers' side searching through a trash barrel. Directly in his view was another man leaning on the building; the stranger wore a long dark colored trench coat.

The two young men paused and stared at him. The man across the street walked toward the car. Jan's hand touched the gun barrel resting on the car seat.

The light changed. Jan sped away. Within five minutes, he was safely in the command station. He said hello to the desk sergeant without slowing. He made a sudden stop at the swing gate, caught off guard by the loud singing.

"For he's a jolly good fellow! For he's a jolly good fellow! Oh how he's a jolly good fel–lowww! But we wish he were a little more mel–lowww! For he might give a loud bel–lowww! And we can all say hel–looo! And he's not a wine–oo, on his twenty–seventh birthday!" bellowed all fifty members of the Johannesburg elite police force.

The group gathered in honor of Linden's birthday. There he stood, all six feet two of him. His face broke into a wide smile. He loved the attention.

"Well," Jan laughed. "I may drown in a barrel of ale but you will never find my body floating in wine."

"The toast of the town to a true Afrikaner," cheered his duty sergeant as he proceeded to gulp down a pitcher of dark ale. It was five o'clock in the evening and he was off the clock. The sergeant had a belly to hold ten pitchers of ale. He held the station's record for being the only officer to down five pitchers within a fifteen–minute span.

"But Jan, my boy, South Africa has made excellent sherry and port for many years, there are many in this room, like me for example, cannot think of a better way to go," said the station's captain. He allowed the fete to take place inside the building on one condition. He wanted to be able to swear to his superiors if word of the party leaked out that he did not witness a single officer on duty drinking. He had six months to go before his retirement, something he looked forward. When it came time to toast Linden, the captain merely removed his thick, rimmed eyeglasses. Without them, he was legally blind. The rest of the officers on duty were ordered toast one drink to Linden.

"Where are my spectacles? Did anyone see my spectacles?" the captain shouted over the noisy men. "I laid them right here, on this desk a few moments ago."

"Officer Linden, have you seen the dear Captain's reading glasses?" the duty sergeant bellowed. His smile was so wide; it was no secret that his mouth could swallow so much ale.

"No! However, I want to thank you! Thank you all! You loony had well better believe that I am proud to be an Afrikaner. I'm also very pleased to be a member of such a fine group of men commissioned to serve law and order," said Jan. The birthday party was the largest social gathering the police squad had thrown for a single officer. Jan was well–liked by his fellow workers, peers, and supervisors.

The huge turnout was in anticipation of news that Jan had been recalled to active duty to serve in the South African Defense Force. Farewell parties were usually the best, there was a purpose to them, he wanted the opportunity to say goodbye to his friends.

He also wanted to say a special farewell to Andrea Krueger, an admission officer on temporary assignment at the station house. She was amongst the crowd. Their eyes met, he grinned at her and enjoyed a thought that was on his mind all day. Andrea smiled back. The magic of her smile made him fall in love with her. Once again, their eyes met. He turned and playfully shook his head. He could not resist the temptation of her body. *She is one hell of a woman,* his thoughts lingered. Once more, he looked in her direction.

Andrea laughed at his silliness. She rubbed the tip of her tongue on her upper lip. She felt Jan was a strikingly handsome fellow. She liked his heavy reddish eyebrows and neatly trimmed mustache.

Her serenity contrasted with everyone else's excitement. She was a tall slender woman, dressed in dark brown culottes. Andrea's glossy auburn hair, plaited into seven rows ended into a bun, highlighting the curve of her neck. She was wearing a thin gold necklace anchored to a petite red heart: a gift from Jan.

Their relationship was a well–kept secret. Whenever they would encounter each other in a remote area of the police station, and Jan tried to get too close, Andrea's favorite response was, *"The department frowns on fraternization."* She would always walk away, brushing up against him in a catlike motion.

Andrea was a cat lover. She had three cats – a Persian, which was a gift from her parents, and two strays. She, like Jan, loved her independence. Andrea had a dominating personality; she intimidated most men by her direct approach. Tactfulness was not one of her characteristics. However, Andrea had many male associates. She considered them only as friends, a view not shared by many women in the clerical pool. She was a person that women either liked or disliked intensely. Those who liked her found Andrea to be a good confidante.

Andrea did not want Jan to leave, but she admired Jan's spunk and it did not bother her that he could also be a conceited bastard at times.

"Speech! Speech! Speech!" shouted the boisterous crowd.

Jan raised his mug towards his colleagues. "I'm proud to serve in South Africa Defense Force. It has been said that our defense forces in terms of leadership, training, technical proficiency and general fighting ability are the strongest in the world!" he shouted. Jan's outburst was quickly greeted with a thunderous approval.

He accepted a bottle of Meerlust Cabernet, a fine wine, from his fellow officers. "Whose idea was this?" Jan asked. "The captain's?"

It was late in the evening when he arrived home. It was a small chalet in northwest Johannesburg, standing at the midpoint of a six–mile crescent of the lake. It was also near the cliff. From the shoreline on a clear day, he could see himself in the limpid lake, where the soft white sand circumscribed the shore.

Jan stared blankly, lost in thought over the problems he faced. He was eager to return to the South African Air Force. His love for flying was first in his life. However, his back injury during the war provided an early discharge. A successful back operation and a few strings pulled by his father earned him reenlistment status. Jan loved his country and hated its enemies. His hatred focused on the African National Congress. In February, an explosion had demolished the rear of the Johannesburg Police barracks while the men were sleeping. One officer killed and nine wounded. His father, a South African policeman and Sergeant Major with twenty–five years of loyal service, had been the lone officer killed. Both of his parents were now dead.

Its leadership vigorously denied certain members of the The African National Congress claimed responsibility for bombing of the barracks that killed many of the police officers along with Jan's father. The ANC had been leading a serious but unsuccessful resistance campaign against the past laws. Up until the bombing, Linden had disagreed with the ANC goals but respected his father's view that the government must improve its working relationship with the black population. Linden's father had felt South Africa was misunderstood by the outside world and he felt that, in terms of economic and military strengths, South Africa was the most powerful country in Africa. He would argue with Jan that one of its strongest weapons was the country's location.

"This apartheid thing will divide our country," Jan's father would say. "Here we sit, at the tip of the continent. We have strategic dominance over the Atlantic and Indian Oceans. This is 1948! We have to join the rest of the world! We cannot hide from change. We have become a country of struggle, conflict, and survival. Just look at the problems the people of Israel are having with its independence. They will one day rise and fight for their freedom and the whole world will take notice and recognize them."

Jan was young and immature enough to resent the outside world's meddling in his country's affairs. His family was one of the first of the Dutch who had settled South Africa beginning in 1652. Starting at the Cape of Good Hope, the Dutch spread deep into the interior. Jan's ancestors were familiar with fighting the blacks, although each group wanted the same thing: To live undisturbed in its accustomed manner. Fierce battles between the Zulu warriors and the Dutch settlers erupted over territory, which each had claimed.

He took exception to the notion commonly shared by outsiders that the blacks were there first and it was their country. South African whites such as the Boers will never give up their country. His ancestors came first to a large area that was once wilderness land, built their homes, tilled the soil to grow vegetables and fruit, formed a strong government, and lived a lifestyle very dissimilar from the neighboring tribes. He and his father did share a common ground, the love for their country. They both loved the country's lofty mountains, subtropical beaches, rolling hills, and fertile valleys. Perhaps this was why Jan felt he had to get away. Jan was filled with hatred for the African National Congress. Hatred was an attribute his father had not taught his children.

Jan's thoughts were interrupted by a familiar voice; it was Andrea. She was untying the bun of her hair and sitting on a couch near the window. "Don't ever leave a woman waiting. The longer she waits, the less you reap. Come on, sit beside me," she beckoned. "You've made a nuisance of yourself, haven't you?"

"I beg to differ. What do you mean?"

"Tonight is not the night for a difference of opinion. Come here!" Jan was seduced by her radiance. It was Andrea's eyes and the way she stared at him that projected an invitation for mischief. She drank the glass of wine in one mouthful.

He walked towards her and rubbed her lips softly with the tip of his finger. "What do you want?"

"Something hard, real hard, yet soft, warm and moist," she answered, nibbling at his finger.

Jan knelt down between her legs. Andrea placed her arms around him. They kissed, their tongues moved fast and searching, each fighting for control. She received he gave. Then he received; she gave. Andrea placed both hands in the center of Jan's chest and tore open his shirt in one movement. Jan's hands were on her breasts, his lips at her neck, working up to her ears, his tongue darted in and out. They fell on the floor and his hands searched for the clip on the bra as he tried to unbutton it.

"Where's the darned thing."

"It's in the front, honey, the front," Andrea whispered. Her hand unbuttoned his pants. She kissed him, her breathing quickening. Andrea found what she wanted. She grabbed his penis with authority. "This is what I want, all of this."

With the bra off, he had no problem with the culottes. Their kisses grew more passionate. Jan's fingers explored the inside of Andrea's thighs, feeling her moistness. She clasped him with her thighs. He ran his other hand over her bare skin, cupping her breast. He sucked the nipple hard and long, causing Andrea to open her thighs, releasing his hand.

"Jan, oh Jan, quit teasing me, please don't tease me anymore."

"Relax honey, the night is just beginning."

Andrea responded like a purring cat. When she is hot from passion, she likes to lick Jan profusely. Unknown to her, this is Jan's clue for penetration. They lay together on the hardwood floor on top of a lap robe. Andre uses her hands to lift up his chest and wiggles her head and body down until she found his nipples. Andrea flickers her tongue around each of them, sucking hard, but lapping softly.

"Mm, Jan, mm . . ." Andrea purred. "Honey, just relax, I want all of you." Andrea's tongue and mouth found Jan's belly button. He tried to comply. Jan could not stand it anymore. He had to be inside her. On all fours, he held himself above her. Andrea reached and toke a hold of his manhood, guiding him in. Jan filled her; Andrea tightened the muscles of her passageway. Their rhythm increased, and then slowed down, as they passionately made love to each other. Jan wanted it to last forever, but the sensation was too much for him. He felt himself about to come. Andrea reached down and grasps hold of Jan's testicles and massaged them with the wetness of their lovemaking. Jan cried aloud from the excitement and collapsed into a climax. They both fell together into a light sleep.

It was one hour later when they awoke. The air turned cool and the night had gathered. "Do you want a glass of wine?" she asked.

"Yes, please," he smiled. "What's for desert?"

Andrea picked up her culottes, folded them neatly, and then threw it at him. She stuck out her tongue, turned and slapped the side of her buttocks. Jan caught the culottes and admired her smooth, rounded butt.

Andrea returned a few minutes later with a warm, wet bath cloth and two glasses of wine. She lay on her stomach, pillow under her chest, legs separated, sipping the wine. She noticed Jan was staring at the ceiling. "Baby, where's your mind?" She snuggled close to his shoulder, placing her hand on his hairy chest.

"My dad. I can't seem to get over the way he died."

She looked at him. "Honey, I know it's been a little over four months. The death of your father was a blow to all of us. Don't let this hatred for the ANC destroy you."

"Andrea, please!" he snapped.

"Damn it, Jan Linden, don't *please* me! You know how I hate that!"

"Andrea, wait a minute. I have something to tell you."

She felt a lump in her throat. "You re–enlisted." For Christ's sake. Why? What in the hell for? If it's not running away, then what is it?"

"Andrea... Andrea... Andrea..." Jan whispered, trying to calm her. He placed both hands on her face.

"You know how much you mean to me. I don't want you to go. You don't have to run away." said Andrea.

Jan pushed her head away. "I'm not running away!"

"Oh, you're not! Then what in the hell is it? Don't tell me you're leaving to go find yourself!"

"Don't patronize me! Members of the African National Congress blew up my father's barracks. Those SOB's have adopted a so–called Program of Action calling for 'freedom from white domination and the attainment of political independence.' For all we know they are probably part of that secret terrorist group of restless blacks rumored to be the organization behind the Mau Mau society."

"That's ridiculous!" screamed Andrea. "The Mau Mau is in Kenya, a thousand miles to the northeast of us."

Jan raised his voice, "Some members of the South African parliament believed the group was trying to spread its terrorist activities into South Africa. Members of Mau Mau took lives of whites and mercilessly murdered their own people who were servile to the whites and..."

Andrea interrupted. "Yes that's true, but the retaliation by the whites was equally brutal. Blacks suspected of participating in this secret society were shot on the spot by white authorities."

"For God's sake, whose side are you on?"

Andrea grasped his hand. She whispered, "Jan, baby, your father was right. Apartheid will divide this country. I condemn those who set fire to the barracks. I will denounce those who destroy and take lives of innocent people, whoever they are."

"That's it. Andrea, the subject is closed. Put on your clothes. Go. Go. I'm leaving tomorrow."

Andrea fumed. "That's it! You are dismissing me! You conceited bastard. Go! Go then! Don't expect to find me sitting here waiting on you when you get back!" She rose from the bed, quickly put on her clothes and walked out the door with her bra and shoes in hand.

CHAPTER FIVE

The Young Lion

U. S. Army Base, Seoul

Fourteen months later and thirty unanswered letters was a bitter blow to Jan's pride. Andrea not only had not written, but she also changed her phone number. Nothing is as it once was. His government decided to enter the Korean War. Jan was captain of the small force, a squadron of South African Mustangs and Sabres assigned to fly with the United Nations force in the Korean War. What he did not like was flying a mechanical prone F–51 jet fighter and he detested taking orders from an American commander. He and his men had just returned from a search and destroy mission. His mind was mingled with bombs, deaths, and people screaming. However, more than anything else he still had his favorite pastime. He was alone in the quiet surrounding of his bunk. He was able to keep abreast of world events, thanks to news clippings sent by close friend of his father. The one item he had brought with him was his father's diary. He carefully pasted together the following headlines.

\-

The year – 1950

> *March 8 – Senator Joseph McCarthy of Wisconsin, accuses the State Department of having fifty–seven officials labeled by the FBI as being Communists.*
>
> *June 13 – South Africa passes the Group Areas Act, permitting proclamation of areas for the exclusive occupation of white and non–whites.*

June 25 – South Korea is invaded by 100,000 North Korean troops with 150 Russian–built tanks.

June 27 – President Truman orders U. S. forces into Korea. He also orders General Douglas MacArthur to send the Seventh Fleet to the Formosa Straits, south of the 38th Parallel.

June 28 – Seoul, the capital of South Korea, is captured by the North Koreans.

September 11 – Field Marshal Jan Smuts, a South African soldier, general, U.N. organizer, and past twice Prime Minister, dies.

September 22 Dr. Ralph Bunche, an American Negro educator, is awarded the Nobel Peace Prize for presiding over the settlement of the war in Palestine.

September 26 – South Korea recaptures Seoul.

Jan added the following in longhand.

September 29 – Captain Jan Linden leads a small symbolic force, a squadron of South African Air Force F–51 Mustangs and F–86 Sabres, to fly with the United Nations force in the Korean War.

The 187th Airborne Infantry Regiment and the 2nd Infantry Division were located on the western slopes in a gorge facing Mt. Namsan, a fact Lieutenant McClendon found slightly unsettling. His idea of a proper command station was on land that was flat, as far as the eye can see. The base supported an assorted wing of F–14 fighter–bombers, South African Air Force F–51 Mustangs, F–86 Sabres and equipment from other European nations. Jonathan was twenty–eight, dark brown eyes with short black hair interwoven and mistaken for curls. His five–feet, nine inches medium frame body blocked the door to the officers' quarters. His back rested between the door's squeaky hinge, his feet was on the doorjamb. His watchful eyes, too rational to be passionate about anything, stared down the large campground. He pulled on the little patch of hair directly under his bottom lip; his mind was not on his latest military victory over a North Korean battalion.

McClendon had led a small task force to seize a bridge site on the Soyang River. He had just returned from a successful ten–day mission. He and his men had pulled off a surprise attack on an advance party of North Koreans and had gained vital intelligence information. He could not help but smile. His white teeth drew attention away from his strong black bushy eyebrows. His gleam was not from his recent victory, but from a picture of his wife and two–year–old son Djhon, whom he had not seen in the past eighteen months. Lieutenant McClendon, stationed in Japan for a little over a year, received orders for combat duty in Korea. A rhythmic knock on the door and a whistling tune interrupted the Lieutenant's thoughts.

"Lieutenant McClendon! It's Sergeant Walters. May I enter Sir?"

"Come on in, Sergeant."

Sergeant Walters gave a side warded salute and smiled. He was a man of Irish decent. "Colonel Gage wants to you to join him at the officers' mess hall."

"You seem to be in a chipper mood, Sergeant."

"Yes sir!" The sergeant did a hop and a skip, followed by a click of the heels of his boots. "We're going home! The reinforcements are here!"

"All right!" laughed McClendon. He put his arm around Walters' shoulders and the two headed toward Colonel Gage's headquarters.

South Africa's military barracks were adjacent to the American Army officers' camp. Jan and his men were playing a game of croquet. One of the men used a long–handed mallet planted a beautiful kiss–off on Jan's wooden ball and knocked it some fifty feet away from the hoop. The ball stopped directly in Sergeant Walters' path.

McClendon and the sergeant came to an abrupt stop.

Jan shouted. "Hey Sergeant, at this rate, I'll never finish this bloody game. It seems the old chap over there wants to knock me to, as you Americans say, kingdom come."

McClendon smiled, picked up the ball, and walked towards Jan.

"Captain Linden, apparently you and your men did not hear the news. Nine months in this place is more than enough for any one man. The reinforcements are here. I may be back in the States in time for Christmas."

Jan frown and stared at McClendon. He found it difficult accepting the fact that he was fighting along the same side with black officers.

"My dear Lieutenant, are you aware that Colonel Gage only received orders to ship the 7th Infantry regiment back home? My men and I are scheduled to fly another mission at daybreak."

McClendon was apologetic. "I'm sorry. I thought..."

Jan interrupted, "not as sorry as I, but it's not shocking at all when you think about it. South Korea, nearly on the brink of defeat, was invaded by 100,000 North Korean troops with 150 Russian–built tanks. Now Pyongyang, abandoned by the UN forces."

"Yes, that was true, but surely you heard that South Korea had recaptured Seoul."

"So what. Intelligence sources are predicting that North Korea and Communist China will combine their forces to try to break through the UN lines along the 38th parallel. If it's true, you know what will happen. Your General MacArthur wants all the flying military aircraft he can get his hands on."

McClendon stood motionless; the exuberant smile slowly disappeared from his chapped lips. "A recapture of Seoul," he whispered. "If intelligence is correct in their assumptions, then good luck, Captain."

"Lieutenant, the luck apparently is with you. Now, give me back my bloody ball."

McClendon snapped to attention and saluted him. "All right sir."

Jan returned the salute and watch McClendon's as he departed. "Not a bad fellow," he muttered.

McClendon continued towards Colonel Gage's headquarters. "Sir, is Captain Linden correct in his assumptions?" asked Sergeant Walters.

"I don't know Sergeant, I really don't know. I have had my share of fighting for now. This war is a no—win situation. I wouldn't be surprised if within the next forty to fifty years that this country will not unite as one again. I'm not going worry about it, tonight I'm going into the city to collect some more souvenirs and tie one on."

Later that afternoon, McClendon borrowed a jeep and drove across the Han River through Itaewon, an area adjoining the United States Army base. Seoul Central Mosque was crowded with souvenir shops, bars, and dance halls. The city was heavily guarded and the military police walked in pairs. Some buildings were devastated and in ashes. McClendon drove down Chongno Street, the main shopping center of the city. The sun had set. Seoul had experienced three cold days followed by an unusual three warm days. McClendon pulled up to the side of the street. He was fascinated by the 500—year—old bell after which, the street was named. Since the Korean liberation in 1945, the bell had rung at midnight on the last day of the each year. McClendon stared up at the bell pavilion, admiring its structure. Without thinking, he drove on.

"Look out!" shouted a woman with a bag of groceries.

"Oh my God!" McClendon cried. He jammed on the brakes, but not quick enough as he saw the body of an old black man roll on top of the jeep and fall off on the passenger side. He jumped from the jeep and ran back to where a crowd has gathered encircling the victim. Ten yards from the accident scene, a crowd of South Koreans parted. There laid an old man. The people turned and stared at McClendon.

"I did not see him!" he shouted. "He walked into my path." Two young Korean boys helped the old man to his feet.

"Relax my son, I'm not hurt." His speaking voice was Korean, his accent specific and localized his diction precise.

He was relieved when he heard him speak. The old man was gray—haired, but lean and athletic in appearance. McClendon helped him brush off a neatly knitted and decorative blanket that matched the pattern of the dashiki he was wearing.

McClendon knew a little Korean and spoke to the old man in broken phases. "Thank God, you're okay! I, I, didn't see you." He continued to brush gravel off the old man's blanket.

"Relax my son; an old man is but a paltry thing."

McClendon smelled a peculiar odor coming from the old man's garment. He wondered what the man was doing there. "He couldn't be part of the Armed Services entourage. And what is he babbling about?" He looked at the old man. "I'm sorry sir, what did you say?"

The old man slowly turned his head and stared at him.

McClendon returned his stare, his thoughts wandered. "It as though he is looking past and through me into another place, perhaps the past, perhaps the future."

"It's time for me to depart, my son," said the old man. He walked away and never looked back.

McClendon stood dumbfounded. He wondered who was the old man and what was he doing in Korea.

CHAPTER SIX

Halt! Who Goes There?

Montreal, Quebec – Three weeks later

The congratulatory messages had begun arriving at the hotel two days earlier. Dr. William Riley received the Nobel Peace Prize for his study and findings on the biological, genetic, and cultural environments of different societies' migrations through parts of the world. Jan was invited to Canada to be the key speaker for the International Society of Economists.

He stood five–feet, six inches, late thirties, slightly bald and forty pounds overweight. Riley leaned on the front desk in the lobby of the old Ville Marie hotel. He was weary from the long bus ride. His hand, heavy from all the greeting and handshakes, tingled from poor blood circulation. Dr. Riley's poor eyesight caused him to adjust his thick spectacles to see the small writing on the bundle of messages. He glanced quickly at the small pink slips of paper, recognizing some familiar names with an occasional smile.

"Dr. Riley. I am Rossi. Dr. Frank Rossi.

"Yes, it's a pleasure to meet a renowned economist and a student and follower of economist John Maynard Keys. I read your paper on the Innovation Theory.

"Congratulations on winning the Nobel Peace Prize," said Dr. Rossi. "I'm curious, if you would pardon me; your graduate work at M.I.T. would seem to indicate a preference for the academic life."

"Thank you, Dr. Rossi," Riley said gravely. Then his face broke into a grin. "I wasn't always in the academic world, Dr. Rossi, but yes, I was a professor of economics while working on my second doctorate."

"You must have spent a fair amount on the research?"

45

Riley nodded. "Yes, there were many long hours at the campus library researching genetic and biological cultural backgrounds on various races of people."

"Excuse me Dr. Riley, I was referring to the massive amount of money it must have taken in personal funds – in addition to the grants – for you to travel so extensively for your research. Quite unusual for a man of your race."

Riley looked somewhat perplexed by Dr. Rossi's comments. "How so?" he asked.

"You must either be fortunate or have some influential friends," continued Dr. Rossi.

Riley arched his brow. The wrinkles around the eyes enlarged. "Yes, Dr. Rossi, I was indeed fortunate to obtain the grants and to convince some friends and colleagues to believe in my research. Excuse me; I believe it's time to go back to the ballroom. The program will start in five minutes."

Dr. Riley walked in the direction of the Queen's Province Room. A waiter in a tuxedo pushing a room service table smiled at him. Their eyes met. Something was wrong. The smile on the waiter's face contrasted with his cold glassy stare. After the man passed, Riley stopped and turned towards him. He had noticed the man before near the science laboratory. "Why is he watching me?" Riley asked himself. "No, he must be Security. That's right, Security. There are a lot of important people in this hotel," he thought.

Dr. Riley entered the large banquet room and proceeded towards the podium. He looked around the head table for his nameplate.

"Over here, Bill. You are sitting right here by me," said his good friend, Dr. Browne and Toastmaster for the event. After a very long accolade and a restless Riley, Dr. Browne said, "Ladies and Gentlemen, it's with great pleasure that I introduce this year's Nobel Prize winner, Dr. William Riley!" The crowd stood and applauded.

Riley thanked them. His acceptance speech was short and to the point, because he empathized with the crowd. The conference had lasted longer than expected. It was near dark. The scientists dispersed quickly and a small group followed Dr. Riley. He was on his way to meet some friends for a small and private celebration at the Delta Montreal.

A stranger wearing tinted dark glasses with a mirror, followed Dr. Riley; watched him get into a new 1950 black limousine and drive away. The stranger quickly motioned to a man in a gray sedan parked on the other side of the street to follow Riley.

The limousine and the gray sedan drove by 2 Place Ville – Marie. The limousine driver, in an effort to create conversation, remarked how beautiful the city was at night.

"Monsieur, Montréal, un soir." Dr. Riley ignored him. His mind was elsewhere. "Ah, chez vous," said the driver. "Monsieur Riley, Delta Montréal."

"Thanks driver, meet me in the front of the lobby at 10 p.m., and if I'm not out here, have the doorman ring Mr. Matthews' room."

"Oui Monsieur. Aurevoir."

Riley walked to the lobby entrance and stopped He had an uneasy sensation in the pit of his stomach.

The valet greeted him by opening the door. "Bon soir, Monsieur. Dr. Riley. Sir, it's sure a pleasure to see you again."

Riley just stood there; he felt the presence of someone watching him. He turned and saw the silhouette of a person at the end of the block created by the contour of the building.

"Monsieur, pardonnez–moi. Is there a problem?" asked the valet.

He ignored the valet. The silhouette grew smaller. An old man appeared. He was a wearing dashiki. Riley turned and questioned the valet. "How long has that man been standing over there?"

"Monsieur Riley, what man?" asked the valet.

He turned and pointed in the old man's direction. "That man," he answered. "Oh, where did he go?"

"Monsieur, you must have had a bad day?"

"Forget it, it's just my imagination. It's been a long day." Riley walked into the hotel and passed the elevator, his mind wondered if paranoia was beginning to set in. He realized his error and returned to the elevator.

"Floor please," said the elevator operator. Riley took the elevator to his friend's room on the sixth floor, his thoughts wandered back to the oddly–shaped figure that seemed to be staring at him, and back to his speech. He had a funny feeling someone was watching. *"Of course I was being watched, I was the key speaker!"* he reasoned to himself. Things had not been the same for the doctor and his family for the last two and a half years.

The elevator jolted slightly as it reached the sixth floor, and brought his state of mind back to the present.

"Sixth floor! Watch your step!" shouted the elevator operator. Odd numbers to the left! Even numbers to your right!"

Riley smiled at the man. He had on a clean–cut, black tuxedo suit with a white ruffled shirt. The elevator operator's black shoes shined so clearly that he looked down and adjusted his own tie.

There was a noise coming from Room 618 and the familiar voice of a colleague telling one of his favorite stories brought a smile from Riley.

Mrs. Matthews, a small but chubby woman with heavy makeup around the eyes, was hosting a small get–together for Riley. She heard the elevator, glanced at the clock and knew that it had to be Dr. Riley. He was the guest of honor, and he was late. She opened the door at the same moment that he reached for the doorbell.

"Bill! Honey, Bill's here!" shouted Mrs. Matthews. She kissed and gave him a warm hug. "Thank God, you made it. I thought the ceremony would last forever."

Riley finally laughed. "You were not the only one."

"I hope you plan to stay a couple of days and enjoy Montreal. I've made plans for tomorrow."

"Oh, what sort of plans."

"You and I are going to see the Notre Dame Cathedral and on the way we will stop by Olympic Stadium."

"Hold on. I understand it's one of the world's most spectacular sights, but please spare me some time to see 'The Man and His World' exhibition."

"Sure, no problem." Mr. Matthews took him by the hand and introduced him the guests. He shook one hand after another, and

48

exchanged kisses with the wives of his friends.

"Hello, Dr. Riley!" A slender woman in a red cocktail gown kissed him on the cheek. "How are you?" she said, adjusting her black choker. The woman saw an approving smile on Riley's face as he looked at her.

"You are a very lovely woman."

"Why, thank you. I am Helen McClendon. We met at the agency over two years ago. Jon's, out near the balcony..."

Riley became agitated and interrupted her. "Yes, yes. Excuse me; I prefer not to discuss the agency. I hope you and your husband understand." Riley hurried his reply and then he walked away.

Mrs. McClendon followed him and grabbed his arm. "Of course," said Helen somewhat puzzled by Riley's actions. "Where is your wife? I'm surprised she's not here."

"She's at home with our son. Michael has the chicken pox."

Helen was sympathetic. "Oh, that poor boy, I know how he feels and how helpless your wife also feels as a mother. Djhon, our son, had just finished his bout with the chicken pox two weeks ago."

"Yes, yes, I know what you mean. Your husband is a fine officer and I believe he is a major by now? You can be proud," said Riley.

"Oh I am, indeed, he was just promoted to a captain. Jon has big goals; he wants to attend the War College. I am glad to have him back home. Thank God, he's out of Korea, we haven't seen each other in nearly sixteen months."

Riley felt a tug on his shoulder.

"Dr. Riley! I am Jonathan McClendon. Honey, why didn't you let me know that Dr. Riley had arrived? How long have you been here?"

"Just a few minutes. It's nice to see you again, Captain, especially since we have so much in common."

"Congratulations on winning the Nobel Peace Prize. If anyone deserves to get it, you certainly do."

"Thank you, Captain McClendon."

"Please call me Jonathan. When someone wins the Nobel Peace Prize, what does he do next?"

"I'm interested in studying the plight and country of the South

African people. I'm planning on spending two or three years of research in and around the villages," answered Riley.

McClendon looked perplexed. "South Africa! Surely, you are aware of that country's race relation problems. I wouldn't think the government would be interested in your exploitation of the plight of the blacks in South Africa."

Riley was aghast at McClendon's choice of words. "Exploitation! Why would you say that?"

Jonathan apologized. "I'm sorry, exploitation, from the Pretoria government's viewpoint."

"If you would pardon me, there's an old friend over there that I haven't seen for several years. As usual, his arms are around two women." Riley departed and made his way over to his old friend.

Mrs. Matthews had reserved the largest suite the hotel had to offer, it had three balconies overlooking the city. Riley and Mrs. Matthews were on one of them.

"A full moon really does this great city justice. Look over there, see how the Washington monument illuminates the water," said Mrs. Matthews, pointing to her left.

"Yes, I agree. It's a beautiful sight," replied Riley.

"And over there, see, see, the White House. My God, what is that man doing there? He's sitting there on the side of the street on a blanket, under the streetlight. It's a shame to see homeless and hungry old people in this country of ours. The government should do something about it," said Mrs. Matthews.

Riley looked towards where she was pointing. "It's the old man! What is he doing down there?"

"Dr. Riley, do you know the old man? He's looking up here."

"That man is neither helpless nor homeless!" Riley was angry. "I want to know why's he's following me."

Jonathan saw that something was wrong with Riley. "Is anything the matter? What's all the commotion about?"

Mrs. Matthews pointed down at the street. "It's that man down there, for some reason has upset Dr. Riley. He thinks the old man is following him."

"Well I'll be a monkey's uncle," said Jonathan. "The question should be, is he following me? I met the old man in Korea three weeks ago. There's something strange about him."

Riley looked pointedly at Jonathan. "Were you at my award ceremony?"

"No, I was not," he answered.

"Then, he's following me. He was there," snapped Riley.

"If that's the case, why don't we both go down and ask him," said Jonathan.

The two men ran quickly for the elevator, leaving behind a room full of puzzled guests. Jonathan pressed the elevator buzzer. The two waited.

No elevator.

Jonathan pressed the buzzer again for an extended period. Thirty seconds passed.

Still no elevator.

"Where's the operator?" asked Riley.

"Let's take the stairs, it's only six floors," said Jonathan.

Three floors down, Riley stopped and gasped for air. His back rested against the rail. Jonathan was at the base of the first floor when he looked up at Riley. "Go! Go! Don't wait on me," he shouted.

Jonathan lowered his shoulder and burst through the exit door. He turned and ran to the corner. He stopped abruptly. His eyes searched left, then right and up towards the six floor balcony, and once again to the spot where they first saw the old man. He took a deep breath, a bead of sweat rested on the tip of his nose. He saw Riley coming out the exit door. Jonathan ran towards him grabbing his shoulders. The force of his thrust caused a tired Riley to lose his balance.

"He's gone," both men whispered within a half second of each other.

CHAPTER SEVEN

A Far–fetched Theory

March 1952 was a cold gusty winter day in South Korea.

Jan took a deep breath and exhaled. He watched the vapor slowly disseminate around his face. He pulled the sheepskin collar of the heavy overcoat around his ears. He cupped his gloved hands together and blew into the small opening between his thumbs. His hands were almost numb. His left knee joint aches from the blizzard that brought forty mile an hour winds and two feet of snow.

He looked at the right airplane's engine, then to the left. Thin layers of ice covered both engines. The early morning bright sun rays had not yet intensified to thaw the plane wings. Jan rested his head on the headrest, his thoughts drifted backed to the winter of 1939. It was colder than this winter, but he could not remember suffering from the cold. He looked down at the navigator and wondered how the standing in below zero temperature could maintain his composure; he flailed his arms against his side, maintaining a firm grip on the corrugated baton.

Jan's F–51 Mustang was in the front of the squadron. He was worried. The plane had a history of icing problems. Sitting in the plane in freezing temperature seemed to last an eternity.

The colonel stared out the cloudy window from the warm comfort of the tower, and ordered the navigator to run the plane engines a full fifteen minutes before take–off. The navigator finally gave Jan the take–off sign to leave the runway. He radioed to his men in the F–86 Sabres to follow his lead.

Jan's plane sped down the runway as it had done over a hundred times; however, he felt something was wrong. He did not like the sound and roar of the right engine. Twenty seconds into the take–off, the right engine caught fire. Flames three feet in diameter sprouted from the engine housing and casing. The plane began to vibrate and caused the steering wheel to shake. He grabbed the handle and tried to hold the plane in place. His thoughts heightened. "My God, what should I do? Am I too far along to abort take–off?" Breathing heavily through his nostrils, Jan made his choice. He shut off the engine and paid the price.

Twelve weeks he lay on his stomach in the hospital. He severely injured his back when the plane tumbled on its side. He spent another sixteen weeks in physical therapy learning to walk again. His top three vertebrates were fused together. The doctors also inserted a two–inch pin in his right hip. He was lucky. The rescue squad pulled him to safety moments before the place exploded. No longer able to fly, he left the Air Force, however this time, a war hero.

Jan packed his clothes to return to Johannesburg. A small box of news clippings had just arrived. He sorted through the articles and was not happy with the racial problems he was reading about, especially those concerning Nelson Rolihlahla Mandela, leading over 8000 people in a campaign of defiance of apartheid. Mandela was arrested. The government gave him a suspended sentence and banned from political and social activities. He went through the small stack and was saddened at what he was reading.

The year – 1952

January 7 – Rioters in Jerusalem demonstrate against the decision to negotiate with West Germany on compensation to be paid for personal injury and suffering by the Jewish people at the hands of Hitler and his followers.

February 6 – King George VI dies in sleep at Sandringham. Elizabeth, Queen at 25, Flying from Africa.

February 15 – On all the islands of Britain, at two o'clock in the afternoon, all activity stops for two minutes of silence and prayer. The coffin of George VI comes to the door of St. George's Chapel at Windsor, traditional home of the royal family.

June 26 – The African National Congress with its membership of over one hundred thousand mounts a passive resistance campaign against the South African government. They are successful in launching a series of demonstrations and protests using Gandhi's passive resistance techniques. Nelson Mandela was arrested and experiences his first night in the South African police cells for holding a meeting past curfew time.

November 4 – General Dwight D. Eisenhower wins the presidency and carries the Republican Party to victory in both houses of Congress by using the campaign slogan of "Communism, Korea, and corruption."

November 13 – South African courts declare illegal the High Court of Parliament Act, permitting Parliament to override all other courts. The Act took 48,000 voters of mixed blood off the common election rolls and placed them on a separate list.

December 8 – Several whites have joined forces with the African National Congress, and the son of a former Governor General of South Africa is arrested for taking part in the organized defiance movement. Race riots in several towns develop. Some forty people, including six whites, were killed.

Jan added another entry to the list.

December 17 – Captain Jan Linden ends his military tour and returns home to Johannesburg, South Africa.

Six weeks later on February 7, 1953

Jan walked, deep in thought, his eyes on the building in front of him, ignoring the rain, wondering why headquarters had chosen him for this assignment. He sighed, "Tough shit." His face bore an expression of frustration and boredom. He was sent to London to learn riot control techniques from the British. "This is worse than the military," he thought.

The South African National Police organized into three branches:

The Uniformed Branch, The Detective Branch, and the Security Branch. Since the Uniformed Branch is where the bulk of the force is located and employed, the commander felt someone from the Uniformed Branch should be in London learning riot control from the British.

Jan personally did not like taking orders from the British. His ancestors had fought against the British in the Anglo–Boer Wars. After two weeks in London and surrounding townships, Jan felt that he was a prisoner. He did not agree with the decision but a patriotic man such as himself must serve his country and do what is best to protect it.

He stared at the sign on the building marked CID – Central Intelligence Department. He glanced up the street and smiled at a bobby walking his beat. Foul clouds threaten and the cobbles of the old street glistened with raindrops consumed by the cold air. His military service ended six weeks ago and he was glad to be back with his old South African police buddies.

Jan's beloved country, South Africa was now besieged by race riots. The blacks had begun migrating from tribal homelands in large numbers and were settling in surrounding cities. The jobs grew scarce and wages dropped around the white–operated farms, and later in the diamond and gold mines. The white government reacted by enacting harsh and restrictive laws to control the urban tide of increasing black population. This led to isolated race riots in the black townships.

He knew the trip was political. The South African government had been receiving pressure from world leaders on the amount of violence the police, especially his regiment, were using to control the race riots. To pacify the critics, the South African government chose one of their top police officers to send to London to learn race riot techniques.

Jan felt his government was too easy on the handful of so–called black leaders who are stirring up trouble; however, he agreed to obey his government's orders and go to London to learn a more tactful way of stopping or controlling the riots.

The class training was over for the day and he decided to go for beer and skittles at one of the local pubs called George VI. It was crowded as usual; the local Bobbies considered the pub to be their second home. He muscled his way through the crowd and found an empty spot at the far end of the bar. He ordered a pint of ale. He overheard a conversation between two Bobbies seated directly behind him.

"An odd thing came across the teleprompter, something that happened over four and half years ago," said one of the Bobbies.

"What's so bloody odd?" asked the second Bobbie between a sip of dark ale.

"Ah, some African chieftain was on trial for conspiracy and the chief prosecution witness was found dead with his head on a spear," answered the first Bobbie.

"Yes, I remember that. A friend of mine told me it was a gruesome site. However, that was over four years ago. Ah man, why would something like a dead blackie with his bloody head staked on a spear be of any interest to intelligence?"

"Hell, I don't know. Maybe it has something to do with that Mandela fellow. He has caused the South African government a lot of grief. Ah, but the ministers are also concerned that the violence doesn't spread into our neighboring colonies, and the African chieftain on trial was one of the bigwigs."

Linden approached the two men and raised his mug. "Here, here, to the Queen."

The Bobbies responded in jest and well other several other British officers. "Yes, our Queen," shouted the first Bobbie.

"Excuse me gents, my name is Jan Linden and I couldn't help overhearing your conversation and..."

"Foreigner if you ask me. Wouldn't be anyone local," interrupted the first bobby. He looked at his friend and pointed his thumb down at Jan.

The second Bobbie grabbed his partner's hand and turned his thumb upward, then looked at Jan. "The gent's not all bad. He saluted our Queen."

The first Bobbie slowly agreed. "Ah, what can we do for you?"

"Corporal, I'm a police lieutenant from South Africa on assignment here in London and am attached to your station. Any news from my country is of great concern to me. You can check my credentials with your Captain O'Riley at the CID."

The Corporal gulps his ale. He burped and wiped the foam from his mustache. "I see. How long have you been in London?"

"Three days, ten hours, and twenty–two minutes," Jan answered, looking at his watch.

The second Bobbie took his whistle from his shirt pocket and blew two short, clear, shrill notes. The noise got everyone's attention in the pub.

"Do any of you gents know or vouch for this here fellow?" shouted the second bobby.

A large burly gent with five stripes on his uniformed shouted, "Ah, yes, he's the fellow from South Africa. It seems his government feels they need a lesson in controlling the blackies back in his country. The police are shooting most of the blackies and their government feels if they keep shooting them, there will be none left to work the mines and fields."

The room filled with laughter. Jan's face reddened. He tried to control his frustration and restrain his anger with what he thought was idiosyncratic behavior on the part of the British Bobbies.

"Please, there's not much coverage on South Africa in the local papers, and I would deeply appreciate any news concerning my country."

"I'm not sure what I saw came from intelligence, and those boys don't take too kindly to leaks," said the corporal.

"Come on, Corporal, was the message restricted?"

"No!" He looked around and saw several of his fellow officers staring at them.

Jan shouted back, "Then what's so bloody wrong with sharing it with me!"

"Lower your voice or I will tell you nothing. Sit down."

"All right, all right, what did it say?"

"The message said something about an African chieftain who was arrested and held on trial for crimes against the South African government, and the chief witness was another blackie with enough damaging evidence to hang him." He paused. His eyes search the room.

"Go on, go on, tell me more," he demanded, tapping the table.

"All right, hold your bloody tongue. The day before the trial, he was found dead with his head cut off and placed on a spear in the center of the room."

"Iklwa." Jan whispered.

"Aye, what did you say?" The corporal looks puzzled.

"Iklwa, that's the name of a particular assegai blade used in such killings to demonstrate a point to other native blacks."

"Wait a minute, there was no mention of such a blade."

"I know, but was there any mention of a Chieftain Gowon?"

"Ah, yes, he's the one that was on trial. Who is this Chieftain Gowon?" replied the second bobby.

"South African government had him under surveillance for some years. We feel he was a leader in the terrorist group called the Circle," Jan answered. "But, why now the interest? He's been dead for four years."

"Ah, I read about that group two years ago. I thought the government executed or jailed all the members," questioned the first bobby.

"We did. However, there was not enough evidence to hold Gowon. Who was the man killed?"

"I don't recall," answered the second bobby looking at his friend. "Do you?"

"It was a funny name for a black..."

"It had to be Nigel?"

"Yes, that's it!" answered the first bobby, pointing at Jan. "Why the interest after four years? Many blackies have died or been murdered by the police or their own people.

Jan was convinced that the way in which Nigel was murdered was something of a signal to others. It was a method of killing one's foe used many years ago by the Zulus. His mind raced with several thoughts. "What have the Zulus to do with Chieftain Gowon's death? He is a member of the Sotho tribe. Something funny is going on. I've got to wire back home for permission to return and see what the Zulus and Sothos are up to."

Jan thanked the two Bobbies, gulped his ale, and rushed out of the crowded pub. Once outside, he realized he could do nothing until morning. Everything was closed. His clearance into the station was from 8 a.m. to 6 p.m.

The following morning Jan left the boarding house and started walking straight to the London Police Headquarters. He was some two–hundred yards from Scotland Yard before he considered how he was going to explain to his superiors, both here in London and in South Africa, the reason for his request to leave London. His viewpoints were well known by others concerning his London assignment.

Jan had no concrete evidence that there was a connection between Nigel's death, the Sothos, and Zulus, but he had a gut feeling and wanted to investigate the murder. His explanation for wanting to send a wire over the teleprompter to Johannesburg received less than lukewarm response from Captain Lodge.

"You want to do what?" bellowed the Captain.

"You heard me correctly the first time, Captain."

"Is this your way of not completing the training?"

"No Sir, I believe that I'm on to something."

"Very well, send the wire! It will not do you any good. You're here to learn how to deal with race disturbances in an effective manner in order to avoid a full scale riot."

"There's only one way to put down aggression and that is to jail or hang the leaders for conspiring against the government," Jan said with a bit of sarcastic.

"Both the British and South African government know your views quite well," answered the Captain.

Jan sent the wire and kept inquiring throughout the day as to whether his people had responded. Later that day while on the training grounds, he could see Captain Lodge walking briskly towards him with an envelope in his hand. He was smiling broadly. The look in the Captain's eyes convinced Jan that once the training was over he would have to take the matter in his own hands.

"Mr. Linden, I'm afraid you will be spending the next six weeks studying riot control techniques. Your superiors in South Africa responded with a single word, 'Preposterous!'"

Jan was disappointed but determined to follow up on his theory as soon as he was back in South Africa.

CHAPTER EIGHT

A Beastly Little Man

Spring 1953

Jan's return to Johannesburg and his further investigations proved fruitless. The department's policy towards the blacks had not changed.

"It amazing me that the general belief among all the people I contacted, including those in high government positions, is always answered with the same three words, 'Ludicrous! Preposterous! Absurd!'" Jan whispered to himself. He was unable to find any clues about Nigel's death. He was now beginning to doubt himself.

Three years had passed and the year 1956 was a turbulent one. Racial violence played against a backdrop of cold war politics. Jan's diary continued to grow as the years passed. He was at home in his study scanning data from newspaper clippings, personal notes, and copies of police files on various known anti–apartheid leaders. The room was always locked. Jan's father's treasures, now his, contained memorabilia collected over the years. His father did not allow Jan's mother access to his collection. They were his private diary; now it belonged to Jan. The family tidings continued to give the diary a personal touch.

The year – 1956

February 1 – South Africa government orders the Soviet Union to close all its consulates by March, amidst charges of spreading Communist propaganda among the black and Indian populations.

February 6 – Autherine Lucy, University of Alabama's first

Negro student, leaves the campus under police protection. The University officials suspend her until the order can be restored.

April 23 – Soviet leader Nikita Khrushchev states the U.S.S.R. will make a guided missile with a hydrogen bomb warhead capable of hitting any target in the world.

The United States Supreme Court rules that segregation on intrastate buses violates the Constitution.

May 18 – South Africa's Supreme Court upholds the removal of 40,000 "colored" (mixed) voters from the voting register.

July 26, Egypt seizes control of the Suez Canal and President Gamal Abdel Nasser announces its nationalization.

October 30 – Great Britain and France vow to send troops into the Suez Canal unless Israel and Egypt withdraw their forces ten miles from the Canal.

October 31 – British bombers attack military targets, sinking an Egyptian naval frigate.

November 5 – The Soviet Union announces it's prepared to use force (Soviet volunteers) to restore peace in the Middle East.

November 6 – President Dwight D. Eisenhower and Vice President Richard M. Nixon win re–election by a landslide, again defeating Adlai Stevenson.

November 16 – U.S. Under Secretary of State tells the United Nations that the United States would "act" if Soviet "volunteers" go to the Middle East.

December 2 – Fidel Castro, with an invading force of 82 Cuban exiles trained in Mexico lands on Cuban soil. He initiates a guerrilla campaign against Cuba's President, Fulgencio Batista.

Jan carefully inserted between the dated clippings his promotion.

On May 18, 1956, Jan Linden was promoted to Captain of Detectives. Waiting to get a haircut in a Johannesburg police barbershop, he read a newspaper article on the refusal of the

South African Supreme Court to stay a lower court ruling on the removal of 40,000 "colored" (mixed) voters from the voting register when the news of his promotion reached him.

It had been eight years since Nigel's death. As each day passed since Jan's trip to London, he was now convinced an organized terrorist group was plotting to overthrow the government. He made numerous inquiries for information on known anti–apartheid organizers. Each led nowhere. Jan's refusal to discontinue his quest for the truth brought him a storm of ridicule from colleagues. He continued to pester fellow workers, superiors, and other members of South African police in nearby cities, for more information to support his theory. However, Jan was concerned with rumors of how members of the secret society called the Circle were financed.

"Proof is what I want, Captain Linden," shouted the chief of detectives. Do you have any proof? Do you? What is the nature of this proof?"

Jan took a step backward. He coughed to clear his throat. "Chief, how can you turn your back on the truth?"

"Ha, the truth is only useful if it's convenient to those seeking vengeance," smarted the chief of detectives.

Jan swallowed hard. He looked at the chief and strode back and forth across the small wooden office floor. "Chief, I have reason to believe..."

"I don't give a fuck what you believe; this mission of yours has to stop. For Christ sakes, you haven't come up with one thread of proof in four years."

"But what about Nigel's death, the way he was murdered," Jan insisted.

The Chief threw his hands in the air. "Oh give me a break! A group of tribal chiefs gets together and a damn black's head ends up on a spear, and you think a conspiracy is brewing. Hell, many in this department feel the blacks are not intelligent enough to mount a successful organized campaign against each other much less the government.

Jan ran a sweaty palm over his head to slick back his full–bodied red hair. He stared at the chief. "Sir, if this conspiracy ring have access to tremendous amounts of money, then my God, there's trouble ahead. The key to any rebellion is money and money is power. If properly used, and carefully placed in the hands of the right people, a successful revolt could be launched."

The chief shrugged his shoulders. "All right Linden, let's assume you're correct. Then who are they, what do they want and where are they getting the money?"

"The money I don't know, but I have some..."

The chief interrupted. "Hell Captain, even if we knew their identities, has it ever occurred to you that the South African police were perhaps the most well–trained police force in the world. They have had years of experience in controlling the blacks and keeping them off balance. Now apartheid gave the police unlimited powers." The chief ended the discussion to attend to matters that are more important.

It was early afternoon when Jan arrived home for a quick lunch. He lay on the sofa to rest his eyes. His three brothers and baby sister never really understood him. All of his brothers were married. He was the uncle to eight kids. He did not particularly like kids, and refused many opportunities to go to family outings. His brothers felt this was the reason for his not taking a wife. Whenever Jan visited the family, they teased him about breaking the family tradition of marriage and a large family. Marriage had never been on his mind. He knew that his natural good looks afforded him certain amenities.

The only woman that touched his heart was Andrea. However, Andrea was true to her word, and did not wait for him. She married an engineer from Capetown. He still carried a torch for Andrea. He often had warm thoughts of her in his dreams. The dreams were usually sexual and surprisingly vivid. He dismissed his feelings as purely sexual, nothing more. Jan felt he was indeed carrying on his family's tradition. His great–grandfather, grandfather, and father each served their country as South African police officers. Like them, he had made it his career, something his brothers could not boast.

Their father was also a Regimental Sergeant Major during World War I, and Jan, a commissioned Lieutenant, served his country as a fighter pilot during the Second World War.

Jan looked at the clock and suddenly realized he had thirty minutes to get to work.

"Good morning, Sergeant Fisher."

"Good morning, Captain," replied the night station sergeant, looking up over the paper he was reading.

"You must have had a slow night to have completed all of the paperwork and be reading the paper with almost an hour left on your shift," said Captain Linden.

"Sir, it's been a very busy night. I had the usual number of drunken brawls, a cat burglar, domestic disturbances, and the usual problems with the blacks. I put the last one in the cell fifteen minutes ago and I am training the young corporal on the paperwork procedures.

He is in that office with the closed door. I told him to have everything finished ten minutes before quitting time."

Jan smiled and asked, "What does, *The Star*, have to say to us this morning?"

"Oh, nothing much. The Constitutional Court upheld removing those colored folks from the voting rolls. The government should have done that years ago," he said, handing Linden the paper.

"Yeah, I agree." The night sergeant had a fetish for old newspapers. Night duty was sheer drudgery to the sergeant. In the corner of the room, the papers were dated the first and eighth of each month. Eighteen was the Sergeant's lucky number. The Sergeant would throw the papers away at the end of each year and start over with the New Year. Jan once asked him, "Why not keep the eighteenth?"

"Two papers are better than one." was his response. Jan passed the stack of old newspapers. He stopped suddenly, staring at an article on the top front page.

Johannesburg Star
Monday, December 10, 1956
@ A Pretoria government owned newspaper
South African government ordered the Soviet Union to close consulate by January 1, charging that it has been used to spread communist propaganda and material among the blacks and Indian population.'

"So they found another source to back their activities." Jan muttered. He grabbed the newspaper and stormed into his superior.

"I have read the newspaper article and I don't want to hear it."

"But, let me explained...."

His superior shouted, "Out! Out! Get the fuck out!"

Jan turned towards the door, his head lowered and for a few moments, he gradually sank into a beastly, purposeless existence.

CHAPTER NINE

The Old Peddler Carried a Cudgel

December 1956

The next morning Jan awoke from a deep sleep, drenched from perspiration. He had an unpleasant dream. He could never forget the brutal beating Rogers inflicted on him. It was more, it seemed, than he had decided in his lonely, inward way, that he could forget. Jan was proud of his manhood. After all, he once was a cocky young police officer, a military officer, and a war hero, yet he came home and was beaten unmercifully by a gay flamboyant stranger. He shrank at the thought of his colleagues snickering laugh. He told his superior that Rogers and two other men had caught him off guard and inflicted his wounds.

During the past four years, his taste for beer and fresh roasted peanuts had caused his belly to protrude slightly over his belt buckle. Not proud of his beer belly, he concealed the additional weight by wearing tailored uniform shirts, which met the middle of the pants pockets.

Jan still had a safe haven – his diary. The collection of news clippings, created a need for him to start a new binder. He searched the mini–markets until he found a 15 by 18 inch rectangle replacement. He had the word 'TIDINGS' stenciled on the center front cover. He started the year with articles on segregation, race riots, human rights battles and Vietnam, which plagued the sixties.

The year – 1960

February 19, 1960 – Queen Elizabeth gives birth to a son. Prince Andrew, the first child born to a reigning British sovereign since 1857, is the second in line of succession to the throne.

March 21 – South African police, equipped with Saracen armored cars, open fire on an unarmed crowd numbering several thousand, which had gathered outside the police station at Sharpeville. The crowd is demonstrating against the South African pass laws: Sixty–two Africans are killed and 191 wounded.

April 9 – South Africa's Prime Minister, Verwoerd, is shot twice in the head at an agricultural exhibition in Johannesburg. Verwoerd is expected to recover. His attacker is understood to be in protest against the policies symbolized by the Prime Minister.

April 25 – Race riots breaks out in Biloxi, Mississippi, after some forty negroes attempt to use the city's "whites–only" beaches.

May 1 – American U–2 reconnaissance plane is shot down over Soviet territory. Francis Gary Powers, pilot, is held in exchange for Rudolf Abel.

May 27 – Israel agents kidnap former Gestapo chief Adolf Eichmann in Argentina and smuggle him back to Israel to stand trial for Nazi war crimes.

August 23 – Johannesburg, five months after it had been proclaimed, the state of emergency declared after the Sharpeville shootings had ended.

October 5 – A special referendum is held among the white population of South Africa. Approximately 850,000 people are expected to vote to transform South Africa from a constitutional monarchy accustomed to being loyal to the British crown into an independent Republic.

October 20 – Chief Albert John Lithuli, Zulu Chieftain and President General of the African National Congress is named co–winner of the Nobel Peace Prize.

November 8 – John F. Kennedy is elected President, with

Lyndon B. Johnson as Vice–President.

November 11 – A brigade of South Vietnamese soldiers attempts to oust its President, Ngo Dihn Diem – accusing him of corruption and suppression of liberties.It was twenty–five minutes past eight that Monday morning when the district commander confronted Jan. He was concerned over the number of unsolved cases assigned to him. He also knew of Jan's drinking problem. The Commander removed his spectacles from his ears and frown at him.

There was a moment of puzzled silence before Jan wondered why the commander was at his precinct. The commander was twice his age. He was a fatherly figure to the men in his district. He had the reputation for covering up for his men's mistakes.

The district commander had always liked Jan, he himself, was a lieutenant when Linden joined the department. He walked up to him and put his arm around Jan's shoulders. The two of them walked slowly away from the rest of the men. "Jan, my boy, they tell me that you have become obsessed with what you call *strange circumstances* regarding Nigel's death."

Jan shrugged his shoulders. "Sir, I am even more convinced that Nigel's murder was the act of conspirators.

The commander stop and removed his arm. He looked at him and noticed his bloodshot eyes. "Jan, Jan, my boy. You are going to destroy yourself and your career if you don't stop pursuing an idiotic idea."

"Sir, they, the ANC, killed my father."

"Jan, I knew your dad and this is not something he would be proud of. He would say, no personal feelings and be a police officer first. Proof show them proof."

"I know commander, but the ANC and their members are clever, quite clever."

"Jan, if there was such a conspiracy, we are vastly superior in weapons and intelligence. The black natives and their man–made weapons, dancing, spiritual singing and lack of unity, are not even a

69

smitten no match for a superior force. Hell, just look at what happened to them at Sharpeville. They were no match for a well–armed police force."

The two men departed unable to sway each other convictions. A couple of hours later Jan leaned back in his upright chair and closed his eyes. In his head, he continued to go over repeatedly the pretrial testimony regarding Nigel's comments about membership in the Circle.

"Three tests one must pass and Nigel failed the 'test of life.' What is the 'test of life?'" Jan thought to himself.

Jan heard the noise of someone moving a chair. He opened one eye and saw a black reserve police officer assigned to police the black townships surrounding major cities in South Africa. It suddenly hit him: "Tomar! Tomar Mangopela, he is the one known by his fellow black police officers as "Unwabu," the chameleon," Jan shouted, rubbing his head. He lowered his voice. "He would know the three tests one must pass to become a member of the Circle and especially the *test of life*. Tomar is a person who possesses the cunning to convince both the South African police and his own people that he served their interests."

Jan heard that the police were told how Tomar cherished the rewards of being selected to protect the South African government. He also was persuasive in assuring his people that being on the police force provided inside information and protection for his fellow black natives. Neither party completely trusted Tomar. They knew he was only looking out for himself. If either side offered something worthwhile, Tomar would sell what was left of his soul.

Jan shouted at the man with the pear–shaped head and tobacco stained teeth standing by the desk, "You, there, come here boy."

The black reserve police officer slowly walked towards him. "Yes captain, can I be of service?"

Jan stood and stared into his face. "Where can I find Tomar?"

"Who, Sir?" he answered.

"You heard me the first time, don't play dumb with me. I want to know where Tomar is."

The black police officer lowered his head. "Tomar is not working tonight, Sir."

"I don't care if he's working or not, where in the hell can I find him?"

The man looked at Jan. "He lives in a small concrete house in Soweto on Kagiso Street, Sir."

Jan ordered a couple of the young police officers to follow him to Soweto. It was late in the evening when they arrived and there were no lights in the concrete house.

"Sir, it's my understanding that Tomar lived alone," said one of the young police officers. "He may be at the local hangout that most black policemen favored."

There was no answer when Jan knocked on the club's door. The young police officer then went around the back to look in the side window and saw the glint of something in the darkness on the floor. He returned to the front and reported to Jan what he had seen.

Jan nodded to the second policeman to kick the

door down. Tomar had stepped unknowingly into his death. There was no sign of struggle, or battle, no attempt to escape, no warning. The shiny object was a knife pierced in the center of Tomar's chest through his heart.

"Is anything missing?" Jan asked. He stood over the body, feeling the neck, trying to determine how long it had been since Tomar was killed. He saw a piece of paper clutched in Tomar's left hand.

"It's hard to tell, sir, his wallet is lying on the table with $R3000 folded and stuck in the side. It doesn't look like anything was taken. What's that piece of paper in his hand?" answered the young police officer.

Jan carefully pried open Tomar's hand to pull out the torn piece of paper. The young officer looked over Jan's shoulder as they both stared at the writing on the paper. The paper, partially torn down the center and to the left, was a square–shaped piece.

"What does it mean?" asked the second eager police officer.

"I don't know. It appears to be in one of the native languages. Go outside and round up several of the near–by black natives. I want one of them to tell me what these words mean."

The two young police officers went outside and did as he ordered. Jan was relieved that he was finally on to something. He had a deep–rooted feeling that Nigel and Tomar's deaths were related. Somehow, there was a connection between members of the Circle, the Mau Mau, and the murders.

He felt more confident that if he could prove the connection, his superiors would believe him and convince top officials that some sort of conspiracy was at work. He was also convinced that a Zulu murdered each victim. He was only disgusted with himself. It had taken him twelve years to figure out that the key to Nigel's death was a man working right under his nose. Now that man was dead.

"Sir, this is Tomar's neighbor, he's a peddler and he claims to be versed in several dialects," beamed the eager young police officer.

"Bring him over here," Jan ordered.

He gave the old peddler the crumpled and torn piece of paper. The words, "Qaphela, Kulu–nye, Ngadla," appeared, smeared lightly with Tomar's blood.

"Ngadla!" the peddler said, frightened. He dropped the piece of paper. The look of fear embedded in his eyes. "The – sign – of – death – to anyone who speaks," he stuttered. The old man stood there, petrified with fear."

"What in the hell is he mumbling?" Jan demanded.

"Speak in English," the young police officer shouted at the old man.

The old peddler stared at Jan. "The message says 'Beware. Greatness. I have eaten.'"

Jan shouted at the peddler. "I have eaten? Don't you lie to me, old man, or I'll lock you up for withholding information vital to a murder investigation."

"Qaphela – Beware. Kulu–nye – Greatness. Ngadla – I have eaten," whispered the peddler.

"Eaten what?" asked the young police officer.

The peddler walked towards Tomar's body, knelt down and touched Tomar's head. "There's an ancient tribal saying among the old natives that there once was a great Zulu warrior..."

Suddenly, the peddler fell forward on top of Tomar's body. A short spear lodged deeply into his back. Guns drawn, the two police officers ran toward the opened door. There was no one in sight. Even the group of natives, which had gathered outside the house, had disappeared.

The peddler was still breathing. Jan yanked the spear from his back and turned him over. "My God, why, why you? What did they want to kill an old peddler," cried Jan. He cradled the peddler in his arms.

"The... Circle." He gasped for air and grabbed Jan's shirt, pulling him closer. "They are the ones known as Beetle. The Circle will rule..." His head fell to the side and the final breath of air left his body lifeless.

It was a night filled with darkness. All the lights in all the houses were off but one. The two police officers were unable to see, crouched to their knees as each slowly crept around the sides of the house. Finding nothing, they returned to see Jan with the dead old man still resting in his arms.

"Nothing, sir. There is not a soul in sight. What's going on here? We haven't had two killings in the area in years," said the young police officer.

"I don't know, but I'm sure the hell going to find out. Someone is going out of his way to prevent me from learning the truth. Three killings, all done with a Zulu weapon and style. I wonder what the connection between Nigel and these killings is."

The next day at Police Headquarters Jan stopped at the water fountain. He felt nauseated, his stomach felt as though it was tied up in knots. With his right hand on the left side of the stomach, he took a deep breath before proceeding into the Commissioner's office.

"Sir, I believe there's a conspiracy to overthrow the government. The blacks have formed some sort of organization called the Circle and are plotting this very minute to organize themselves against us."

"Captain Linden, do you honestly believe that those people, considering their lack of intelligence, can skillfully organize in such a manner as to overthrow the South African government? For Pete's sakes Captain, we had to teach them how to used modern lavatories. The blacks were so intrigued; they stole the toilet paper to use as bandages for healing wounds."

"Sir, twelve years ago, a man named Nigel was going to testify against a Sotho chieftain called Gowon . .."

"Captain Linden, I'm very familiar with that case, and I am also aware of your obsession with identifying members of the so called Circle group..."

Jan interrupted. "But sir, I..."

"Let me finished!" shouted the Commissioner. "I've checked and found the Mau Mau society was heavily active in the Kenya area. The Kenyan government defeated and executed the key members. The blacks in Kenya are not as obedient and trained to respect the government as our South African blacks. The Kenyan government was too lenient with the blacks. Its lack of a strong ruling party and a hard hand led to the formation of that damn society."

"Sir, last night a black registered policeman called Tomar was killed when a couple of other officers and I had gone by his place to question him on Nigel's death."

"Captain Linden. Why after eight years did you decide to question this Tomar? How did you know he knew or had anything to do with your own private investigation. Especially since the government closed the case on Nigel's death? Two months later, the man responsible for the murder was executed. The woman that was also killed was the murderer's mate. She shunned him and he had lost face before the tribal members because Nigel was from another tribe."

Jan became agitated. "Sir, I did not then and I don't now, believe the man executed was responsible for Nigel's death. The police officers in the area were embarrassed that someone could get to and kill a key witness. They reacted to the first suspect available so that they could save face with the government."

"Captain, I must warn you, those accusations could get you in serious trouble. There is no basis or fact to substantiate those claims."

"Sir, Tomar had a piece of paper crumpled in his hand with several key words which could be clues."

The commissioner rubbed his forehead. "Clues, oh yeah, they are clues alright; but maybe clues to his death and not clues to some conspiracy."

"Sir, one of the officers found an old peddler and he was in the process of translating the words when someone threw a spear into his back."

"I beg to differ; I still don't see the connection. The old peddler could have been killed because whoever murdered Tomar thought he left something, or that piece of paper contained evidence linking him or them to Tomar's death. Which still does not lead me to believe the South African government has reason to re–open the investigation Nigel's death, much less Tomar's death. Two unrelated murders."

"Sir, I disagree. Let us not underestimate the black natives. This anti–apartheid thing has created unrest among the blacks, especially the young men. There is more uneasiness than I anticipated. Our government can not afford a well–organized conspiracy, should they ever unite."

"Unite! Unite! Captain Linden, have you lost your bloody mind? It will be a cold day in hell if the plurals ever unite or form any semblance of a unified force. Ha! The Sotho don't trust the Zulus, the Xhosa dislike the Tswana and the rest are off doing their tribal dances, customs or just doing enough to get by."

"Sir, all I need is a few men and an allowance to travel to..."

"Captain, you won't get any funds to pursue such an idiotic mission for your personal ideological purposes. Permission denied! I have work to do! If you keep the blackies in your district from gathering in groups of three and make sure any one working there has a pass, then there will be no conspiracy. The government has agreed on apartheid, and you, my dear Linden, must enforce it. Get the hell out of my sight! You're dismissed."

Jan's facial expression was obvious. He too was disgusted. The discussion had created an inflammatory situation. His high–strung temper always got him in trouble. "Commissioner! You don't understand the gravity of the situation! I have evidence..."

"Captain Linden, I said you were dismissed! Now get the hell out of my office!"

"Yes sir!" Jan turned and walked towards the door, he muttered, "You idiot."

"No wait one god–damn minute," shouted the commissioner. "What did you say?"

"Jan stopped, turned and gave the commissioner a meek look. "Nothing sir."

"Nothing, my bloody ass. You are suspended for three days. "Now go soak on that."

Two days later, Jan was cold. Still darkness engulfed him, the pain was severe, his stomach ached, and his mouth was dry. A dark oddly shaped figure came forward. A thin film of light provided a confusing illusion. The face staring at him was horrible. On the side of the bed was a cockroach the size of a rat. "What did I do to deserve this?" he thought, trying frantically to move his body from its path.

"Relax, honey, relax." The voice was soft and

reassuring, yet familiar. The figure's hand touched the side of his face. He tried to reach and grasp the hand, but could not move. His hands tied to the bed. He struggle to release himself, he tried to rise. The figure placed both hands on his shoulders with authority and gently lowered him back to the bed. "Jan, relax, please, you will break the stitches." The voice belonged to Andrea. "You, my conceited bastard, had a rough night."

He was surprised. "Andrea? Andrea?"

"Yes, I don't know why I'm here, but it's me."

"Where am I?" he asked.

"Johannesburg Central Hospital. You evidently had an appendicitis attack. It happened while you were driving. Somehow, you managed to avoid running into another vehicle and crash into an embankment. The duty sergeant called me. The guys at the station figured you needed someone to hold your hand for a few days."

"Honey, you can hold my hand anytime. What about your husband, he may have a few words to say about that?"

"Don't worry about my husband. After the nightmare you just had, coupled with the wreck and operation, you need some rest. The nurse gave you something for the pain." Andrea sat in a chair by the side of the bed. She untied his left hand and caressed it softly. Jan slipped back into a deep sleep.

PART TWO

THE TIME IS NEAR

CHAPTER TEN

A Loss So Precious

Friday, 5:45 p.m., December 18, 1960 – Washington D.C.

Helen took a sip of wine and looked first at her watch, then across the crowded bar. Three men had offered to buy her a drink, one made a direct pass, thinking she was a high–class hooker, and the other two just quietly walked away when she said her husband was due any minute.

Jonathan was late, exactly fifteen minutes late and counting. He was supposed to meet her at their favorite club, frequented by middle class blacks and very few military officers, just the way he wanted it to be.

The club was located in the heart of the city, a block north of Fourteen Street and Avenue U. Helen worked for the Smithsonian Institution, in the liberal arts section; her specialty was pre–1700 history. Helen normally car–pooled with two neighbors, but on Fridays, she would drop Jonathan off at the Pentagon. After work, around five, Jonathan would take the shuttle from work and the two met at the club. They both recapped their week to unwind and laughed at some funny situations encountered on the job. It was their time out away from Djhon and the pressures of work.

Today, however, did not seemed to be a good day to meet for drinks; sixteen inches of snow had blanketed the city three days ago. The streets in the downtown area had been cleared but some of the roads leading to the suburbs were still icy. Jonathan wanted to go straight home right after work, but Helen insisted on getting together, because it was a special day – it was her birthday.

The bartender tapped Helen on the shoulder and told her she had a phone call. He pointed at the end of the bar. Jonathan knew the bartender and had called the club.

Helen smiled. "Jon, where are you? If you don't hurry up and get over here, a good looking man may pick me up and carry me out the door.'

Jonathan laughed. "Yeah, sure. That smooth rascal had better be me."

"Then hurry up and get your fine self over here. I want my man and I want him now!"

"Baby, I'm sorry, but General Gage called a high level staff meeting. In fact, we're set to start in a few minutes."

"Damn Jon, why didn't you call? You had me sitting in this bar with high hopes and..."

"Helen, I couldn't get away. I have been in a briefing since we found out. Maybe it's for the best. The weather bureau is predicting a hard freeze tonight. Go home before it becomes too dangerous to drive. Drive slow and careful."

"Oh, all right, but you better makes it up to me when you come home."

"Honey, you know I will, Just keep it warm."

"Jon, warm will be an understatement. I am not going to pick up Djhon. He is spending the night with Craig. Besides, it's going to be so hot under the blankets; you are going to scream for relief. When I'm finished with you, you're going to come so hard, there will be nothing left for you to shoot."

"That's the way I like to hear it, baby, I won't disappoint you."

"How long will the meeting last?"

"I don't know, but the Colonel thinks it won't last more than a couple of hours."

"Do you want me to pick you up?"

"No! Not in this weather. I can bum a ride from Phil; he lives a few miles from us, near the Fillmore Shopping Center. Just go home and drive carefully."

Helen hung up, feeling strangely uneasy about Jonathan's repeated remarks about driving carefully. However, she was disappointed. She had planned something special for Jonathan.

Helen really looked forward to this particular night. She had a surprise for him. There was a God, The doctors were wrong. She had a rare blood type considered to be Rh–negative. Helen's Rhesus factor and the lack of certain antigens in her red blood cells caused an inability to donate blood but, most importantly and dear to her, caused her to have a miscarriage. The doctors told her that she would not have any children. At least that's what she thought and what everyone believed. She couldn't wait to get home. She did not know when to tell Jonathan, before or after they made love.

Helen quickly left the club and walked briskly back to the car. "Whew, it's cold." The sun had set. She searched in her purse for the car keys when something wet and mushy fell on face. "Darn, it's starting to snow."

Traffic seemed extremely light considering it was a Friday. The projected weather forecast caused many people to leave early from work. Helen was crossing the 14th Street Bridge when she noticed the car seemed to swerve to the left. The road had already begun to ice. She remembered Jonathan's repeated warnings and slowed down.

Helen quickly turned her head. The oncoming car's bright lights gave an optical illusion of countless illuminating miniature stars and they seemed to get closer and closer overshadowing her with their radiance. Suddenly there was a crashing roar followed by the direct hit of the steering wheel into her chest. Her head snapped backwards and then with a forward thrust, jettison through the windshield. Death was instant.

CHAPTER ELEVEN

Beauty Tames the Lion

Twenty months later – 1700 hours

Houston, Texas, a city with a reputation for being hot and humid. The cool air and brief rainstorm that suddenly besieged the city during the early morning hours had moved quickly to the north. The bayou city was viewed as a large metropolitan area, yet rural in some parts, with cattle breeding within the city's inner loop or beetle. One day it was cool, the next day it was hot. The metropolitan area and the residents have experienced 54 straight days without rain before the thunderstorm hit. A heat wave had blanketed the city with temperatures of 99, 102, 101, 104, 103, 105, 104, 107, for 8 straight days, setting another record for that time of year. Relief was near; the local weathermen had predicted a northern cold front was heading towards the city, unusual for the month of August.

A few miles south of the city, a black sedan stopped at the checkpoint before entering Ellington Air Force Base. The MP on duty promptly saluted after recognizing its occupant, Major Jonathan McClendon. At thirty–nine, Jonathan was a rising spit–and–polish officer with a promising career and friends in high places. He was proud of the circular patch of gray hair on the right side of his head, just above the ear. He sat upright, chest extended, a definite tribute to his military training. His plans included making General before he was fifty. He was now a highly ambitious fellow with a taste for war and vengeance. Jonathan had been lobbying hard for an assignment to Vietnam. He had a feeling that the time was ripe for Hanoi to launch an offensive attack on South Vietnam. The U.S. had no choice but to protect its ally and he wanted to be right there in the thick of battle to further his political and military goals. He was a proud and stubborn man with high ideals as his performance reviews so indicated. He often was cited for his military genius and his leadership flair. Jonathan was nursed by his mother through the first seven years of his life. He was a weak and sickly child who was kept alive only by the relentless care and devotion of his parents. By the age of nine years, he was a slim, fragile boy involved in fights with a bully intent on taking his money, lunch, and personal belongings. Jonathan grew up with the reputation of a fighter determine not to be pushed around.

As a father, he was also extremely proud of his son, Djhon, whom he raised in a strict and disciplinarian environment. His son tried very hard to please him; he also shared goals and high expectations of his own. At the age of twelve, Djhon had achieved every award that a Boy Scout can acquire. His goal was to become the youngest boy to achieve the rank of Eagle Scout.

The past year since Helen's death had been hard on both of them, but leaving Jonathan extremely bitter toward life. The closeness between Helen and Jonathan was more than one can describe. They shared the same thoughts, the same goals, and the same likes and dislikes.

Jonathan during the last two years had preached military concepts and strategy to Djhon, explaining in detail Napoleon's conquests, Custer's battles, and Hitler's victories. He took great care to explain to his son the reasons for Napoleon's battle losses and Custer's tactical mistakes at Little Big Horn and Hitler's military collapse.

Jonathan was on his way to join General Samuel Gage and his wife for dinner at a small family–run French restaurant, called La Tour D'Argent of Paris. He wanted to try to convince the general to use his influence in Washington to get him assigned to South Vietnam. He needed the General's assistance because his MOS, Military Occupational Specialty was Infantry. The U.S. was only assigning advisors to Vietnam with non–tactical specialties.

Military men typically spoke of certain officers that they would follow to hell and back. General Gage was just that sort of man, as far as Jonathan was concerned. He had first worked for the general when the two were assigned to Korea, and again at the General Officers' Branch at the Pentagon. Samuel Gage, then a colonel, was the branch Chief Administrative Officer when Jonathan was a captain. He had been looking forward to his first assignment to the Pentagon. Their duties at Branch required reviewing personnel files of the top officers in the Army and recommending to the DCSPER, Deputy Chief of Staff for Personnel commanding officer a list of officers meeting the requirements for fulfilling top positions.

The three–star general in charge of DCSPER required them to submit three names to the Chief of Staff. One name was submitted to the Secretary of the Army.

Jonathan and General Gage worked late at night together on many occasions trying to narrow the field to six names, which was a routine requirement of their boss. On numerous occasions, the list of qualified officers was long and the two did not always agree on the final selections. General Gage admired Jonathan for his outspokenness and spunk, and took a personal interest in his career development. Unknown to Jonathan, Gage's wife, Kate, had arranged for a special guest to join them for dinner; a blind date for Jonathan. Samuel felt that for Jonathan to make the colonel's list, required at minimum was the demonstration of a stable marriage. The General and Jonathan discussed remarriage, but Jonathan still carried a picture of Helen in his wallet. His life now revolved around his son and the Army. This was the only way Jonathan could control the sexual urges he experienced from time to time.

The ride to the restaurant from Ellington Air Force base was at least forty minutes, so Jonathan took the time to rehearse his justification to the General. As he was approaching the downtown exit, traffic was congested for at least a mile. Jonathan, somewhat familiar with Houston streets, exited onto Almeda, cut through the side streets, and entered the downtown area from Third Ward. He glanced into the rear view mirror and could not help from smiling as he saw a car following him on the "shortcut" through the city's streets. Jonathan pulled up in front of the restaurant, checked his watch to discover he was running fifteen minutes late. He opened the door before the valet parking attendant could reach for the handle, and slid out. The cool air of the evening had helped to clear his head, but he was still a little nervous about asking the General to pull a few strings on his behalf.

Jonathan reached inside his suit for a cigarette, lit it, drew a series of short puffs, and flipped it to the ground. He looked up. Out of the right corner of his eye, he noticed the same two–toned Chevy that had followed him, parked across the street next to a fire hydrant. An oddly–shaped figure dressed in a dashiki stood in the shadows created by the setting sun.

"That's strange," Jonathan thought to himself as he walked into the restaurant. For a brief moment, his thoughts flashed back to Washington D.C. over ten years ago. He stopped and turned around. "Naw, no way," he muttered.

He walked into the restaurant and looked past the maître d' towards the woman seated with General Gage and Kate. Jonathan saw several men with smiling faces staring at the woman. He quickly agreed with their assessment, just to see her had a startling effect.

Her long, black hair cascaded down over the front of her white satin dress. He admired how the dress was cut with the slit midway to her thigh. Sitting down, she appeared to be a tall woman with a diamond choker around her neck. The smile on her face coupled with the dark eyes completed the look of a devilishly beautiful woman.

The maître d' interrupted his thoughts. "Sir table for how many?"

"I see my party," Jonathan answered, never once taking his eyes off the beauty in his sights.

"Hello, General Gage. It's nice to see you again." Jonathan picked up Kate's hand and softly acknowledged her. "Ma'am," he said, trying not to stare at the woman whose eyes and smile were just about to leave him speechless.

"Come on, my boy, drop the General bit. Jonathan, since you have been staring at her from the moment you walked into this place, we would like you to meet the daughter of a good friend of Kate's. Jonathan McClendon, meet Phyllis Johnson."

"My pleasure," Jonathan responded. He grabbed her hand, softly without letting go.

"I've heard an awful lot about you. Kate and my mother speak very highly of you," said Phyllis. "You look exactly as I've imagined."

Jonathan smiled. "I'm afraid you have me at a disadvantage. It seems you know more about me than I do about you."

Phyllis chuckled. "As soon as you release my hand and by the time the evening meal is over, your military prowess will enable you to obtain enough information to put you more at ease."

The General and Kate laughed. Jonathan smiled and sat down.

They all chatted about everything from when Phyllis was a child to Jonathan's school days to current events to wine tasting and the General's latest assignment.

All during the meal, Jonathan and Phyllis were in and out of the conversation without really participating. They had their own private discussions going on with their eyes and minds.

Kate suddenly looked at her watch. "Honey, it's almost 2230 hours. Let's not forget about the prior engagements you have early in the morning, especially since we have to drive across town to drop Phyllis off at home."

This was Jonathan's cue to offer his assistance. "Samuel, Kate, I want to thank you both for inviting me to dinner and of course for bringing Phyllis along. I would be honored to escort her home."

"I've been trying to arrange this meeting for the last four months, but Phyllis was off to South Africa on one of her hunger crusades and when she was in town, you were always working on some key military project," responded Kate.

"South Africa?" queried Jonathan.

"Now, now, I thought we'd agreed not to mix business with pleasure. I haven't had such an enjoyable evening with close friends in quite some time," interrupted the General as he lit one of favorite cigars.

"You're quite right, of course. However, sir, I would like to discuss something of a personal nature with you tomorrow at your office."

"I have an idea of what you have in mind; I'm not quite sure I agree. Tomorrow around 1300 hours will do," said the General, looking at a somewhat surprised Jonathan.

General Gage's sedan was the first to be brought up by the parking attendant. Jonathan and Phyllis waved good–bye and shared a sigh of release that they were now alone.

"I know of a nice quiet cozy place on the other side of town where we can order a nice bottle of wine," suggested Jonathan.

"My time is precious, and I must savor every minute that is afforded me when I'm not involved in my work." Phyllis smiled as she once again stared at Jonathan with her light brown eyes. She knew her eyes were the best weapon she had against such a formidable opponent. "I have a vintage bottle of wine at my apartment."

The ride to the apartment seemed short, although it was really twenty minutes from the restaurant. Jonathan did not care, for his mind was totally on Phyllis. He almost forgot that his son was expecting him home before midnight. Jonathan called and arranged for a very good wartime buddy, living next door, to go over and spend the night with Djhon.

The inside of Phyllis's apartment was decorated in deep, earth tone colors with various souvenirs, painting, and relics from her travels to South Africa. She excused herself and returned a few minutes later dressed in a violet kaftan with a slit on both sides. She carried two glasses of white wine.

"Mm, this is very good. What is it?"

"T.J. 39." Phyllis smiled.

"T.J. 39?" asked Jonathan.

"Twee Jongegezellen, 1939."

"Spell it, please."

They laughed and she sat down on the sofa with Jonathan.

"T–w–e–e Jon–ge–ge–zel–len."

"Where is it bottled?" Asked Jonathan.

"South Africa. It means 'Two Young Friends,'" responded Phyllis as she leaned over to top off his wine glass.

Jonathan could not help but admire how low the kaftan was cut in the front. Phyllis set the wine bottle down on the coffee table and stared at Jonathan. Her seductive eyes made Jonathan a little uncomfortable. She sipped the wine and rimmed the top of the wine glass with the tip of her tongue. He could not resist the temptation of her rosy lips.

Jonathan coughed. "And, er, you can purchase the wine here in Houston?"

"No."

"I see." Jonathan tried hard not to stare at her body. "You brought back several bottles on the trip back from South Africa?"

"No." Phyllis smiled and continued to stare at Jonathan.

Jonathan loosens the top collar button of his shirt. "Oh, I understand, you purchased the wine in another city?"

"May I call you Jon?"

Jonathan was no longer smiling. Looking down, he realized that only one other person ever addressed him by that name. He slid back and looked to his left.

"Jonathan, are you all right?" He did not say a word. "I said, are you all right? What's the matter?"

He nodded. "No--I mean yes." Jonathan quickly responded. "Yes, by all means, you can call me Jon." He looked at her with a radiant smile.

"Relax, I won't bite. You can lower those shields Major McClendon." Phyllis leaned her head towards Jonathan. Before she knew it, his arms were around her, drawing her to him, and he was kissing her hard, very hard.

"Whoa! I did not order the reinforcements. I only want the man leading the charge." Phyllis separated herself and stood up.

"I'm sorry. I--I don't know what came over me."

"Ssh, don't say anything. You talk too much. I'll be right back." Phyllis walked over to the lamp, dimmed the light, and slowly returned to the sofa.

He reached for her hand, inviting her to the sofa. Phyllis pulled back hesitantly in a teasing manner, all the time still smiling. His hands around her waist, he was surprised to find her very soft buttocks.

She shivered as Jonathan's hands slid from her buttock and explored between her legs.

She gave a small laugh. "What do you think you're doing? I'm not an easy lay."

"I'm pretending to be a forest ranger, clearing out the thick bushes, so the small tree can have room to flourish."

Phyllis sat down on the sofa, looked at Jonathan and firmly asked, "Do you have a considerate amount of experience clearing bushes?"

"A little, not very much," he answered. Their lips met, her mouth was full and soft beneath his. Their tongues met each other, each searching to be dominant over the other, and neither giving ground.

"What about you, have your bushes been recently cleared?"

Phyllis pushed him back and snapped. "When was the last time, you cleaned someone's bush?"

"Must we fight? It's been almost twenty months ago," Jonathan whispered.

Phyllis smiled and leaned back into the depths of the cushions. "Then, it'd been fifteen months and one day since my bush was cleared."

Jonathan also smiled and his mouth came down on hers with a kind of furious passion. Soon he had slipped the kaftan down from her shoulders as he kissed his way down to her breasts.

"Your mouth is hot," she murmured, "suck hard, baby."

Jonathan obeyed her command, sucking both nipples until Phyllis let out a loud cry. Jonathan boasted a smile for his accomplishment.

"My turn," she said. Before he knew what was happening, Phyllis ripped open his shirt and sucked his nipples hard. Jonathan cried out when she bite him.

Phyllis pushed him upward. Jonathan obliged and reached for his belt buckle. "Leave your pants on honey. I am not as easy as you think. You may have cleared many bushes, but this is one bush you will not clear tonight. I don't believe in one–night stands. I want to get to know you better, before we jump into bed." She rose and walked to the chair.

Jonathan, dumbfounded, caught his breath, and then grinned. "You, Phyllis Johnson, are a formidable opponent."

She smiled. "Only when I choose to be."

"How about breakfast tomorrow?" he asked.

"Major McClendon, I would be delighted to have breakfast with you," said Phyllis. "Here's your coat and hat. Time to go, its 11:45pm."

"Fine, let's makes it at 0800 hours. I will pick you up.

"No, 0830," responded Phyllis.

Jonathan saluted her. "Yes, ma'am, your order will be obeyed."

CHAPTER TWELVE

Beware! Not All That Glitters is Gold

Houston, Hobby Airport – 1200 hours.

It was nearly midnight when without warning, it turned cold. A strong bitter wind whispered through the mobile home park, rattling the patio enclosures, then rose sharply and suddenly ripped limbs and branches from the small trees near the runway.

A DC–7 airplane reduced its air speed to prepare for landing when a loud rumbling noise, accompanied by a lightning discharge, scared the small child sitting in his mother's lap; his arms wrapped tightly around her neck. The woman's eyes could not hide her fright; her voice quaked when she tried to comfort the boy. The plane sudden drop in altitude caused several passengers to use air bags to ease the queasy sickness thrust upon them. Trans world Flight 102 battled the wind shears during the last twenty minutes of its journey. The jolt of the wheels finally touching the runway was heaven to the shaken passengers, including the crew. When the aircraft taxied to gate 18, they wasted no time disembarking the plane.

Far behind the other passengers, an old man with a large forehead and deep–set, dark brown eyes walked stiffly down the empty warm concourses of Hobby airport. An uncomfortable amount of relative humidity caused the old man to clear his sinuses with a tainted cloth. The air conditioners were not working and the unventilated air inside the airport contrasted with the temperature outside.

A tall immigration officer stood next to entrance for foreign visitors. A large white sign with red letters that read 'Customs and Immigration' hung over another officer seated in a booth. The tall officer watched the old man walk slowly towards him. He noticed the old man's weary eyes.

"Purpose of the visit?" asked the officer seated in the booth. The tall officer stared at his new arrival and focused on the old man's facial expressions.

"Vacation," the old man replied as he looked up at the ceiling. He admired the pre–Renaissance sculptures suspended in mid–air.

"Your passport states that you are a South African native. However, your paper indicates your previous destination was Leningrad, Russia. What was the purpose of your visit there?" demanded the officer in the booth.

The old man flicked the officer a rueful smile. "Vacation, a well–deserved vacation." His speaking voice was English, with a southern accent; his diction trained and precise.

The immigration officer looked at his counterpart. The tall officer motioned to his superior seated in a glass office, drinking a cup of coffee, and reading the newspaper.

The superior, a large man weighing at almost three hundred pounds, put on his hat and walked towards the opened door; he paused and stared at the old man. He could not help but notice that the old man seemed familiar. He walked towards the old man, stopped and sniffed several times. He approached the old man and smelled a peculiar odor coming from the his clothes. The supervisor extended his hand.

"Passport." He looked through the passport and noticed frequent visits to and from the U.S. and Russia. "Step aside, Mr. Williams, and follow this officer to the waiting area?"

A Negro janitor pulled his mop back to allow the old man and immigration officer to pass. The old man grinned and winked at the janitor. The janitor smiled and whispered in a low–keyed voice, "Umbiki," when the two turned and left into the glassed enclosure.

Inside the glass enclosure, the two immigration officers studied the old man's passport and papers. "What do you think, Sir?" asked the tall immigration officer.

The Supervisor shrugged his heavy shoulders. "I don't know, his papers seem to be in order. His baggage. What about his baggage?"

"Nothing but some smelly clothes and some old strings of beads."

"Something funny about the old man, and I can't put my finger on it." The Supervising officer removed his hat, blew on the attached silver insignia, and rubbed it with his elbow. He whispered to the tall officer. "Let him sweat for a while. Let's finished processing the other passengers." The two men left the room and walked over to a third officer.

Two hours later.

"Who is he, really?" asked the officer seated in the booth. I don't buy the vacation bit, especially for a Negro. What was he's doing in Russia?"

"I don't know," answered the Supervisor. "Take his luggage into the other room and search it once again, thoroughly."

The old man sat on the hard wooden bench. He closed his eyes and leaned his head back against the wall. His mind wandered, recalling the story his father told him of 'The Lifaquane.' His father's voice seemed as vivid as yesterday...

'My son, during the time Shaka was building his empire, destructive wars took place in the interior plateau of South Africa in our homeland of Lesotho. These wars overwhelmed the clans in the Caledon River Valley, and groups of hungry invaders from the northeast appeared on the scene to raid and destroy. It was the time of the 'Lifaquane' called the 'hammering' by the wandering hordes. The invasions began when 'Ma–Nthatisi, a chieftainess of the Botlokoa, they were the people of the wild cat and the one–eyed female warrior. She led her people to raid the peaceful and prosperous Sotho clans. They devoured our crops and practically destroyed our people. The Sotho clans were broken; thousands of our clans disappeared forever.'

'Moshoeshoe, know also as The Shaver, built a new nation from the remnants of the old and new inhabitants, drank his joala and boasted loudly after each drink.'"

The old man reminisced how his father, originally named Lepoqo, was also nicknamed Moshoeshoe, told him how he stole his first cattle as a young man on his first warrior exploit against a neighboring chief, Ramonaheng. He justified the name by saying he had shaved off Ramonaheng's beard. The name, Moshoeshoe, represented the sound of shaving.

The old man was startled from his dream when the supervisor shouted, "On your feet, Williams! Williams! That is an odd name for a native from South Africa. Especially, someone with your deep Negroid color. What's your real name?"

"Williams," replied the old man.

"I mean your natural name."

"Leopold Williams! As indicated on my visa, passport and other documents you and your comrade have so carefully examined." His facial expression and the tone of his voice indicated that the old man was growing weary of the questions.

"All right Mr. Williams, what's the extent of your visit in Houston and don't you dare say vacation."

The old man smiled, looked at the superior and noticed a silver bar on each shoulder. "Vacation, my dear sir, vacation!"

The Supervisor threw the passport at the old man; it landed a few inches from his face. "Vacationing where, you black son of a bitch! And, what was the reason behind your visit to Russia?"

Silence filled the room. The immigration officers stared at the old man. The old man smiled once more, exposing his white teeth. "I always wanted to see Leningrad; I'm an avid reader and admirer of Russian literature and paintings, particularly of Marc Chagall. His painting 'The Father,' on display at the Russian State Museum in Leningrad was marvelous! 'The Mirror,' is a priceless work of art, and 'The Promenade' is a blend of realism and fantasy."

The two immigration officers stared in disbelief. The old man marveled on. "Your Museum of Fine Arts here in Houston has on display the paintings by Chagall during his stay in your country from 1941 to 1946, from his private collection left to his wife. They have never been shown anywhere outside of the United States."

The supervisor handed him the papers.

"Sir, your courtesy will be remembered," said the old man. He walked towards the glass door.

"Get your things and get the hell out of here!" shouted the Supervisor.

The old man picked up his bag and walked down the long corridor. He passed the janitor leaning against his mop handle. The janitor winked as the old man passed.

CHAPTER THIRTEEN

The Secret to the Riddle

0830 hours

When Jonathan arrived the next morning, Phyllis was standing outside the apartment steps. Her hair rolled in a large bun and she was wearing a blue blouse and a checkerbloom wrap around skirt.

"Right on time. I had you pegged," said Phyllis.

"I'm sorry, what did you say?" Jonathan asked as he got out to open the car door.

"Oh nothing," smiled Phyllis.

Breakfast with Phyllis was more than Jonathan bargained for. She questioned his childhood, his decision to attend George Washington University, why he joined the Army and how and where he had met his wife. Jonathan liked her personality and directness. The two talked for several hours. Jonathan decided to show Phyllis the sites of Houston. They toured NASA and Busch Gardens. Later in the day after leaving the museum, Jonathan and Phyllis locked arms and walked to where the car was parked.

"Some local merchant must either be opening up a new shop or have a sales special going on," said Jonathan. He reached to lift what at first appeared to be a sales flier. The paper was folded once, with his name and military rank addressed on it.

"Who would be leaving a note addressed to you on your car?"

Jonathan shook his head slowly. "I don't know... I can't make it out. It seems to be written in another language."

Phyllis grabs the note. "Let me see it. That is odd; this note seems to be written in Swahili. No, not Swahili, the vowels are slightly different. It's either Xhosa or Zulu."

Jonathan's brow arched with surprise. "Zulu. You've got to be kidding."

Phyllis nodded. "These words don't make any sense." She tried to read aloud the note."*Qaphela! Khulu −nye dlula isehlo... ncane umfana woza, sina emacaleni onke wag'−n−bietjie umuthi. Ngokuba guga indoda kanti ubuthakathaka into umqondo sukuma pha amandla ethula isishiyagalombili ufakazi memeza Ngadla!*"

"You were in South Africa, not me! Maybe it's intended for you."

"No, this is definitely for you."

"Who, besides Kate and the General even knows you were here?"

"No one," answered Jonathan."

"Someone sure the hell does! Wait a minute, you and the General worked together at the Pentagon? Are you involved in the C.I.A.?"

"C.I.A., don't be ridiculous," protested Jonathan. "Let me see that damn note again. It's madness, this doesn't tell me anything."

"Then, why in the hell are you so upset?"

"I'm all right. Do you have any idea what it says?"

"No, but I recognized some of the vowels."

"Hell! Give me the darn note. Let's go."

They got into the car and headed north. The inside of the car was silent. The foreskin at Jonathan's temple was wrinkled as though he was in deep thought.

"Jon, please talk to me."

"What?"

"I said, please talk to me. What's the matter? You haven't said a single word to me in the past five minutes."

Jonathan turned the car into a small shopping center directly in front of an Italian place. "Let's have lunch," he said. He got out of the car and left Phyllis sitting there. He walked thirty feet before he realized that she was not by his side. He turned and saw Phyllis; she fixed him with a piercing glance. Jonathan walked back to the car and offered a sheepish apology.

The two walked to the restaurant and neither spoke a word. Once seated, Phyllis ordered a fettuccine and scallops dish and Jonathan ordered his all−time favorite, spaghetti with meat sauce and meatballs. Jonathan ate quickly. Phyllis meekly played with the scallops, twirling the fettuccine around the fork; seldom taking a bite.

Jonathan finally broke the silence. He looked at her curiously. "Do you think the central library will have the books?"

Phyllis smiled. "I don't see why not. A city as large as Houston with three or four universities and colleges, must surely have someone who has done a research paper or something worthwhile on the languages of South Africa. Besides, we could call some language translation specialist and pay for his services if it's really that important to you."

Jonathan gently held her hand. "It's important; however, I must ask for your confidence, and we cannot get anyone else involved," he insisted.

"Jon, you have had my confidence ever since I noticed how much this meant to you."

Jonathan lit a cigarette and inhaled a large amount of smoke, turned his head and exhaled to the side. "After we translate the note and depending on what it says, then I'll tell why I'm so concerned. It may be nothing, just a coincidence."

Phyllis was silent for a moment studying Jonathan. "What's the coincidence?" she asked. "Trouble?"

"Yes." Jonathan lowered his voice. "Something from the past."

"Does it have anything to do with South Africa?"

"I don't know," Jonathan replied somberly. "They were of African descent."

"They?" queried Phyllis.

"Nyerere and Rhosida."

"Who?" Phyllis again asked, puzzled.

"Let's translate the message to determine if it's not just my imagination."

"Were you ever in South Africa?"

"No!" answered Jonathan forcefully.

"All right, all right. Let's go to the main library and decipher the darn message," snapped Phyllis. The walk back to the car was a silent one. Phyllis could see something was troubling Jonathan. She had decided Jonathan was worth getting to know and she was not going to pressure him at this point. She wanted to go with the flow and see where Jonathan would take her; after all, she would be gone in four days, and the first day with him certainly was not dull.

They got into the car and headed downtown. Phyllis stared at Jonathan. Neither said a word.

"Jon, please talk to me."

"What?" His mind was elsewhere.

"I said, please talk to me. What's the matter? You haven't said a single word to me in the past five minutes."

Jonathan took a deep breath. He cracked the window and lit another cigarette. "Wait until we get to the library."

Phyllis sighed. The longer he drove, the harder it was to keep her attention from wandering. The man she met less than twenty–four hours ago had too many secrets.

"Excuse me, where's the social science department?" asked Phyllis.

"Around the corner to the left," replied the library clerk.

"You look under South Africa for..." began Phyllis.

"South Africa?" queried Jonathan, "Why South Africa?"

"Because, you dummy, Swahili is the language of the Bantu–speaking people over much of East Africa. We already ruled that out. Xhosa and Zulu are the languages of most of South Africa."

"What do I look for?"

"What do they teach you Army fellows? Books on Zulu – English or Xhosa – English translation." Phyllis started thumbing through the card index file marked "XYZ" looking for Xhosa–English translations.

"'*The Rise and Fall of the Xhosa People,*' *Xhosa Culture and Life Style,*' '*Xhosa Music,*' '*Xhosa Women.*' Darn, everything but Xhosa – English translation," she whispered. "Hopefully there's something under Zulu," Phyllis was again mumbling to herself. "'*Zulu Boyhood,*' '*Zulu Men,*' '*Zulu Music,*' '*Zulu War,*' '*Shaka's Army,*' '*The Rise and*

Fall of Shaka.' Nothing!" Phyllis whispered, somewhat rejected.

Phyllis looked across at Jonathan; they were separated by four or five people. She hoped his luck was better than hers was. She decided to go over to him and offer her assistance.

"Any luck, Jon?"

"Do you know how much is listed under South Africa? We're not going to find anything here."

"Did you look for official languages?"

"Yes!" snapped Jonathan. His response drew stares from the people around them.

CHAPTER FOURTEEN

Heed the Words

The same morning – 0915 hours

A heavy raindrop fell on the old man's face. He tilted his head back and looked up over the tall pine trees scattered throughout Memorial Park, and noticed the dark clouds. It came in a sudden outburst, ricocheting on the sidewalk. People around him were scampering for cover. The old man stood still, mesmerized at the shower of raindrops falling onto his wrinkled forehead. He was smiling; the rain reminded him of his tribal homeland. He was coatless and soaked but did not seem to mind. He was known in America, Russia, Britain, Israel, and other parts of the world as Leopold Williams. In South Africa, he was also known as Lamizana, 'Umbiki,' the messenger.

He stared at two young boys hovering together under a covered picnic table. He had kept them under his observation since an Army sergeant dropped off his son and Djhon at the park to pursue a Boy Scout project of studying natural elements. The rain showers were violent and brief. After the rain stopped the two boys, giggling at each other's attempts to stay dry, proceeded with their project.

The sergeant's boy was the first to see it. He stopped and stared at the object. "Somebody lost a medallion," he said.

The old man stood, at least twenty yards away. Djhon playfully pushed his friend. "Aw, come on, nobody lost the medallion. See, it had been carefully placed, not dropped, and it's resting upright against a tree. Obviously, someone had placed it there. Perhaps a jogger; the park is a common exercise grounds for local residents." He reached down to pick up the medallion. They admired its artistic workmanship when the old man suddenly stood before them.

"The owner of such a fine medallion would probably be disturbed when he returned and it was missing." He startled the two boys.

"We, er... we sir, were just admiring it," stammered Djhon.

"Things of beauty are to be cherished and not parted with. You, young man, must be Djhon McClendon?" The old man smiled and rubbed the other boy's head.

"Yes sir, but how did you know my name?"

"I know many things about you, my son. I have known you since you were born. I have come from a very far place to make sure that you are prospering as we intended."

"Sir," said Djhon, "then, you must also have known my mother before she died? And also my dad."

"Yes, I know of your dad, and I am a great admirer of your father."

"What about my Mom? I don't recall either of them speaking of you. By the way, sir, what's your name?"

"I'm known as Leopold Williams. Your mother was an understanding and strong–willed woman. Your Mom was a good wife to your dad. I understand you want to be the youngest person to achieve the rank of Eagle Scout. How many ranks do you have left to go?"

"Three," said Djhon proudly," First Class Rank, Star Rank, and the Life Rank. It was easy; a piece of cake."

The sergeant's boy agreed. "Yeah, he breezed right thought it. He slaughtered the rest of the boys going for the same thing. He achieved it faster the anyone in the state's history."

"When you go after the Life Service Rank, don't take it lightly. It will play a major part in your life when you are an adult."

"I don't understand," said Djhon.

"When I was twelve, your age to be exact, I started to work in the coal mines of South Africa. I worked in the summer months and went to school in the winter months. During certain periods, when times are really rough for my parents, I also worked during school months..."

Djhon interrupted the old man. "But my Dad makes plenty of money. I don't have to go to work after school."

"Son, money is not so clearly and uniquely the culprit when it comes to the real problems of our times. One day you will ask the question, does money buy happiness?"

Djhon looked more confused. "What do you mean?"

"You will, when the time is right. I must move on, there are many places I have to visit."

The old man reached out, tousled Djhon's hair, and shook the boy's hand.

"Djhon, it's time for me to depart. Look for me in the future."

"The future," said Djhon. "Well, whatever."

"Mayibuye Africa!" The old man left the two boys scratching their heads. He had six more visits to make before he could return to his home. He fingered the fragment of the stone, which hung on a thin piece of string around his neck. The edges appeared jagged, yet smoothed, polished, and fitted precisely into a puzzle.

The stone had certain mystic properties. It was irregular and yet constructed perfectly. To the eye, to the touch, anyone could see its craftiness: A series of miniature–smoothed planes met and turned in tiny angles to form a strange but beautiful tool of some kind. Williams' face was just as puzzling as the stone. It was impossible to guess his age or background. The face was unlined, the hair still dark, the eyes glowed with an intensity that was his own personal magic.

There was nothing else memorable about the old man until he spoke; he could pass for a well–seasoned waiter or an old shoe–shine man, or even someone's grandfather. He often dressed in nondescript khaki pants and a faded blue work shirt. The old man appeared to be sixty or seventy years old. He wore a dashiki covered with allegorical pictures and emblems of his homeland.

The old man was a master of many languages and understood many cultures, but as to where he had acquired the knowledge, no one knew. It seemed likely that he spent time in foreign lands as a soldier, and learned the lands as he learned the languages. His seemingly aimless wanderings across the world belied a specific purpose, which he followed throughout the years.

The old man labeled a suspicious character years ago by C.I.A., when the bashing of communism was commonplace. Even J. Edgar Hoover's FBI boys eventually accepted the man as a traveler who would never be caught breaking the law or customs of the places he visited.

CHAPTER FIFTEEN

He Too Has a Secret

Washington, D. C. – 1100 hours

Dr. Riley put on the tan overcoat and gray scarf. He reached down to pick up the gray hat, which had fallen onto the closet floor, next to his tie rack. He was in a hurry. He had earlier arranged for special passes to the Senate chambers, the White House and the FBI building. He was on his way to pick up his wife, Carol, and son, Michael, at the library.

Dr. Riley was invited to other speaking engagements, but this time before newly elected members of Congress. He promised Carol and Michael he would get the tickets.

They had parked the car at a parking lot on 14th and E Streets and decided to walk to the Capitol.

"Dad, I hope it doesn't rain," said Michael, adjusting his glasses.

"Yes, I do too," replied Riley. "I don't like the look of those clouds."

The guide showed the tourists one room after another and filled them with various tidbits of history surrounding the Capitol. The family, especially Michael, was most interested in the Senate Chambers. Michael had received permission to miss a couple of days of school so that he could spend a short vacation with his dad. The teacher gave him a project of reporting to the class on a live Senate hearing or filibuster, if one was in progress.

Dr. Riley had become a world–renowned authority, and traveled quite extensively giving lectures. He served as a director on several corporate boards. His expertise on the economy was considered a valuable asset to many corporate chiefs.

"Dad, let's go. The Senate is about to discuss allocating more funds to the South Vietnamese."

"Relax Michael, there is plenty of time," responded Carol, fondly scratching Michael on his thick head of hair.

"Your mother's right, Michael. The Senate has several key issues to resolve and is scheduled to be in session until 6:00 p.m., besides, there's plenty of time."

"Aw Dad, this tour is boring, I want to see the real thing. I want to see the senators in a heated dispute."

"Michael, this is the real thing, this is where it really started," said Carol. "This is where the government began, how history became part of what we know it to be."

"But Mom, Dad's book on the economics of scale and society reactions, says that there are too many fish in the pond and that it takes a few strong people to control and direct the events of time."

"Bill! Our son is too darn mature for his age."

"Honey," Bill laughed, "Michael is a very intelligent boy."

"Yes, I know, but I want him to be a boy first, and enjoy the fruits of childhood."

"Dad, there are some people talking about a heated debate going on in the Senate. Let's go!"

After walking up and around the spiral stairs leading to the Senate chambers, they finally reached a checkpoint to turn in cameras. Carol had her purse inspected.

The Senator from Idaho was arguing with the Senator from California on proposed farming budget cuts from the pending budget bill.

"Mom, this is really neat. I bet you the Senator from Idaho wins the votes necessary to stop the farming proposals from being cut from the new budget."

"I think you may be right son, there's a lot of sympathy for the Senator from Idaho's side. This has been a bad year for farmers."

They listened to the senators argued and debate the issues. Riley decided that he had enough and wanted to head back to the car. Michael stopped to take a picture of the Capitol. When he pulled the camera out of the bag, he noticed an envelope.

"Dad, did you put an envelope in my camera bag?"

"What envelope, son?"

"It's an envelope with your name on it."

"Let me see it."

Riley stared at the envelope and opened it.

"What is it, dear?" asked Carol.

"It doesn't make sense; it seems to be in a foreign language."

Carol, herself, was curious. "Well, what does it say?"

"I can't. It appears to be written in cipher or some foreign language of African origin.

Carol looked at the note with Bill. They were each at odds to decipher its meaning.

"Bill, what does it mean?"

"Relax Carol. I have several colleagues versed in foreign languages. I will get one of them to translate the note. Get in the car and wait for me. I'm going back to where we checked in the cameras to see if the clerk has any idea who may have put the note in the camera bag."

"Bill, there's something you're not telling me. If there's nothing to the note, then why are you going to walk six blocks back to the Capitol just to find out who put that the note in the camera bag?"

"You're right, honey, I'm making too much out of this; it's probably nothing. I'll have it translated in the morning."

CHAPTER SIXTEEN

Your Secret is Safe

Back at the library – 1600 hours

Jonathan and Phyllis were having very little luck finding either an English–Zulu or Xhosa–English dictionary in the reference section of the main library. There was nothing listed either in the reference or foreign language sections for Xhosa–English and English – Xhosa. Phyllis decided to play a hunch and looked at the regular books with same numbered section as the referenced books.

"I found it! Damn it!" she exclaimed.

"Phyllis, what's the matter?"

"There's an English – Zulu dictionary, but no Zulu – English translation. This will not help us."

"It's a small book. Let's see if anything explains the language. Maybe from the description we can get close enough to decipher the message," said Jonathan.

"Okay, it's a start. Let's find a table to work at."

"You go ahead. I have another idea. I'm going to find the oldest library clerk and seek her assistance on other possible avenues."

Jonathan and Phyllis each went in separate directions. Phyllis found a table and settled down to read the contents and preface to the dictionary. She was having some difficulty in understanding the Zulu vowels and the relationship to the English language.

Meanwhile, Jonathan was successful in finding an elderly library clerk in the social sciences department. She pointed him to the travel and entertainment section under foreign countries. Together, they found an old, worn and damaged English – Zulu, and Zulu – English lexicon, all in one book.

"Phyllis, ask and you shall receive," said Jonathan. He held up the book so that the title was in plain view.

"Where did you find it?" Phyllis asked in an astonished, low whisper.

"The only true authentic authority is a library. The elder statesman, however, in this case, is a political leader. Where's the note?"

"Right here. What's the first word?" asked Phyllis.

"Look under q–a–p–h–e–l–a."

"Q–a–p, here it's, 'watch out for.'"

"Watch out for, for what?" asked Jonathan.

"I don't know! What's the next word?"

" K–h–u–l–u."

"Damn, there's one, two, three, no four different translations. One is an adjective meaning great, big, large or important. The other three are nouns meaning hundred, nobleman, or person of rank, and the last one is size or greatness."

"Watch out for; great or large; hundred, nobleman, or person of rank," said Jonathan. He tried to reason the interpretations.

Phyllis whispered the words, "Watch out for, great, large, hundred, nobleman, some, different, bladder. Bladder! No, not bladder. Let us throw out that meaning. What was the last translation?"

One hour had elapsed before the words began to make sense. "I agree. What's the next word?" asked Jonathan.

"Wag'–n–bietjie."

"Spell it again, please."

"W–a–g hyphen n hyphen b–i–e–tjie," said Phyllis.

"No such word, add it to the list."

"I hope we don't come across too many more words with no apparent English translations. Try u–m–u–t–h–i."

"It says umu is a prefix, let me look up t–h–i. Jon, there must be seven t–h–i's, all with different meanings. Try defect; act nearly; poison. Ah ha! Thi, u–m–u–thi, means a tree."

"Then Wag–in–biet must be some kind of tree."

"The next word is I–n–d–o–d–a."

"Man, adult man. Is the message making any sense now?"

"Let's see what we have translated so far. Watch out for, a great nobleman or person of rank, oneness or unity, which will either pass or die, small boy, grinning, dancing, or celebrating something, all, whole or quantity, wag—in—biet tree, because, ill, sick, man."

"Jon, this doesn't make any sense at all. So far, we have a very important person or someone of noble status, who will die because he is a sick man, and the boy is dancing or celebrating near some darn what—you—call—it tree."

"You're right, honey, I know it doesn't make any sense, but I still would like to try to translate this message for its true meaning."

"What do you mean its true meaning? What is it you are not telling me? Why are we in this stupid library translating a piece of paper with a note written in Zulu of all things? And who the hell are Nyerere and Rhosida?"

"It's Nyerere and Rhosida. They are the parents of my adopted son, Djhon."

Phyllis was dumbfounded. "Djhon, your son, is adopted?"

"Yes, I don't know why I'm telling you all this. No one else knows, not even the Army, friends, the General, and my parents died when I was in my teens. It all happened when Helen and I was trying to have a child. It was also the low point of my career as a young officer. I was stationed in Zaire, working for the U.S. Embassy. Helen always wanted to go to Capetown and Johannesburg so that when we returned to the States, she could tell her family and friends all about South Africa. I also wanted to go, but after the baby was born. Anyway, by some streak of luck, my name was chosen to deliver a package to the British ambassador in Johannesburg. Since it was in the middle of the week, I took the extra days off and ended up with five free days before I was due back. Helen was overjoyed and we scrounged up our extra pennies and flew to South Africa in a military cargo plane.

"Wait a minute," said Phyllis. She pointed her finger at Jonathan. "You're telling me that you flew all the way from Egypt to South Africa, in the back of a cold military cargo plane, with a wife six months pregnant."

"Yes. Helen appeared to take the trip well. After delivering the package, we began enjoying our short vacation. Johannesburg was not what I imagined. I had heard how advanced South Africa was, but I thought that a country with eighty–five percent blacks consisting mostly of natives, and I mean backward black tribes; well, we expected to see our history, our ancestors' country. We did not expect tall buildings, trolley cars, and modernization. Helen was a history major and her specialty was the pre–1700's era. She knew this was not really South Africa and she wanted to visit some of the black townships and villages. I tried to discourage her, mainly because of her pregnancy. Helen was somewhat just like you; hard–headed, stubborn, and knew what she wanted.

Phyllis placed her finger on his nose and pushed. "Stubborn, hey!"

Jonathan did not smile. "Let me finish. On the third day, we went to Soweto, a black tribal township, consisting mostly of Zulus. That is where it happened; we were visiting in the hut of a Zulu chieftain when Helen started experiencing sharp contractions, so severe that she could not stand up. The Zulu chieftain shouted something in his native tongue and within seconds two women appeared and took charge." A tear rolled down Jonathan's cheek.

Phyllis reached forward and rubbed the teardrop. "Honey, thank God they were there, they were probably mid–wives."

Jonathan continued. "Yeah. We were ushered out of the hut, and I was acting nervous, blaming myself for bringing Helen on the trip with me. I was also scared. I had seen women in labor before, but this was different, Helen was experiencing sharp, sudden, violent pains and contractions. The Zulu chieftain, a large man, with a piercing look, spoke. Warriors jumped at his commands, not from fear but respect. He put his hands on my shoulder, and told me it was now in our God's hands. Several hours passed and finally one of the women surfaced. Her name was Rhosida, she spoke in Zulu to the chieftain, but I needed no translation. I knew either Helen or the baby was dead. I rushed to the hut and saw Helen still perspiring and moaning something. The other Zulu woman was covering a small figure. I reached over and grabbed her hand. I wanted to puke, it was the first time I had seen death, especially a baby. He was so tiny. My parents' death were different. Their bodies were cleaned and mom was dressed in her favorite dress that my aunt made for her, and dad, well, there was only one suit for him. This was different; there laid a small baby, wrinkled, bloodied, with the umbilical cord wrapped around his neck. I later found out it was a boy." Tears started to roll down Jonathan face.

Phyllis reached over and placed both hands on the side of his face. "Slow down, honey. I know it has been bottled up inside of you and you want to let it go. I'm here and I'm not going anywhere."

Jonathan kissed the palm of her hand. "Helen was saying, 'I'm sorry, I'm sorry.' I sat there holding her hand all night. I thought how much she and I both wanted this child. We had difficulty with two previous miscarriages and had even considered adoption. Once she had passed the critical period we even celebrated and could not wait until the child was born. We had so many plans. The next morning I was awakened by the sound of a baby crying. Helen was nursing a child and there stood the Chieftain, smiling and Rhosida with another man she introduced as Nyerere, the husband. The Chieftain told us that Rhosida had given birth four days ago to a son, and they wanted us to have him. I was dumbfounded; flabbergasted, but Helen was smiling. Nyerere and Rhosida had eight kids and food was scarce in the village.

Phyllis sat upright. "They gave you their son. Just outright gave you their son!"

"Yes! I know it's hard to believe. At first, I objected strongly, and so did Helen. Nevertheless, the Chieftain explained how food was scare in the village and the children were dying from lack of food and proper nourishment. There were so few jobs for so many blacks. He told us that one hundred and twelve infants died last year in the village, most suffered from malnutrition. He felt that we would love and take care of the child.

"Jon, but that's what the Chieftain said. What about the

parents?"

"Nyerere and Rhosida were glad to see their son get a good home and a chance for an opportunity to live and prosper in America." Jonathan paused and looked at Phyllis.

"That was very considerate of Nyerere and Rhosida. Apparently, they had to get the Chieftain's permission. Who was he, what was his name?"

"I don't know. We called him 'Inkosi,' meaning, chief, as everyone else did. On the way to the restaurant the other night, I felt someone was following me. At first, I thought it was the traffic jam, but after reaching the restaurant, there was the same car parked across the street and a man dressed in similar clothing as the Zulus were wearing in the village. Then the next morning there's a message written in Zulu placed on the car and specifically addressed to me, that's too much of a coincidence."

"What do you think he wants, surely not your son?"

"I'm not sure. Let's finish translating this message and see where it leads us. Turn to the Ks and look up k–a–n–t–i."

"Just a minute, Jon. You and Helen brought the baby back as your own. What about the records, the Army, and her family?"

"We told everyone the child was delivered by a Zulu midwife and the Army naturally certified the birth certificate."

Jonathan and Phyllis spent the next hour translating the rest of the message.

"We may have something here. Listen, 'Watch out for, a great nobleman or person of rank, who will die...'"

"Okay, here we go. 'Watch out for,' wait a minute, the first word is followed by an exclamation. Therefore, the first words are, 'watch out for,' period. Phyllis, what's another way to say, 'watch out for?'"

"Beware!

"That's right, beware!"

"Beware of what?" said Phyllis, now sitting upright and leaning forward towards Jonathan.

"I'm getting there. Great nobleman, or great oneness will pass or die, happen or experience. Greatness is a passing experience!"

shouted Jonathan.

"No Jon, I read somewhere that greatness is a transitory experience!"

"You're right. 'Beware! Greatness is a transitory experience. Small boy come, small boy come.' This doesn't make sense, look!"

"Reverse the words, Jon. 'Come small boy, or come boy.'"

"That's it. 'Beware! Greatness is a transitory experience. Come boy, come boy, grinning, dancing, whole, all wag−n−bietjie tree.'"

Phyllis grabbed Jonathan's hand. "The boy is celebrating something by dancing around the wag−n−bietjie tree. How many times when we were kids have we danced or played games around a tree? But what is he celebrating?"

"Honey, your guess at this point is as good as mine; however, the next word was easy, if you remembered, we didn't have that many. He was dancing around the tree, 'because.'"

"Because?" asked Phyllis.

"Yes, Phyllis, 'because,' it's so."

"Don't be facetious, Major McClendon."

Jonathan smiled, kissed his index finger and placed it lightly on Phyllis's lips. She also smiled, reached up with her hand to grab his, and rested the side of her face in the palm of Jonathan's hand.

"Why was the boy dancing, Jon?"

"Because, an ill or sick feeble man with a declining will to live will rise and give present strength." Jonathan paused.

"And what?"

"That's as far as we have translated."

"Jon, wasn't the translation for man referring to an adult man?"

"Yes, I believe you are right."

"Then, an adult man can be interpreted as mature or of age, or he could be an old man. Isn't this the place where the word 'into' was?"

"I believe you're correct," said Phyllis, "its right after an adult man."

"An old man is a feeble, sick, thing. No! An old man is a paltry thing who shall rise and give strength."

"Not strength, Jon, what about POWER! Insert the word and

read it from the beginning."

'Beware! Greatness is a transitory experience. Boy come, boy come, and dance around the wag'–n–bietjie tree. For an old man is but a paltry thing who shall rise and give power unto eight witnesses, who shall shout, 'I have eaten.' Come on Phyllis, you have to do better than that. They are shouting something, and it's sure as hell not, 'I have eaten!'"

Phyllis laughed. "I agree, so why don't we leave that word as is for now, and try to decipher what the message is really trying to tell us. Obviously, someone is telling you to be on your toes, but I don't understand what the boy has to do with it and why he is dancing around some particular kind of tree. And the old man, what kind of power does he have to give, and who are the eight witnesses?"

"I don't rightly know, maybe I was jumping to conclusions in thinking it had something to do with my son, but it's too much of a coincidence that the note was written in Zulu. What about the man who was following me dressed in the same clothing as some of the Zulu men? This is not getting us anywhere, and I am tired and can't think straight. Let's go back to your place so we can relax and review what we have translated."

It was 1800 hours in the evening before they arrived at Phyllis's apartment. Jonathan made a quick phone call to check on Djhon. He arranged with the Sergeant to pick his son up the next morning around nine. While he was on the phone, Phyllis made a pitcher of cold iced tea.

"Here, drink this. I forgot to check the mail. Oh, how's your son?"

"Thank you, Djhon's fine. He as usual, is having a good time."

"I'll be back in a couple of minutes," said Phyllis, "make yourself at home."

Jonathan drank a big gulp from the glass and rested his head back on the sofa. His arms extended on the back of the sofa, his inner thoughts were on Phyllis, fondly, longingly, and the more he did, the more excited he became. When Phyllis came back into the apartment and walked by the sofa, he caught her by the arm, pulled her to the sofa, hugged and kissed her.

"My God, is this the kind of affect I have on you when I leave the room for a few minutes?"

Jonathan said nothing. Phyllis, now secured in his arms, brought his mouth to hers. Her head tilted, her eyes closed, her lips slightly parted; her mouth was warm when their tongues met. Phyllis began to suck his tongue and licked his ear. She then whispered in his ear and kissed him again. Jonathan smiled and whispered something in Phyllis's ear. He began covering her face and neck with an abundance of soft warm kisses.

Phyllis laughed. "Naughty, naughty, naughty." She pointed her finger at him and placed it on his lips. "You brought the cavalry. I feel like I'm being kissed by a hundred men."

"No baby, only one. The commanding officer," said Jonathan. He sucked on her finger and gently cupped her breast. His hand fumbled with her blouse buttons.

Phyllis laughed. "No, not here, not on the sofa. I want to enjoy all of you. No quickies with this lady."

Phyllis grabbed Jonathan's hand and led him to the bedroom. She slowly unbuttoned the blouse and peeled off her bra. Phyllis undid her wraparound skirt and let it slide down her thin waist and large thighs to the floor.

Jonathan quickly undressed, throwing his shirt to the the floor and his trousers and boxer shorts to the small armchair. The two stood in their naked bodies and slowly admired each other's treasure. The two slowly walked towards each other; their bodies embraced and their mouths entered into a deep prolonged kiss.

Jonathan slowly backed Phyllis onto the bed without breaking the kiss. He kissed the corner of her upper lip, the side of her neck and gently caught the nipple of her breast between his teeth.

"Oh! Oh! Jon," she groaned and felt a pleasurable pain.

"Am I hurting you?"

"No Major, you haven't broken any regulations yet."

Jonathan let go of her nipple and sucked on it, then around the breast. He worked his way over the other breast and licked under it and along the side of the nipple. He kissed and sucked Phyllis' chin, throat, and neck. For about fifteen minutes, which to Phyllis seemed like an eternity, she moaned, panted, and enjoyed the foreplay, admiring Jonathan's patience.

"What a man," she thought. Jonathan took hold of her hand and introduced it to his manhood. Phyllis an adventurous woman, unafraid of risks, boldly caught hold of his semi—hard penis and massaged it. He separated Phyllis's legs and cupped her pubic area surrounded by a mass of thick black hair. His fingers explored through the massy bush and opened the vagina lips to allow entrance. She was extremely wet as Jonathan's middle finger slowly eased into her until the cheeks of her ass rested on the base of his hand.

"Damn you Jon, you are good," said Phyllis. She arched her back and demanded, "take me, take me now."

"Baby, I'll do anything you want me to," said Jonathan, now stiff and hard, gently easing himself into the waiting orifice of her genital canal.

Phyllis groaned and arched her back again. She spread her bent legs as wide apart as they would go, allowing Jonathan to feel the wetness of her inner lips.

Minutes later, their bodies were slick from heated moisture. Phyllis uttered a low moan, gasped and went into a trembling orgasm. Jonathan waited a few moments, withdrew and rolled Phyllis on her belly. Slowly and assuredly, he rubbed his penis up and down between her firm cheeks until he became engulfed by her wetness. He moaned and bucked feverishly, shouting, "Two years honey, two damned years! Oh, you feel so good, oh so good! No! No, No, oh shit, oh, no! I don't want to come, not now!" Jonathan collapsed on Phyllis soaked in sweat and exhausted.

Phyllis smiled. She conquered her man. Her thoughts were on Jonathan. "The man is mine for the next three days." Her conceited smile went unnoticed by Jonathan. The two embraced and quietly entered into a deep sleep.

The sun glaring through the partially opened curtain awakened Jonathan. He could feel the warmth of Phyllis's thigh touching his leg and smiled as he stared for a moment at the curve of her back. Phyllis was sleeping soundly and did not hear or feel Jonathan getting out of bed to close the curtain.

He made his way to the kitchen, looked into the icebox for something cold to drink besides water. He found fresh orange juice and started going through the cabinets searching for a glass.

"Hi, you find what you're looking for?"

"Most definitely," retorted Jonathan.

"What's that silly grin mean?" asked Phyllis.

"Oh, I just was thinking how long it's been."

"Well, how long?"

"My, you are a nosy little..."

"Now, now, now, let's not let your male ego gets in the way of a beautiful relationship."

"You're right baby, I'm sorry."

"Now, how long ago and when was the last time you had such a good romp in the saddle?" asked Phyllis softly.

"Two years."

"Care to make up for lost time?" licking her upper lip once again.

"You know, honey, I don't know why I find you so appealing. You are so different from Helen. She was a reserved person and so dependent on me. You, Phyllis, are so sure of yourself, adventurous, and challenging."

"Jon, I decide on what I want, and then I go out and get it."

"What do you want from me?" asked Jonathan.

"I'm only here for a few days, let's not get mushy. There is nothing in the apartment worth eating. Get dressed and buy me an early lunch."

CHAPTER SEVENTEEN

Asked but Will You Receive

The following morning – 0900 hours

"Morning, Major McClendon," said Staff Sergeant Cynthia Bell. "I haven't seen you since the Pentagon days. It's nice to see you again. You look terrific."

"No complaints," Jonathan offered immediately. "Sergeant Bell, you're the one that looks so good, you can make a grown man cry."

She blushes every time Jonathan compliments her. "Major, please call me Cynthia. You don't have to play military when we are alone."

"Sergeant Bell, I think it would be in both of our best interests if we continued to address each other by our military titles. That way, you and I will both stay out of trouble. Is the General in?"

She stared at him, at first not knowing if he was pulling rank, and then burst out laughing. "Speak for yourself, sir. I won't tell if you don't."

"Jonathan smiled. "That's the problem. I could not keep it a secret. I have a bad habit of talking in my sleep."

"Shush! Yes, General Gage is in; however, I don't believe he was expecting you and the schedule is tight. I believe you were scheduled for 1300 yesterday."

"That's correct. I called the General at home the night before and canceled the appointment. The General told me he would see me for a few minutes if you were able to squeeze me in."

"Oh, how would I like to squeeze you in?"

"Sergeant Bell! I would like to see the General, please."

"Major, you should be nice to a NCO, especially one that works for a general and has authority to set and control their appointments

119

for any given day."

Jonathan smiled, lifted the sergeant's hand and caressed her palm. "You're right, Cynthia. Please see what you can do to fit me in."

"Fitting you in would be no problem, Jonathan. The General just happens to have fifteen minutes free just before his next appointment. Let me announce you."

"Thank you, Cynthia."

"General Gage," she said. "Major McClendon is here to see you." She held the intercom button down with the left hand and announced the Major as he continued to hold her other hand.

"The General said to give him a couple of minutes, then you can go in. Please let me know if I can be of any service to you."

"Sergeant Bell, when I need further service, I certainly know where to come." Jonathan smiled and walked towards the General's office.

"Good morning, Sir," he said, saluting the General.

"Jonathan, how many times have I told you not to salute me when we are alone and not in the presence of other officers, unless you have been summoned on official business. Relax; sit down, son.

"Thank you sir." The General shouted, "Sergeant Bell, please bring the Major a cup of coffee." He walked around the desk and sat next to Jonathan. "When you called the other night, you said personal problems concerning Djhon prevented you from keeping the appointment."

"Sir, I originally set the appointment to try to convince you for an assignment in Vietnam. Since then, some things have happened, and now I wish to withdraw that request. I cannot leave Djhon with his aunt at this time. I want an assignment where he can be with me."

"Well, I'm glad to hear that because I could not pull the strings necessary to get you to South Vietnam or any part of Southeast Asia. The Joint Chiefs and the Secretary feel very strongly that our role in Vietnam should be advisory only. Some of my peers have a feeling things will heat up and at that time you will get your chance."

"When do you think things will heat up?"

"In two to three years," replied the General. "In the meantime, let me look in my side drawer and see where I can send you for the next two years. The last time I checked your file, you needed some intelligence experience. Mm, that's General Allison's area. Jonathan, I think you and your son will like Germany. If you keep your nose clean, you can come back as a Lieutenant Colonel. If my hunch is right about Vietnam, that's just the right kind of experience. The boys at the Pentagon charged with selecting Lt. Colonels, like to see officers who have this type of background."

"Thank you, Sir. You don't know how much this assignment means to me and Djhon."

"Jonathan, may I ask what kind of problems you are having with Djhon?"

"None at all. We just need to spend some time together. Since Helen died, I had to play both mother and father and this assignment in Germany is just what the doctor ordered."

"Good. You and Phyllis certainly hit it off the other night. Kate finally did a good job of matchmaking, considering all of her previous attempts had failed."

"Yes, Phyllis is quite the young woman. She is intelligent, very inquisitive, and certainly has a mind of her own. I never thought I would fall for another woman and certainly not in a matter of a couple of days."

"Fall for? Jonathan, you can't be that serious about her. Are you, son?"

"Sir, I'm in love with Phyllis and I'm going to ask her to marry me. That is, if she will have me."

The General became boisterous. "Marry! Boy, you do work quickly!" The General reached out and shook his hand. "Forty–eight hours ago, you have dinner with a beautiful young lady, and now you want to marry her. Wait until I tell Kate. She felt all along that Phyllis was the type of woman for you to marry.

"Sir, before you tell Kate, Let's make sure Phyllis will say yes."

"You have doubts?"

"I don't know. I think she feels the same, but she may want to get to know me better. I'm going to try to convince her how right we are for each other."

"All right, if you say so. I'll hold off on telling Kate until you pop the question to Phyllis."

"Excuse me General Gage," Sergeant Bell's voice came across the communication box. "Colonel Lewis and Colonel Walters are here for their appointment."

The General voice grew louder. "Hell, tell them it will be a few more minutes."

He became tickled at the General's reaction to the news. "Sir, once again thanks for your guidance and the continued support." Jonathan sipped the last drop of coffee and rose from his chair.

"Jonathan, you know I have always thought of you as a son. Good luck."

He had arranged to meet Phyllis at Ninfa's for lunch around 12:30. It was a beautiful cool and sunny day. The fresh air and the comfortable temperature in the low 70's felt like it was early March.

The Houston weather was known by some old residents to possess the qualities of a fickle woman. One day, she is boiling mad, lovable and the next, cold and miserable, or humid and damp with tears the following day.

Jonathan decided impulsively to pick up a bottle of Chardonnay, a couple of sandwiches and cheese to have lunch at Memorial park. He thought the idea would put Phyllis in a more amorous mood for him to ask the question. Phyllis thought lunch at the park was a marvelous idea. Once at the park, Jonathan drove around a couple of times until he found a nice isolated place, slightly shaded, and hidden room the normal view of others.

He waited until Phyllis had a couple of glasses of wine. Her head rested on his chest. "Honey, I got orders to go to Germany."

"Germany, what in the hell for?"

"I asked for this assignment. I think getting out of the country and having Djhon with me will be good for the both of us."

Phyllis sat upright. "Oh, I'll be darned!" She snapped. "What in the hell are you doing, running away?"

"No! I am not running away. I just think it's necessary to forget the recent set of events. The message on the note plus the old man's appearance is just too much of a coincidence."

"Oh, hog wash! You were just running away from things by not wanting to find out who was behind the note and what it all means."

"Phyllis, please, today is such a nice day. Let's not spoil it."

"Jon, I think..."

"Shh," Jonathan placed his finger on her lips. Then taking his finger away, he kissed her lightly. She smiled and reacted by resting the side of her face on the palm of Jonathan's hand. Jonathan placed the same hand behind her neck, pulled Phyllis closer as their lips met for a prolonged kiss.

"Phyllis, I love you."

"I love you too, Jon."

"I never believed in love at first sight, or that a person such as myself could fall in love with you or any woman in a matter of two days."

"Jon, when I awakened that morning and saw you lying there in my bed, I felt a twinge. But I thought it was just a fulfilled sexual feeling. Those next four hours together in the library convinced me it was not. In those four hours, I knew your strong points, weaknesses, and the consideration you have for others."

"Honey, I also felt the same. I love you and I want to marry you. I want you to come to Germany with me and Djhon." Tears rolled down Phyllis's face. "Phyllis, why are you crying?"

"Jon, I can't marry you. What about your career, your son, and you know what you want to achieve in life. Your ambition is to become a General, better yet, Chief of Staff."

Jonathan arched his eyebrow. "Why not, you just said you love me?"

"Honey, you found your niche in life. I haven't. I promised myself that until I found out what I wanted to do in life, it would be best that I remain single."

"But Phyllis..."

"Jon, please. Let me finish. I have too much energy; too many things to do. Did it occur to you why I travel so much? Why I am involved in this South African thing and other noteworthy causes? I have been searching since I left college. I am thirty–one years old and don't know what I want in life. When I find it, then it's time for marriage. Honey, I never loved a man so much. I'm willing to see you as much as possible, remain faithful to you, but it must be on my terms."

"Phyllis, you sound so sure of yourself. Is there anything I can do or say to convince you to marry me?"

"I'm sorry Jon, no."

"Well, you can't blame a man for trying. The assignment to Germany is three weeks away, there's still time."

"No, you don't have three weeks. You forget that I leave in two days."

"Two days," snapped Jonathan, "I thought that your leaving was tentative."

Phyllis looks sternly at him. "Jon, nothing I do is tentative. I bought my plane tickets before I arrived in Houston."

Jonathan began packing things up and the two got in the car and headed back to Phyllis's place.

The ride was long and silent as neither said a single word to each for at least thirty minutes before Phyllis broke the silence. "This area has developed quite a bit since my last visit. Look at all the new buildings, gas stations, and homes. Jonathan nodded but she could tell his heart was not in the conversation.

The next three weeks were hard on Jonathan. He tried to change her mind during the first couple of days to no avail. He won every battle he encountered in life, but he was no match for Phyllis. When she left town, part of him went with her. She did not tell him where she was going. Kate knew but she promised Phyllis not to reveal her whereabouts. Jonathan and his son Djhon had almost finished packing for the trip to Germany. They had airline tickets to leave at noon in four days.

Later in the evening around 2200 hours, the doorbell rang and Djhon bounced down the stairs. Jonathan was in the den reading one of his favorite mystery novels entitled, *The Last Unknown Soldier*.

He glanced towards the front door; he could not imagine who it could be at that time of night. He shouted at Djhon to ask who it was before he opened the door.

"Good evening, Djhon. How are you? I'm surprised your dad lets you stay up so late, especially on a school night." Phyllis greeted him with a warm outstretched hand.

"Dad always lets me stay up until eleven, as long as I maintain an A average. It's nice to see you again, Phyllis. Dad's in the den reading a book written by his favorite author."

"Djhon, who is it?"

Phyllis put her finger on Djhon's lips and signaled her wish to surprise his father.

"Okay, he is the living room reading that book for the fifth time, he whispered. Djhon smiled and for a moment thought of the warm touch, his mother's hands always had. He quietly headed back upstairs.

"Phyllis!" said Jonathan, surprised and puzzled. He stiffened to attention.

"Hello, Jonathan." The blood rushed to Phyllis cheeks. I, I don't know what to say. I thought..."

Jonathan interrupted. "Don't say anything. Just stand there and let these bloodshot eyes admire your beauty. You look well. Would you like a cup of coffee?"

"No, but I will take a glass of that brandy. I must have done a good job on myself, considering that I have been up all of last night and was unable to sleep today."

"You, too? I thought by reading this book, I would sleep better tonight." Jonathan poured the brandy into a small balloon glass. As he handed it to Phyllis, their eyes met and neither said a word for thirty seconds.

"Jon, I will go to Germany with you but not as your wife. I know it's not wise for an up and coming officer to shack up with an unmarried woman; however, if you're willing then I'm game."

Jonathan beamed. "Phyllis, baby, I don't care under what

circumstances you stipulate, besides beggars can ill afford to be choosy. However, you are right, but General Gage and the entire Army will have to get used to the idea. Who knows? At least, I'll have time on my side."

Jonathan approached Phyllis, the two embraced, and their lips touched in a prolonged kiss.

"Golly gee, Dad, Phyllis," said Djhon. "There's a minor in the house." Phyllis broke the kiss and gave one of her familiar laughs.

CHAPTER EIGHTEEN

Don't Drink the Tea

Washington, D. C., the following morning

Riley did not place much importance on the note that was mysteriously placed in the camera bag. He thought it was some practical joke or the note was inadvertently put in the wrong camera bag. It was obvious to him since the message was written in some African dialect. However, just to satisfy his curiosity, he was on his way to see an old friend at the institute and to seek his opinion.

"Bill! Bill Riley! My God, what in the world brings you to the Institute, especially at this time of day?" Dr. Browne was elated to see his old research buddy. His peers recognized him, like Riley, he was a renowned scientist and president of the McNair Institute on Foreign Research.

The two men hugged each other. "Russell, when a person wants the definitive interpretation of a language, he seeks out the one and only true expert, even if it's 8:45 in the morning." They had become good friends some ten years ago, while working in London on a grant sponsored by the government to study the cultural environment of different societies throughout the world.

"You are still the same smooth, cunning person," laughed Dr. Browne. "You put your foe on a pedestal, and while he's still gloating from all the superlatives, you slip in the back door, gets what you want and leave him hanging by his laurels."

"But Russell," laughed Riley, "you are my friend, not my foe."

"Thank God, with a friend like you, who needs any enemies? What in thunder can I do for you and how are Carol and that growing boy, Michael?"

Riley took a deep breath. "That's one of the main reasons I

wanted to see you."

Browne could see his friend was disturbed. "Please, Bill, have a seat and tell me what's troubling you."

"Thanks, but I prefer to stand. Riley studied the green window blinds behind Browne for a few seconds, and then looked straight at him.

"This looks serious. Let me get my pipe. I think better when I have something to chew on."

Riley handed the piece of paper to Browne. "I think when we were at the Capitol yesterday, someone either confused our camera bag with theirs or intentionally placed this note in our bag. I want you to translate it for me or have a fellow colleague whose specialty is in that field of foreign language."

Dr. Browne looked at the note. "Mm, that won't be necessary. This is written in Zulu dialect. It carries the same variety and features of phonology associated with the tribes in South Africa. The great Zulu wars and chieftains were once part of my research studies."

Riley finally sat down in the chair. "Did you say South Africa?"

"Yes, old chap, South Africa, and I'm afraid this message is a warning."

Riley leaned back in the chair, his eyes focused on Browne. "Warning, why would someone from a Zulu tribe want to give me a warning? I have never been to South Africa."

"I don't know Bill, but I need to get my research papers. I have translated enough to know this message was intentionally placed in your camera bag. The first word means 'Beware.' and the last word was a favorite cry of the great Zulu warrior and Chieftain, Shaka, who was said to shout 'Ngadla have eaten!' as he pulled his spear from his conquered victims."

Riley laughed at the interpretation. "I have eaten, you've got to be kidding."

Dr. Browne gave Riley a stern stare. "Bill, there's nothing funny here. The legend said Shaka killed some two million opposing tribesmen during his regime. Shaka is said to have developed some type of assegai blade called 'Iklwa.' This blade or spear would create a sucking sound as it was drawn from his victim as he shouted 'Ngadla!' meaning 'I have eaten.'"

Riley sat forward. His mouth dropped. "I don't understand. What does all of this have to do with me: Zulu warriors, spears, and a strange legend of some crazy chieftain? If I didn't know better, that message implies someone is out to harm me or my family."

"Relax and let's not jump to conclusions. Let me find my research papers. This is going to take an hour or so of our time and I only have just that cup of tea left, why don't you go down to our cafeteria and pick up a few bags to brew."

Riley put his hand on Browne shoulders and smiled. "Bill, are you still are hooked on tea?"

"Yes, my friend, tea has nutritional and medicinal properties."

"Okay, okay. I will bring you tea, but I will drink some of that hardening of arteries coffee for me. Where is the gray old thermos of yours that is as old as you are? I need it to keep my coffee warm."

"Bill, I may be an American citizen, but it's difficult for me to erase my British background," said Browne. He looked incisively at Riley over the top of his small spectacles.

Riley grinned. "My friend, if you want tea, then tea is what you will get."

A few minutes later and down the hallway, Riley waited in the long cafeteria line, it moved at a slow pace. His thoughts focused back to the first time, he met Russell Browne. It had been fifteen years ago when the two were part of a research team awarded grants to work on a government project together at a remote site in California. The cafeteria setting seemed remarkably similar to the same one where members of the research team ate every day for six months. He often reminisced about their first encounter.

Riley had introduced himself to Browne as he sat drinking tea. "May I join you?"

Dr. Browne had stood up, revealing himself to be very tall, a couple of inches over six feet with a brownish mustache. "Of course. I am Russell Browne. He extended his hand.

"*Thank you, I'm Bill Riley.*" *He placed his tray on the table before reaching to shake Browne's hand; Riley had noticed him staring at his chest.*

"*Excuse me from staring, but is that button right,*" *asked Browne. Riley quickly looked down at his chest and was embarrassed at a button his fiancée had given him before he departed. It read 'Economists do it theoretically.'*

"*Oh, last night was my 40th birthday and my fiancée coerced me into at least wearing this on the plane,*" *he said, pulling it off and putting it in his side pocket.*

"*Don't worry, I understand, two years ago I went through something similar. My wife decided that she wanted to reassure me the spark was still there,*" *Browne laughed,* "*except it was she who turned forty.*"

Riley smiled as he thought about the good times the two had while working on the research project. His thoughts interrupted by the cashier asking him for money. He paid for several tea bags and coffee. He looked at his watch; it was 9:15 a.m. He proceeded back to Dr. Browne's office. He entered the room to find Browne seated with his head laid back on the chair's thick black headrest. His eyes were closed. There was a strange odor in the room.

"Russell, here as you often say, is your bloody tea." Riley suddenly noticed certain stillness in the room. "Russell, my God! Russell, what's wrong?"

Riley dropped the tea and coffee on the adjacent desk and rushed to his dear friend, only to find his body motionless. He ripped opened his shirt, placed his head on the chest trying to hear and feel any signs of life. He stared at Browne's body and saw blood slowly oozed from his friend's mouth.

At forty–five minutes past nine, the police officer scribbled something on a pad. "Sir, how long did you know Dr. Browne?"

Riley seemed perplexed. "I can't believe he's dead."

The police officer never looked up. "Can you tell me what happened?"

"I was hoping you would tell me."

"We don't know, sir, not until the autopsy is completed. According to the medical examiner, the preliminary prognosis indicates a stroke, perhaps from a ruptured blood vessel in the brain." The officer continued to write and talk at the same time. "I know this is difficult, but how long have you known the deceased?"

"Russell never had any heart problems."

"Sir, please answer the question. How long did you say you knew him?"

"Too long."

"How many years?"

"Fifteen, no eighteen."

"Did you say the body was in the exact position as it is now?"

Riley became agitated. "Officer, for the sixth time, as I told two other officers, yes, Dr. Browne's body was exactly in the same position as it is now, and he did not die from a stroke!"

"Sir, do you have any reason or evidence to indicate that Dr. Browne's death was the result of foul play?"

Riley shrugged. "Err, no I don't, it's just a feeling."

"Feelings, sir, don't solve cases. We operate on facts. What was the purpose of your visit?"

"Dr. Browne and I are, were, good friends. We also worked on a project together for several years."

The officer flipped back a few pages. "What time did you first arrive?"

"Almost nine a.m."

"And what time did you discover the body?"

"I think it was around a 9:15 am."

"Sir, you told the first officer it was 9:25 a.m."

"Officer, 9:15 a.m., or 9:25 a.m., it was around that time. What is ten minutes?"

The police officer finally looked at Dr. Riley. "Long enough to kill someone, sir."

"Oh."

"You told the officer you went to get iced tea and coffee, what time did you leave?"

"Hot tea, officer! Hot tea. I left at approximately 9:00 a.m."

"Mm, the same time you arrived," smarted the officer.

"No, a few minutes later. Officer, I don't know, I'm not having a good perception of time," pleaded Riley.

"Don't know?" the officer asked him incredulously. "How do you *forget* the last time you saw Dr. Browne alive?"

A moment of silence elapsed before Riley responded. Suddenly he had had enough. "Officer, are you insinuating that I have something to do with my friend's death?"

"Sir. Did I say that?"

"No, officer, but you are asking me questions designed to trap me, and I'm getting pretty damn tired of it. You should be trying to find out who kill Russell."

"Dr. Riley, I get a particular feeling that you were here for a purpose, and I want to know what that purpose was."

Riley attacked immediately. "How many times do you get an urge to intimidate a suspect?"

"Touché, Dr. Riley, that's what I call a full circle. However, I did not say you were a suspect."

"Yes, I know, but everyone is a suspect until the murder is solved."

"Sir, no one said a murder was committed."

"Officer, Dr. Browne did not die of a stroke and I believe the autopsy will prove me correct."

"Sir, I believe you are withholding information. I must ask you not to leave the city in the near future. In fact, I'm going to speak to the detective assigned to this case and he may want to question you further."

"I understand," snapped Riley, "you know where to reach me." He abruptly departed the room and headed for his car.

Riley decided to drive home by taking the 14th Street Bridge exit to Highway South One, an extra twelve miles out of the way. He needed the time alone to think to himself on just what had happened. He also had an eerie feeling about the note, Browne's translation, the relation of the legend of a great Zulu warrior and the strange circumstances regarding his sudden death. Riley's mind continued to wander, besieged with thoughts and unanswered questions.

"Why on earth; why? What does the note mean? Why was Russell killed or did he suddenly, die of an apparent heart attack? Who is this Zulu chieftain and what does all of this have to do with me and my family?"

He felt his arrival home was quicker than usual, considering the route taken. Carol was across the street chatting with Mrs. O'Hara, the nosy neighbor. She waved to him. She also sensed by his lack of response and the reaction on his face that something was wrong.

"Bill, honey, wait up," she shouted.

He got out of the car and headed straight towards the front door without looking at her.

"Excuse me, Mrs. O'Hara, Bill's home. I'll share the secret with you first thing tomorrow morning."

Riley finally stopped, reached out and placed his right hand on the side of the house, leaning forward and looking downwards towards the ground.

"Honey, what's wrong?"

"Russell is dead."

Carol stopped suddenly. Her mouth dropped so wide her bottom braces were visible. "Dead! How? What happened?"

"The police think it was a stroke."

"And you don't think so. Why?" she whispered.

He did not answer.

Carol caressed his hand. "Honey, what's wrong?"

He kissed Carol's hand and looked into her eyes. "I believe his death has something to do with the note left in our camera bag. I took the note to Russell to have one of his colleagues at the Institute translate it. However, that was not necessary because Russell immediately recognized the language origin. As he translated it, it said something about 'Beware,' a Zulu Warrior or Chieftain that shouted ' I have eaten' as he drew a particular spear from his victims.

"Zulu warrior, are you sure? What's the connection between a

Zulu warrior and us?"

"I don't know. Russell sent me to the cafeteria for tea and when I returned, he was dead."

"Do the police have any idea who could have done it?"

"None, as I told you, they think he died of a stroke. Oh, where is Michael"?

"He went to the library to research some material for a school project, but he should be home soon. Bill, you look beat, why don't you lie down for a few minutes. Dinner won't be ready for at least an hour."

"Carol, I have no desire for food."

A bus stopped in front of the Riley's home. "Hi Mom. Hi Dad."

"Hi son."

"Dad. What is wrong? You look beat."

"Your dad's best friend just died. Did you find enough material for the school project?"

"Yeah, but Dad, who died?

"Russell. Dr. Russell Browne. By the way, what are you researching?"

"Oh, famous Indian chiefs. Dad, isn't, I mean wasn't Dr. Browne that research buddy of yours, the one you're always talking to on the phone."

"Yes son, he was a real friend. Why Indian chiefs for a project?"

"I thought it would be interesting to study the events that led up to them getting their power and recognition. I had problems finding anything good on Cochise and Sitting Bull, but an old man, Mr. Williams, who said he was once a chieftain, gave me some additional reference material to research."

Helen rubbed him on the head. "Michael, that was great, how lucky that you had a real Indian chief to help in the research project. Did you get his complete name and tribe to use a reference material?"

"Mom, Mr. Williams is no Indian chieftain. Mr. Williams said he was a Zulu chieftain."

Michael's comments filled his parents with awe. "What! Bill, what's going on?" shouted Carol.

"Carol, calm down."

"Mom, what's the matter? Did I do something wrong?"

"No Michael, but we would like to know how did you meet Mr. Williams and what did he look like? Something happened to a very good friend of ours and we both are still a little upset."

"I don't know. It seemed like he was just there."

Carol looked at Michael, perplexed. "What do you mean, just there?"

"Carol, please let me handle this. Go in the kitchen and finish dinner."

"But, Bill, I..."

"Carol, please go in the kitchen. Now Michael, where did you first notice this Mr. Williams?"

She squinted her eyes at Bill. "I'll talk to you later."

"Go on son, answer the question."

"Mrs. Harris told the class about several authors that had written books on Indians and their lifestyle. I was on the first floor of the library in the non–fiction section when I looked up and there he was, just smiling. Then I went to the card index by title and two of the reference books were in the social science department, which is on the second floor. I found one of the books and was having trouble finding the second and there he was again, smiling at me. Then he said, 'Michael, what are you researching?' I asked him, how did he know my name, and he said he knew you and mom, but he said it kind of strange."

"What do you mean kind of strange?"

"He said he knew a lot of things about me since I was born and that I was twelve years old and extremely smart. Then I said you must know my parents. He said yes, that he knew my dad and was a great admirer of my father. Then he said Mom is very pretty, and your mother is an understanding woman. Man, did he have a weird way of talking."

"How old would you say Mr. Williams is?"

"Dad, I don't know, but he looked a lot older than grandpa and he had a strange odor. His clothes smelled funny."

135

"Did you say there was a peculiar odor on him?"

"Yes, but I can't describe the odor."

What happened next?"

"Nothing much, I told him that I was researching great Indian chiefs and he told me he himself was a Zulu chieftain and he knew a lot about the subject. He told me his name was Mr. Williams and gave me the titles and authors of books to read. Before he left, he said research and science will play a major role in my life, and to use the knowledge wisely."

"Michael, go upstairs and wash up, your mother will have dinner ready shortly."

"Dad, who is Mr. Williams?"

"I don't know, son."

"But, he said he knew you and Mom."

"Son, maybe Mr. Williams meant he has heard of me. Very few people actually win the Nobel Peace Prize. The news media has written several articles about my life and family. Now go and wash up."

The next morning, Carol was in the kitchen making coffee when the phone rang. It was a detective working on Dr. Browne's case. He wanted to speak to Dr. Riley. She told him Bill was still asleep. The detective insisted on speaking to him.

"Honey... Bill, Bill, there's a detective on the phone insisted in talking to you." Carol shook him on the shoulder.

"What?"

"A detective is on the phone."

"Ah, okay, tell him it will be a few minutes while I wash my face so I can be a little coherent."

As he washed his face, Dr. Riley was wondering why a detective would be calling so early in the morning. The walk to the living room phone gave him just enough time for the mind to clear.

"Hello, this is Dr. Riley."

"Sir, I'm Detective LaRue. I must ask that you come down to police headquarters. We have some additional questions concerning Dr. Browne's death."

"Sure, when do you want me there?"

"Right away, Sir."

"Detective LaRue, its 6:30 a.m. I have not had my coffee, read the morning paper, or eaten my breakfast. What's so darn important that I must rush to police headquarters?"

"Sir, until we clear the circumstances regarding Dr. Browne's death, you are a suspect."

"Suspect! The police officer I spoke to yesterday was so sure Russell's death was from a stroke!"

"Sir, I understand from the officer's notes, you felt Dr. Browne's death was accidental"

"Accidental, my ass! Russell was killed."

"Dr. Riley, that's why we want you down here, the autopsy report revealed he was injected with a drug, which gives symptoms of an apparent heart attack or stroke. Therefore, I must insist you come down to the station as soon as possible."

"So I was right all along. I will see you at eight o'clock, after I have had my coffee and breakfast. If you want me any sooner, send a squad car to get me."

"Okay, Dr. Riley, eight o'clock, it is."

"Bill, what's wrong?" asked Carol.

"Nothing for you to get concerned about, dear."

"Don't dear me! Jesus, you men are all alike. What do you mean I should not get concerned? I heard part of the phone conversation. Why do the police want you at the station so early in the morning? For Pete's sakes, Russell is dead! The police think he died of a stroke. You said he might have been killed. Someone left us a note saying beware and something about Zulus. Then our son meets a Zulu chieftain! What in the hell is going on?"

"Carol! If I knew, I would tell you. Lower your voice. Let's not upset Michael. Go make us a cup of coffee and settle down."

"I don't want a damned cup of coffee!" she shouted. "What did the detective want?"

Just as Bill was about to explain to Carol, Michael knocked on the bedroom door.

"Come in!" They both shouted in unison.

"Mom, Dad, why does a detective want you to come down the police headquarters so early in the morning?"

"Nothing of any importance, Michael. I'm helping them work on a case involving psychopathic behavior relating to genetic genes." He turned and frowned at Carol.

"Dad, I'm twelve years old. I read at an eighteen–year–old level and my IQ is 180, thanks to private lessons from you. I know Dr. Browne is dead. The walls in this house are thin, and you have not been arguing about genetic genes. Does this have anything to do with the man I met in the library?"

"Son, I really don't know, I sometimes forget how fast you are maturing, but, until I find out, I want you and your Mom to stay in the house. Is that understood?"

"Yes sir."

"Carol?"

"Yes, we hear you."

Bill made himself a cup of instant coffee and read the paper, while Carol cooked him a couple of eggs. He could tell she was still upset. He later assured her everything was going to be all right, kissed her at the door, and headed downtown to police headquarters.

"Excuse me Sergeant, I'm Dr. Riley. Could you direct me to Detective LaRue?"

"He's the tall man with the shoulder holster," answered the sergeant.

"Detective LaRue, I'm Dr. Riley. The autopsy report must have verified my suspicions."

"Sir, please follow me to the Captain's office." The detective turned briskly, to his left without acknowledging Riley. Like a trained dog, Riley followed.

"Dr. Riley, Captain Brooks," said Detective LaRue. He gave Dr. Riley the expression he was not interested in idle chit–chat.

"Please sit down, Dr. Riley," said the Captain. He reached across the desk to shake Riley's hand. "The medical examiner informed Detective LaRue that if it were not for your suspicions, he would not have examined the deceased further."

With a sheepish grin, Riley looked at LaRue and said. "No kidding."

The captain looked at the men and continued. "The preliminary examination showed symptoms of cardiac arrest more closely related to those of a stroke victim. Your comments to the officer on the scene caused the medical examiner and his colleague to extend the examination of the deceased. The autopsy revealed Dr. Browne died from a strange poison.

"Poison, what kind of poison?" asked Riley.

"The poison has a chemical reaction which causes immediate clogging of the artery, which in turn produces a violent reaction of the blood vessels simulating a stoke," answered the captain. "We believe..."

LaRue interrupted. "The poison disseminates from the body within six to eight hours, making it difficult to trace, leaving one to believe the victim died from a stroke or a heart attack. In a city of this size and a backlog of bodies in the morgue, the medical examiner's office is lucky to see a body within thirty–six hours after death. I hope you're satisfied."

The captain stared at LaRue. He did not like his behavior towards Riley. "The only tell–tale sign of the poison is the presence of a strange foul odor, present only after consumption or dilution with a watery base. It's believed this poison exists from the leaves of a tree located in the southern part of Africa. I hope you now understand why we summoned your presence so early in the morning."

"So, Russell died from the leaves of a tree in Africa," said Riley. He looked puzzled. "I can't believe this is happening."

"What is happening?" asked Detective LaRue.

"A message written in a Zulu dialect. My son then meets a Zulu chieftain in the library."

"Sir, please be more specific. What message?" asked LaRue?

"A couple of days ago, we, my wife, my son and I, were visiting the Capitol when someone apparently placed a note, a message in my son's camera bag. It was written in a foreign language. Russell, being a long–time friend as well as President of the McNair Institute on Foreign Research, was fluent in fourteen languages. That was the reason I visited him, Russell recognized the dialect right away. He said the first word meant 'Beware,' and another word was a war cry from some great Zulu warrior or chieftain shouting 'I have eaten...'"

LaRue interrupted. "Sir, if this wasn't a murder case, and if we didn't have the body of a prominent citizen, I would say you flipped your lid."

"I've been in this business, detective, before you were wearing diapers and I've heard and seen all sorts of evidence, statements, and people dying of mysterious causes. Please precede, Dr. Riley.

"Wait a minute, Dr. Riley," interrupted Detective LaRue.

"Why didn't you tell the officer this when... just a moment," he thumbed through his notes, "the officer's question to you was, 'Why were you in this area?' Answer: 'To see the monument.' Question: 'Why today?' Answer: 'An urge.' LaRue then stares at Riley."

"Yes, I said that."

"Someone put a note written in a foreign language in your son's camera bag and followed him to the library. Why were you so evasive in your answers?"

"I didn't know until after Russell's death that Michael was followed! I thought..."

The captain interrupted. "Then why, after Dr. Browne said part of the note said 'Beware' and, 'I have eaten,'" and he tells you part of a note means some crazy Zulu chieftain shouting a war cry. Then you decided to get tea, come back and find him dead. For Pete's sake, Dr. Riley, didn't you think at the time it was too much to be coincidence?"

"Yeah, Dr. Riley. If the note meant so much for you to drive across town, and Dr. Browne to immediately translate part of it, you certainly picked an odd time to go get some ice tea. Where was you curiosity?"

"Hot tea. Detective LaRue! It was hot tea. Russell loved hot tea, especially when he is in deep thought. Besides your own people said Russell died of a stroke. The medical examiner said the poison that killed him would not have been traceable after six hours and the poison gives the same symptoms as a stroke. I had no reason to tell the officer the exact reason I was there. The whole thing is bizarre. It's even too much for me to believe. Look at your captain; he thinks I'm off my rocker!"

"Well, I don't think so," said the captain. "But someone poisoned Dr. Browne and until I find some answers, you are still a suspect."

"I certainly hope you do find some answers. I want Russell's killer brought to justice as much as you do. There is nothing else I can tell you."

"Do you still have the note?" asked the captain.

"No, I couldn't find it. I left it with Dr. Browne."

LaRue throws up his hand in disgust. "Great! Now we have a mysterious note missing."

"Dr. Riley, we are aware that you are a Nobel Peace Prize Winner and have speaking engagements committed. I must insist on a copy of your itinerary and be advised of any changes until we have solved this case or you are no longer a suspect," demanded the captain.

"Yes, I want your schedule today, before my shift ends," barked LaRue.

"My secretary will forward a copy to your office and I will advise you personally, Detective LaRue, of any changes."

PART THREE

Time That Tries Mens Souls

CHAPTER NINETEEN

Panic in the Streets

Four years later, Johannesburg – Spring, 1964

The presence of a nighttime guards patrolling auspiciously around the airport was normal for the South Africa people. The ANC and the government were constantly at odds with each other, both political and armed confrontations.

One of the officers could be seen flirting with a flight attendant, while another was ribbing the porter on the size of his belly and his taste for ale. They traveled in pairs since the bombing resumed. Things were beginning to return to normal, the bombing attacks ceased almost six months ago.

The South African Defense Force and the local police believed the African National Congress suffered a crucial defeat. Most of the ANC heir leaders were now behind; including Nelson Mandela, and the others disbanded, all except one, the old man. No one knew his exact identity; he was known by many names.

A small band of carolers from one of Johannesburg's finest private schools huddled by the newsstand, stamping their feet to the beat of the boy playing the drums and cheerfully singing a favorite school melody. Their young voices penetrated the airport's halls between the busy sounds of baggage handlers, people arguing about seating arrangements and the laughter from passengers ignoring the children.

It was a busy Saturday afternoon at the airport when without warning chaos was set into motion. Terrorists used tactics in each of the prior bombings, to frighten the passengers. The chain reaction of the bombings had the signature and trademark of the ANC. A five-minute fuse, one simply lit with a match detonated first, followed by five consecutive blasts, each one minute apart.

Dr. Riley was also in the airport. During the chaos, he walked back on to the plane and waited until he believed it was safe to exit. His earlier arrival in Johannesburg created a stir when the local newspapers did a feature on the Nobel Prize winner. A black man in Johannesburg, South Africa, with a doctorate and of the notoriety Dr. Riley possessed, attracted attention.

The first blast was always several sticks of dynamic carefully placed in a white's–only rest room stall, which sent screaming half–dressed women running down the concourse. A white woman shrieked when she saw a black woman crawling on the floor without any hands, blood oozing from her decapitated wrists. Screams echoed from the crowd.

A voice shouted! "Oh my God! Please help me."

People stared at each other in total disbelief. The explosion frightened them. Someone shouted from the startled crowd. "They killed her! Those bastards kill my wife!"

Another explosion, one minute apart and fifty yards away in the kitchen of the airport eatery caused a group of hysteria people to trip and fall over each other in a futile effort to escape the flying debris.

The crowd turned into a confused sea of faces. People ran in all directions, trampling each other. A couple of reporters returning from a trip stared in disbelief; one ran outside to find their mobile van. The other one stayed to take pictures.

All nearby communication lines were busily occupied. Police officers arrived. "Don't run! Please remain calm." Their orders smothered by the screaming voices.

More screams followed. An elderly man fainted.

A large woman wearing a silver cross began shouting the Holy Scriptures. "The Lord is my shepherd, he makes me..."

Two minutes later from the initial blast, the third bomb exploded in the passenger's loading dock, killing the reporter standing by his mobile van. Bewildered airport security yelled at each other.

"It's the lady's bathroom in Corridor B," shouted one officer.

"No, damn it. The explosion came from the eatery on Corridor

C," yelled another officer.

"No, you fool! Call for help, the bombs are everywhere. Don't you see the ANC is blowing up everything?"

A minute after the third explosion, outside the swinging doors, a government limousine burst into flames killing its passengers. The shriek of tires and cars crashing in front of the airport had many people running for safe ground.

"Attention all officers. Attention," shouted the security chief. "Secure your area. Repeat, secure your area."

Police car and motorcycle sirens crisscrossed the street at a furious rate of speed. Medical wagons and personnel scattered to aid the injured.

Five minutes later.

On the runway, a small twin–engine airplane, owned by the SADF also burst into flames. The blasts shot upward, horizontally and jettison the pilot's cockpit at several hundred per second. The rebellion continued and the ANC's fight against the government was reborn.

Just as quick the explosions started, five minutes later, they stopped. The casualty scene left its toll. Twenty–five dead. Forty–two wounded. Among the dead were several elderly and handicapped people. The death scene of the children was too much for the young flirting officer to bear. Two young girls were dead. A dead boy had his head crushed by a large piece of a cement pillar.

Three months earlier in the year, Dr. Riley applied for and received a grant from the federal government to continue his research in South Africa. He wanted to study the black population movement throughout South Africa. He believed it held to key behind their economic status and plight. Dr. Riley wanted the answer to Russell's death and the secret to the riddle. If someone wanted him dead, he would not wait for it to happen. He preferred to face the killers, head on, in their native country. It also gave him the opportunity to travel to Africa and study the cultural differences between East African blacks, their progress in society as compared to South Africa blacks.

The trips to Africa were frequent and troublesome. He and Carol decided it was best for Michael to continue his education in the states while he was away on research.

Jan Linden became suspicious of Dr. Riley during his stay in South Africa. He became interested in Riley when he ignored South Africa's Pass laws and ventured in an area reserved for whites. He was concerned about why the Nobel Peace Prize economist wanted to study South African blacks, especially considering the problems of the Negro movement in the United States.

Riley drew Linden's curiosity when he interviewed some blacks in the same village where Tomar was killed. When he arrived back at his hotel's room, the clerk handed him a note. '*Go to the lounge and order a Tom Collins from the bartender.*'

"Excuse me sir, did you see who left this message?"

"No sir," replied the clerk. "When I came on duty, it was already in your slot."

Riley went into the bar. It was crowded and noisy. The only place to get a drink was at the bar.

"Yes sir, what's your pleasure," asked the bartender.

Riley paused. "Err, give me a Tom Collins."

"Did you say a Tom Collins? Sir, I'm unfamiliar with that drink."

"Oh hell, what am I doing," stammered Riley, "Just give me scotch and water.

The bartender looked at him and smiled. A couple of minutes later, a man walked up to the bar and ordered a Tom Collins. The bartender apologized again and asked how to mix the drink. Riley looked at the stranger. The stranger smiled at him. Riley acknowledged his smile.

"Excuse me sir," said the stranger. "Do you have a lite?" Riley reached into his jacket, pulled out a lighter and lit the man's cigarette. "Thank you."

A woman suddenly appeared. "Honey, our table is ready. Let's go, I'm starving" The glow from Riley's face transformed into a somber stare.

"Dr. Riley, here's your Tom Collins," said the bartender.

"I thought..."

He winked at Riley. "Ssh," whispered the bartender. He looked around to see if anyone was listening or looking. "I have the answer to the riddle."

"What riddle?"

"Don't be coy with me. You didn't travel all this way to my country to study some economic bullshit."

"Okay. Okay. But how do I know that you're not the one trying to kill me?"

"Don't be ridiculous. Nobody's trying to kill you. It's your son they want."

Riley grabbed the bartender's shirt. "Who is trying to..."

"Get your hands off me or I will tell you nothing. What's wrong with you? Are you trying to get their attention? Man, you will get me killed if they found out."

"Found out what?"

"Enough! Finish your drink, and get the hell out of here. I get off in fifteen minutes, meet me in room 610 in exactly twenty–five minutes, and make damn sure you're not followed."

Riley held his glass with both hands and slowly shook his head. Twenty–five minutes seemed like an eternity to Riley. He took the stairs and stopped at each flight to see if anyone was following him. Once he reached the sixth floor, he paused, took a deep breath and wiped his sweaty face on his coat sleeve. He looked down the narrow hallway. It seemed extremely quiet to him. Riley found room 610. He knocked softly. There was no answer. He knocked again, slightly harder. Still no answer.

Riley opened the door and nearly smacked into the worried face of the bartender. He was pacing the floor, walking back and forth to the window, piercing through the blinds. He just happened to be near the door when Riley opened it.

"Jesus Christ," whispered Riley, "what are trying to do, scare the hell out of me."

"What's the matter, you don't trust me?

"I don't trust anybody in this country."

"Hell, come in and shut the door."

When Riley started to shut the door, the draft from an opened window slammed the it shut. The overhead light fixture in the center of the ceiling shook back and forth. He stared at the light for a moment and then at the bartender. "By the way, what's your name?"

"My name is unimportant. The information I have is of the utmost importance to you and your son."

"Why is someone trying to harm my son? What is the significant of the riddle?" And why are you helping me?"

"Wait. Not so many questions. I have my reasons. This country..."

Suddenly there was a noise outside the window. It was the sound of someone rubbing a scrub board. Darkness filled the room. Someone kicked the door in. The light of the full moon displayed the silhouettes of three figures on the walls.

"No, no. please," cried the bartender.

Riley felt an excruciating pain. He grabs the side of his head, felt something wet, and saw the bartender on his knees, begging for his life before he passed out.

It was almost nine hours later before Riley awakened. He had a splitting headache. He touched the back of his head and rubbed it. "Ouch," he cried. Riley looked at the palm of his hand, and noticed it was filled with blood. He grabbed the back of a chair and slowly rose to his feet. He braced the muscles in his legs and used the chair to lift himself. His vision was blurry. He saw the image of what he first believed to be a man; however, the man's figure seemed strange. He had a long thin frame and a head too big for his body.

He rubbed his eyes, hard, several times. His vision was now clear.

"Ugh! Ugh." Riley emitted a loud burp and grabbed his mouth. He could not stop the violet fluids secreting from his mouth. He ran to the bathroom, leaving behind trails of vomit on the floor.

He filled the sink with a green colored retch. A few minutes later, he returned to the center room. He nearly vomited again. There anchored on a spear in the center of the room was the head of the bartender. The word '*Ngadla*' was written in blood on the floor beneath his head.

A few minutes later, the hotel security arrived with the police.

"Dr. Riley did you know the deceased."

Riley sat in a chair, his face buried in his hands. His stomach growled. "No, as I told the other officer, I didn't know the bartender."

"If you didn't know him, then why were both of you in Mr. McGladdery's room?"

"Who's McGladdery? I thought this was the bartender's room."

"The bartender's room, now that's a new one. Since when did a local Blackie bartender rent a room in one of Johannesburg finest hotels?"

Riley looked up at the detective. "Why is that strange? I'm a colored man," he smarted, "and I'm staying at this hotel."

"Yes, very true, Dr. Riley, however, you are a visiting guest of the all mighty United States, and of course a Nobel Peace Prize winner. My government must pay its due respects to such a man, regardless of your color."

"Detective, I didn't get your name. Who are you?"

"Oh, please excuse me, Dr. Riley. I'm Detective Jan Linden."

After two days of intense questioning by Linden, Riley left Johannesburg and traveled back to the United States. It was near Christmas and he wanted to be with his family during the holidays.

Jan and his fellow detectives did not have any clues or evidence to show Riley killed the bartender. One week later, he arrived at work, tired and exhausted. His mind churned with doubts about Dr. Riley, he went straight to his superior.

He had accumulated eight weeks of vacation time. He decided to use this time and followed Riley back to the United States to find out everything he could about him. He prepared himself for the trip.

Jan stood at the window of his home overlooking the lake. The late afternoon sun rays bounced off the still body of water. The light made him squint and the reflection through the window added a glittering luster to his gray sideburns. He had experienced a rough day; there was a resurgence of black resistance to the pass laws. Tired from the gruesome day, he decided to retire to the study and update his journal of news in South Africa and world events. Linden started his third binder and over the years, he became more selective in news clippings.

The year –1964

January 9 – Viet Cong guerrillas overrun two strategic hamlets in South Vietnam Pleiku Province, 250 south of Saigon.

January 28 – Soviet fighters near Erfurt, East Germany attack and shoot down a U.S. Air Force T–39 training plane. The American pilot fails to respond to warnings that he was entering Soviet air space. All three crew members are killed.

February 25 – Cassius Clay, at the age of 22, a 7 to 1 underdog, wins the world heavyweight, boxing championship in Miami Beach with a seventh round TKO over Sonny Liston.

March 10 – Soviet air defenses shoot down an unarmed U.S. Air Force RB–66 jet reconnaissance plane over East Germany. All three crew members parachute to safety. This is the second attack in six weeks where a U.S. plane has been shot down over East Germany.

June 12 – South Africa's Supreme Court sentences Nelson Mandela to life imprisonment on charges of conspiring to promote a revolution. Captain of Detectives, Jan Linden, is instrumental in gathering evidence against others involved in the plot.

July 13 – U.S. sends 300 more special forces troops to Vietnam, bringing total American military manpower up to 16,000. Major Jonathan McClendon leads the group.

October 22 – Martin Luther King, civil rights leader, wins the Nobel Peace Prize.

November 3 – President Johnson scores a landslide victory over Republican Senator Barry Goldwater.

December 11 – South Africa announces a new amendment to the current law strengthening apartheid, which would give the seven million blacks living in white areas the status of "temporary dwellers."

December 19 – South Vietnam's ruling political government is overthrown in a military coup headed by Air Commodore General Nguyen Ky and Brigadier General Nguyen Van Thieu for conspiring with French agents in a plan for the neutralization of South Vietnam.

The morning light broke over the rolling mountain as pockets of mist could be seen floating up from the river outside the city. It was late December and tensions escalated throughout South Africa as anti–apartheid sentiment gathered force. Nelson Mandela's followers and ANC forces were still outraged over his life sentence.

The South Africa government amended and strengthens Apartheid. The new law took away the blacks' rights to land ownership by classifying over seven million blacks who are living in white areas with the status of temporary dwellers. Demonstrations created violent police responses that intensified when five white gunmen shot and killed fifteen blacks and wounded forty more in an attack on striking workers at an iron and steel factory west of Johannesburg. In retaliation, the following day, five people, including a white priest were killed when shooting broke out as a funeral procession passed a squatter camp in a nearby township.

Jan and his men were the first to arrive. He gasped when he saw the bullet–ridden body of a small young boy, twelve or thirteen of age lying beside toppled wooden chairs. He turned and saw a woman weeping, her face buried in the grass. He recognized the young boy; he was the precinct houseboy. He gritted his teeth; he was so angry the veins stood out on his forehead. "Damn, what a waste. Will they ever learn this is one battle they cannot win?

Something Precious is Lost

Washington D.C. – April 1964

Dr. Riley had just received an honorary doctorate from Howard University. The doctor continued to impress his colleagues and peers with his research. He had written several books on the subject, which became required reading material at the undergraduate and graduate levels at many of the leading universities.

His son Michael was about to reach his sixteenth birthday. Riley gave him the keys to his own car. He was extremely proud of his dad, and his grades indicated an equal intelligence level. The argument he had earlier with his Dad tarnished his day.

School officials wanted to advance Michael to a senior this September to graduate two years ahead of his class. Michael was opposed to the idea. He was looking forward to the summer months and wanted to remain with his friends and classmates as long as he continued to receive high marks.

Riley insisted on Michael graduating two years ahead of his time, which would make it easier for him to receive an academic scholarship to Harvard University.

Across town, the phone rang in the precinct office.

"LaRue! Telephone!" shouted one of the detectives.

Linden waited until the detective had finished his phone conversation. LaRue, leaning back in the chair had one leg rested on the desk. He noticed a solid brass bald eagle that the detective used a paperweight.

"Detective LaRue?"

"Yes, what can I do for you?

"I'm Jan Linden, Captain of Detectives, from Johannesburg,

South Africa. Here are my credentials."

"You're a long way from home Captain, how can I help you?" LaRue motion with his hand and offered him a seat.

"Thank you, I prefer to stand. It was a long plane ride. I am here in your country investigating several murders committed in my country. I believed the murders are connected to a conspiracy to cause harm to certain governmental officials in South Africa."

"Captain Linden, I don't understand why your government would send you all the way to Washington, D.C. for crimes committed in your country."

"I believed the conspirators are funded by a man named Rogers. I followed his trail to Paris but he escaped me once again. He is quite an elusive fellow. I had about given up the hunt until I saw a picture of your Dr. William Riley shaking Rogers' hand at a speaking engagement. In addition, I have information from verifiable sources that Rogers is now somewhere in Washington D.C."

LaRue sat upright when he heard Riley's name. "You did say, Dr. William Riley?"

"Precisely sir. Dr. Riley was also in and out of South Africa the past two years."

LaRue frowned. He positioned himself in the chair. "Yeah, yeah I know. The damn federal government gave him a grant to do some research on the economic problems of the colored people."

"Precisely," replied Linden. "The doctor came to South Africa to study the Blackies' economic plight. There are more than enough problems in the United States with the blacks for plenty of research material."

"Hey, speak for yourself," snapped LaRue. "At least we don't restrict their travel. From what I read, your country got those damn Pass Laws, and that's the majority of your country's problems with them."

"My dear fellow, I believed the Blackies' freedom to move about in the United States is a matter of interpretation. Besides, I did not sit on a long bumpy plane ride to debate my country Pass Laws.

"Then what in tarnation brings you to me? Why didn't you

follow Dr. Riley to see if he could lead you to this Rogers person?"

"I don't have the manpower at my disposal to put Dr. Riley under surveillance nor do I have jurisdiction in your country."

"What makes you think I would assign men to help you track Rogers?" laughed LaRue. "Hell, for all you know, Dr. Riley probably shakes a hundred hands at a speaking engagement. There must be a countless number of press and other well-wishers taking pictures."

Linden gave him a stern look. "Because Dr. Russell Brown was killed with a poison made from the leaves of a wag'-n-bietjie tree combined with leaves from a hemp plant. Since Rogers lived in South Africa, he could have obtained access to the leaves and visited any Zulu witch-doctor for the concoction. I understand you never quite believed Dr. Riley's story as to why he was there. However, you had no evidence to link him to the murder."

LaRue stared at the man from him. He was telling the truth. LaRue stood. "You know an awful lot about the case, Captain Linden, where's your source?"

"Good question."

"I don't believe the Washington Post is printed in South Africa."

"As one good detective to another, I make it my business to get all the facts. Now if we can compare notes, you may have enough to re-open the investigation." He provided Detective LaRue with enough information to convince his superiors to assign a team of surveillance officers to watch Dr. Riley. The two men agreed to meet again later in one hour, after he checked into a hotel.

Linden had not come to the United States alone. Andrea came with him. After twelve years, her husband had abruptly terminated their marriage. He had celebrated his 45th birthday by declaring his independence and giving Andrea hers. The woman who once decided not wait on Jan found that he had waited for her. When she learned he was going to Washington D.C., she practically insisted on coming. Andrea had been to the U.S. Capitol on several occasions on official business for the South African embassy. She was no longer a police officer but an official representative for the South Africa government.

Andrea was given the task of improving government relations

among its principal trade partners: Britain, West Germany, Japan, Switzerland, and the United States. Andrea wanted to be his official guide.

Jan for the first time in his life was not his grouchy self. He smiled more, a lot more, the glow to his face had returned. Andrea had a way of bringing him out of his shell. He knew it would take LaRue a little time to set up the surveillance team, so he promised Andrea as soon he and LaRue set things into motion, he would leave the station so they would spend the rest of the day together. This gave her time to unpack, take a bath, and get into some fresh clothes. Andrea had planned everything from renting a room with a private bath in an old Victoria house in Georgetown to obtaining passes for a special tour of the White House from the South African Ambassador.

Andrea walked into the bathroom and dropped her panties. She became conscious of her naked body, displayed in the huge mirror. Her breasts were small, but firm: Her nipples, somewhat large, considering the size of the breasts. The stomach was flat, the buttocks firm but soft and the thighs supported her tall slender figure. Andrea had no problems finding the right man. She had not mellowed; she was still aggressive, outgoing, and demanding. Nevertheless, sometimes, she wanted the confines of a marriage, especially the companionship of a wonderful and caring mate who accepted all of her faults and still loved her. Jan was this man. She had never stopped loving him.

She immersed herself in the bubble bath, relaxed and let warm water engulf her body. An hour later, she dressed herself in a blue jumpsuit, one which he loved so much, especially the view from the rear. She was reading a magazine when she heard a key in the door. It was Jan.

"Hungry?"

"Not really."

"Good. We will just pick up something to kill the appetite. I have plenty to show you in a short period. Tonight, we can go to this fabulous restaurant on the Potomac near the yacht basin. The rainbow trout stuffed with crab meat is excellent. You can make a pig of yourself later. Let's walk, it's a beautiful day."

"Anything you say, honey, I'm all yours."

"You won't be completely mine until I get you into bed. I love to hear you growl."

"I'll make a point not to make very much noise tonight. You know there are three other rooms rented."

"Don't worry, Jan, the walls are awfully thick and I made a point of selecting the room near the end with its own private entrance and bath. There will be a full moon tonight."

Jan took her by the hand. The two clung to each other as though it was their first date. They visited the Capitol and toured the Supreme Court building. He wanted particularly to tour the FBI building before seeing the White House.

"Jan, let's not try to see all of Washington, D.C. in one day. It's late and I don't think with the crowd of people that we are going to tour the FBI building today. And the White House, you can forget it, as they say in America, no way, Jose."

He smiled and placed his hand on her cheek. "You're right Andrea, but you do know that this trip was no vacation. I'm here on business and I let you convince me to bring you along."

"But you promised to spend at least two or three days with me. I will hold you to that promise. Please don't let this crusade of yours ruin our reunion."

"As they also say in Mexico, no go, Jose." Jan laughed and squeezed Andrea's hand.

Later in the evening after a quiet dinner, they arrived back at the hotel.

"Let's take a shower together," said Andrea. She grabbed Jan's hand and led him to the bathroom. As soon as they stepped into the bathroom, she closed the door.

He was not surprised by her bold move. "Do you mind if I take off your clothes first?"

She pushed him back against the bathroom door. "Lean back and relax, I will undress you after I find what I'm looking for."

She unzipped his pants, unbuttoned his boxer short and

searched for his semi–hard penis. Her warm hand grabbed his testicles and maneuvered his penis out of the pants. It protruded from the opening in his pants. Andrea watched it become thicker and continued to grow until he was fully erect.

"My, my, what do we have here? Did I ever say you look really good?" Andrea's hand was around the tip of his penis; she kissed him softly on the lips.

Jan smiled and placed both hand on Andrea's face, her head slightly tilted. "Thanks, we middle–aged men also need a little reassurance from time to time." He kissed her softly while Andrea massaged him. He moaned. His hands let go of her face and unzipped her jump suit down to the crotch. He slid his hand into the opening of her lace panties. The warm touch of his hand caused her to squirm. He knew where to touch her. The area that caused her to purr like a kitten. Andrea breathed harder and she intensified the massage.

Jan started to sweat. "Andrea," he whispered, his hand drawing her close to him. "Only you can do this to me, I love you. I have never stopped loving you."

"Oh Jan, why did we waste all those years? I've always loved you." Andrea opened her mouth to kiss him allowing their tongues to twist together. She held the kiss. The intensity of her hand rubbing his manhood caused him to let out a mild groan. Andrea kissed him harder, grabbed his testicles in the palm of her hand, and carefully inserted a finger into his rectum.

Jan groaned louder, his body sloped forward; his fingers explored her wet thighs and the soft darkness between them. Her body trembled – his shuddered, together they both let out a loud cry.

Andrea's head rested on Jan's chest, his face on her shoulder. Their smiles were an indication of complete satisfaction. Five minutes elapsed without a word being uttered between them. They quietly removed each other's clothes. She squeezed his hand and the two walked with her hand around his waist into the shower stall.

The following morning she had convinced Jan to spend the next day together before he resumed his hunt for Rogers and Nigel's killers. He agreed to take her to the White House, the Lincoln

Memorial and the FBI building. They were acting like two young lovers, held each other's hands, kissed many times throughout the tours, and exchanged, "I love you's."

They walked by the Smithsonian Institute when Andrea noticed a small group of snack shops on the corner. It was an ideal time to rest their feet.

"So, this is a hot dog," said Jan. "It's not bad."

Andrea wiped the mustache off his mustache. "It's all right to kill an appetite."

A small girl approached them. "Excuse me, sir," she said. "We're running a special on Napoleon ice cream. Here is a small sample to see if you like it. It's very good." The girl handed Jan a small paper cup of ice cream.

"Napoleon ice cream," laughed Linden. "Oh, these Americans, anything to make a dollar."

"Let me try it," said Andrea, reaching across and taking the cup from Jan. "Mmm, it's delicious, thanks little girl."

"Child, how much do I owe you?" Jan asked.

"It costs seventy–five cents for a pint."

"Oh, a pint is too much, but here's twenty–five cents for the sample." Jan looked at Andrea. She had almost demolished the cup of ice cream.

"No, I'm sorry Jan, you can't have any, and I don't want to spoil your appetite for the wonderful dinner you're going to buy for me later. Come on honey finish your hot dog. These passes are for 3:15 p.m. and we only have twenty minutes to get to the FBI building. We may have to take a taxi. Wait, there's a carriage. Hey driver! Driver, over here! Come on honey." Andrea grabbed his hand. The two ran across the street when Andrea suddenly fell to her knees.

"Andrea! What's wrong!" cried Jan. Her body went through a series of violent convulsions as though she was having an epileptic attack. Her body arched upwards and then suddenly dropped quickly to the pavement. Jan looked around. "Is there a doctor around? Please! Will someone call a medic?

Jan felt helpless. He bent over her. He touched Andrea's cheek. She lay still on the cold pavement. He opened her eyelids. Her pupils confirmed her death. Jan touched her temple feeling no pulse.

Tears flowed down Jan's cheek. The only woman he loved was now dead. "The ice cream. It was meant for me," he muttered. "No–oo!" The sound of his voice was heard for miles around. His outburst of remorse startled the innocent bystanders. His enlarged eyes and face displayed his anger.

Jan jerked his head and looked around for the ice cream vendor. He saw the small child that handed him the ice cream. He ran towards her.

Startled by Jan sudden actions, the little girl asked. "What's wrong with the lady mister?" He grabbed the girl by the arm. "Ouch! You're hurting me," cried the girl.

"The ice cream! The Napoleon ice cream you gave us. It contained poison."

The girl's father grabbed Jan by the arm and turned him around. "I beg your pardon, sir! There is nothing wrong with our ice cream. We are running a special today. I must have sold three vats of Napoleon today. The people next to you were eating ice cream from the same container. Your young lady must have died from something else."

"Then someone put something into the ice cream!"

"Daddy, a man bumped into my tray when I was handing out the cups. He knocked me down but somehow caught the tray before it fell. He apologized and said he was very sorry."

Jan grabbed the girl's shoulders. "What man?" he demanded.

"I don't see the man," said the girl, "but I saw him running when the lady fell down."

"What did he look like? Tell me!" Jan's grip on the girl's shoulders tighten.

The girl became frighten. "Daddy, daddy, he's hurting me."

The father pulled away one of Jan's hands. "Mister, let go of my child!"

Jan stared at the man, then the girl. "I'm sorry honey; I didn't mean to hurt you. Please, tell the man what the man looked like."

The girl looked at her father, and he nodded.

"He was a colored man, sir. A tall colored man."

"The Circle!"

CHAPTER TWENTY ONE

The Jackal Meets the Old Man

Two hours later

He watched from across the street as the coroner's personnel lifted her and zipped her body into a black body bag.

"God damn it! Why her and not me?" he shouted.

I'm sorry Captain Linden," said Detective LaRue, blowing his nose, "but I must ask you some more questions surrounding the bizarre death of your fiancée. As a police officer, I'm sure you understand." The pollen in the air during the fall season had always been a problem for him.

Jan sighed. "Go ahead and ask your questions."

"Since you are Captain of Detectives in Johannesburg, I will get straight to the area of my concern. What's the connection between Andrea's murder and Dr. Russell Brown's death?"

"I don't know, LaRue. I really don't know."

"I'm sorry, but I cannot accept that answer. You are thousands of miles away from your country. You just decided to visit the nation's capital. The first thing you do after arrival was to drop by the precinct to ask me some questions regarding Dr. Brown's death. Then you show me a picture of Dr. Riley shaking the hand of a man named Roger's. Give me a fucking break! Now, what in the hell does Rogers have to do with these murders?"

"Damn it, LaRue! If I knew, I would find that son of a bitch."

"And do what, Captain Linden! Kill him?"

"No! Beat the bloody shit out of him. And then take him back to my country, so we can hang his ass!"

"Oh, no you won't! We will fry his ass here in the United States for the murder of an American citizen," stated LaRue. "How long are you going to stay in this country?"

"My Visa expires in seven days."

"I will get back in touch with you after the autopsy is done. Don't leave the city."

Jan awakened in the middle of the night. He was restless. Every time he closed his eyes and drifted into sleep, visions of Andrea appeared. It was completely dark in the bedroom but the luminous dial of the clock reflected 1:00 a.m. The more he dreamed of Andrea, the angrier and more obsessed he became with bringing the members of the Circle to justice. Jan lay in bed with tears in his eyes. An occasional smile occurred each time he remembered a scene vividly portraying the good times with her. He rested on his back for a while before passing once again into a light sleep. A short time later, he awakened once again, only this time he was sure he heard something other than the thoughts of Andrea in his mind. He listened intently, thinking someone, perhaps an intruder, was in the room. "But that cannot be," he thought. "I latched the door."

He lay still and listened. Everything was silent, except the ticking of the clock. He was tired and beat. He needed sleep, but his police instincts would not let him drop his guard. He glanced around the small room. Nothing.

"The bathroom," he thought. "The door was cracked open. I closed it, I know I did." Jan reached slowly for his Luger lying on the nightstand. He crawled out of bed and proceeded towards the bathroom. Suddenly he felt a sharp pain in the buttocks. He tried to reach around to rub it, but found he could barely move his arm. Linden felt a terrible numbing pain in his leg.

It was daylight when he came too. He grabbed his head and felt pain. He also had a splitting headache. His vision was hazy. His blue eyes widened and slowly focused on an old man dressed in a dashiki. The room had a peculiar smell he could not identity.

"You, my dear fellow, have been a thorn in the side. It has been sixteen years since Nigel's death and you are still determined to pursue the reason for his death. I admire you, Captain Linden; especially after all the ridicule you have endured from your peers and superiors. You are very lucky. If it wasn't for the ignorance of your people, perhaps I would have eliminated you years ago."

Jan tried to rise. His mind was willing but his body did not obey. "You bastard! You killed my fiancée, Andrea! I will not rest until I see you and all of your allies hanged by the neck until dead."

"You are too wrapped up in emotions to understand. If I wanted you killed, you would have been dead long ago. It would have been swift, before you knew what hit you.

"I don't believe you. I have been close too many times. It's you who's behind this conspiracy."

"Rogers is your foe, not I, nor Dr. Riley. Rogers killed your woman."

Jan tried again to rise. His shoulders move only a couple of inches. "Bullshit! Rogers is a wimp."

The old man laughed a little and pointed his forefinger at Linden. "Yes, but that little wimp gave you a royal beating."

"He works for you. He takes your money. It's you with the power to lead..."

"But to gain power, one need not be violent, for danger is common to all. What we don't understand, we cannot control." The old man stood up and glanced down upon Linden. "Give up your pursuit. You are only creating havoc to yourself and those close to you."

Jan felt a twitch in his hands. "I will not rest until I see you and all of your people hanged."

"The pain in your head, my son, will ease in several hours. Your body coordination will also return. Close your eyes and rest, for no harm will come to you, as long you don't disturb the children of the future."

CHAPTER TWENTY TWO

A Boy Grows Up

May – 1964

"Dr. Riley, Congratulations. Your family and your son must be very proud. You have taught him well," said the old man. He shook Dr. Riley's hand; he was one in the long line of well–wishers. It's been twenty years since the old man wore a coat and tie. His bag of clothing lay beside his feet in a duffle bag.

Dr. Riley gracefully returned the greetings, shaking one hand after another. It was not until he was halfway down the line that he realized a faint but peculiar odor that once filled the room of Dr. Browne's office. He turned his head and looked back. The old man was gone. Dr. Riley's eyes searched the room for the old man, but the faculty, guest, and students, offering congratulations, constantly interrupted him.

Michael, bored by the activities, slipped quietly away to the parking lot to admire his new car. Dr. Riley's award was on the same day as Michael's birthday. Michael sat behind the steering wheel with a broad smile, thinking he could not wait to drive to the local hangout for the teens in his high school.

"Hello Michael."

"Mr. Williams," said a startled Michael. "You certainly have a way of appearing in the oddest of places and times. The last time I saw you we were in Paris, and the time before that in Geneva. For a man your age, one would think you walk on water."

"The secret of walking on water, Michael, is knowing where the stones are."

"That's the problem, sir, I sometimes think only you know where those stones are."

"I appreciate that you did not tell your parents of our previous meetings."

"Gosh, you're the only one I can talk too. My dad is too wrapped up in all of his studies. And mom, she still treats me like a little kid."

"Yes, I know, my son. Michael, it's time for you to move on to greater things. Your dad is right. You should be advanced to the higher grade."

"But, I don't want to. My friends..."

"Michael, listen to me. What have I given you over the years?"

"Wisdom and knowledge."

"It's time for you to increase that knowledge. One should never treat lightly, the power of knowledge. Honor your dad's wishes for one day you will claim title to a great piece of land."

"Oh yeah, Dad always said all the great old wars were over land."

"That's true, little one, but that feat is not your mission. Listen closely. There is a poem by an American poet. His name was Edmund Vance Cook. The first two verses of his poem were called <u>Uncivilized</u>. It will one day have an impact on a great decision you will have to make. Listen to the words."

> *An ancient ape, once on a time*
> *Disliked exceedingly to climb*
> *And so he picked him out a tree*
> *And said, "Now this belongs to me.*
> *I have a hunch that monks are mutts*
> *And I can make them gather nuts*
> *And bring the bulk of them to me,*
> *By claiming title to this tree."*
> *He took a green leaf and a reed*
> *And wrote himself a title deed,*
> *Proclaiming pompously and slow:*
> *"All monkeys by these presents know."*
> *Next morning when the monkeys came*
> *To gather nuts, he made his claim:*
> *"All monkeys climbing on this tree*

> *Must bring their gathered nuts to me*
> *Cracking the same on equal shares,*
> *The meats are mine, the shell are theirs."*
> *"But by what right?" they cried, amazed,*
> *Thinking the ape was surely crazed.*
> *"By this," he answered; "if you'll read*
> *You'll find it in a title deed,*
> *Made in precise and formal shape*
> *And sworn before a fellow ape,*
> *Exactly on the legal plan*
> *Used by that wondrous creature, man,*
> *In London, Tokyo, New York,*
> *Glengarry, Kalamazoo and Cork.*
> *Unless my deed is recognized*
> *"It proves you quite uncivilized."*

Djhon stood in awe. "Sir, that is a great poem. Who was the poet? It's really good."

The old man was disappointed in his reaction. "Djhon, you didn't listen to the words."

"I did sir."

"No, my son. You did not. You only heard the words. A day will come when you will say to an ancient ape that he alone did not make the tree, and the day will come when the young apes will rise in rebellion and all the apes of all origins will share the meats of the nuts."

"Sir, there you go again, always talking in riddles."

The old gave a short laugh. "You too will talk in riddles one day. Now go and do as your dad asked."

"I will do as you ask, for I owe you a lot."

"Good! When you were in Paris, I discussed there would be three things I would share with you. Do you recall what the third one was?"

"Sir, that was four years ago."

"Think boy, think."

Michael closed his eyes and rubbed his eyebrow several times. "I believe it was leadership."

"Fine. I will leave you with a thought until the next time. Knowledge and leadership are like a marriage. Melding the two requires patience. Work on it. The time will come when you will need both." The old man turned and walked away from the car.

"But sir, I don't know anything about being a leader," shouted Michael.

"I will teach you," said the old man. His voice faded in the background of the band's music.

CHAPTER TWENTY THREE

A Time to Fight

West Germany, NATO Headquarters – June – 1964

"Honey, what's so interesting in the Washington Post that has you so intrigued? The last few weeks when the mail arrives from the states, the first thing you read is that darn paper your sergeant buddy keeps sending."

"Sergeant Major, Phyllis. Eddie is a Sergeant Major now."

"So he's a Sergeant Major, what's so important in that newspaper?" Jonathan read the article aloud. '*Despite the still limited nature of the United States involvement in South Vietnam, the so called conflict continues to grow in intensity. More and more, U.S. Special Forces outposts come under attack. More and more, U.S. soldiers are asked to risk their lives in the crucible of battle.*'

"I knew it! I knew it! You must go where the action is! Didn't you get your share of Korea? Why must you always be in the thick of things? Vietnam, the hell with South Vietnam!"

"Dad, did I hear Vietnam?" Djhon asked. "Are you going to fight in Vietnam?" He walked into the kitchen after he heard Phyllis shouting.

"Not yet son, but I have asked General Gage to use his influence to get me an assignment in South Vietnam."

"All right! That's another promotion for you, Dad."

Phyllis's voice was high with rage and shock. "I don't believe I'm hearing this. A sixteen–year–old boy, excited to see his dad fighting. Djhon, do you realize that he could actually be killed or seriously injured?"

"Phyllis, Phyllis. Let us not give Djhon a complex. You knew before we came to Germany that I wanted an assignment in Vietnam.

It has been a long four years stationed here and fourteen years since I have been in any combat action. I am bored! Fighting is in my blood."

"Dad wants to be a General, and it definitely helps to command men in a combat situation. That's why I want to go to West Point and graduate at the top of my class. Sorry Dad, no OCS training for me."

"Vietnam, West Point, OCS, you two believes you all can lick the enemy single–handed. I don't believe this. It's been four years since we were in Texas and I'm still saying y'all." Phyllis gave up the argument as a lost cause.

Jonathan and Djhon both chuckled.

The following month – Frankfurt, Germany

It was July, and it should not have been chilly. Perhaps chilly was too strong a word for the stiff breeze catching almost everyone by surprise. It was a cool day for the city of Frankfurt.

The customers have complained all day about the temperature in the lounge. It felt colder inside than outside. But every man in the place felt the same heated passion as the next man. Heads turned when she walked passed each table.

Lisa was a beautiful woman. The new hairstyle affected a startling change in her appearance. She had a petite body and a shapely figure with long jet–black hair hanging freely down to her buttocks.

"Jack Daniels and Coke, twist of lemon, not lime, light on the ice and half your normal dose of coke," said the woman in red as she snapped her fingers at the bartender.

"JD, a little ice, a splash of coke coming right up, Ma'am," he replied, not taking his eyes off of Lisa. She was standing across the room beside an empty glass tray. Their eyes met, she finally smiled. Rogers smiled back.

She approached the wet bar area for a drink order. His thoughts were interrupted when his eyes became fixed at the wedding ring on her finger. His young darling belonged to another man, a sergeant in the Army. She often boasted that no one had a more lovely marriage.

"I asked for a twist of lemon not lime!" barked the woman as she poured the drink into the tip jar and slammed down the glass. "You would think this five–star hotel could hire competence bartenders!" Her anger exposed signs of a face–lift, especially around the eyes and cheeks. The skin appeared to be stretched to its fullest. The woman wore an elegant lace shawl over a matching embroidered jacket and long, slit skirt.

The woman's facial expression also indicated that she was accustomed to giving orders and demanding service. She was in her early fifties and sat at the bar between two customers; regulars every Thursday night. One was a wide fat man named Eddie, with a medicine ball of a stomach hidden under his pinstriped shirt and the other was a grim–faced man in a dark three–piece suit called Art.

The two men were competitors, they both worked for companies supplying arms and weapons to the military.

The woman was definitely upset at the Rogers' obvious lack of concentration on the task. She adjusted a brown hair comb in her sleek hair and glanced between the clock behind the bar and then at her watch, a handsome piece with a row of eight sparkling diamonds around the crystal. Her hair was in a French twist, and the comb, hardly noticeable until touched, had eight small cultured pearls. She was definitely part of the wealthy German clientele and seemed out of place. They have their own clique and seldom mingle with the average customer and especially this particular bar.

A big grin broke out on the faces of Art and Eddie. They were amused at the hard time she was giving Rogers.

"Say bartenders, the lady asked for a twist of lemon not lime," said Art. He snickered at Rogers.

"Sir, I don't need you to speak for me," snapped the woman. Rogers frowned at her. He disdained her icy aloofness. "Don't stare at me!" shouted the woman. "If you kept your mind on the job, you would have mixed the drink as I requested.

Art made a snide remark and laughed. Rogers walked toward the men and whispered. "Some tough broad." He slowly walked back to where she was seated and wiped the bar with a damp cloth.

"I'm sorry Ma'am, it won't happen again. I am very proud of my profession and seldom make mistakes. I was considered by my peers to be one of the best bartenders in town." He pointed to a signed on the wall behind the counter. "I always carry the placard with me. Look, it simply stated, THE CUSTOMERS ARE ALWAYS RIGHT. THEY CREATE THE BACON. I MERELY CONSUME IT."

Rogers stooped down to open the door to the refrigerator under the counter to look for some more lemons. "Damn, this box is filthy," he whispered. "Old dried cherries, and desiccated orange slices." He sliced the lemon peel and mixed the drink. "JD and coke with a slice of lemon, Ma'am, sorry about the mistake."

She lifted her drink, took several gulps and handed the eight-ounce glass back to him. Her eyes creased into a frown. "It isn't enough." She reached in her purse and pulled out an ostrich skin cigarette case trimmed with gold. The long thin cigarette met her red lips. She waited for Rogers to lite it.

He struck the match tip with his fingernail and lite the cigarette. "Enough Ma'am, what isn't enough?" he said, trying to hide his displeasure at the woman behavior."

She took a long drag and slowly exhaled the strong sweet aroma. "Where's Wingate, he knows that I require at least two ounces of JD in my drinks, and he certainly knows how to make my drink."

"He's off tonight, Ma'am. I will be more than happy to put another shot in your drink."

"Then what's the hell are you waiting for?"

Her retort left him with nothing more to say. He poured the woman another shot without using the shot glass. The woman took her drink and moved to the corner end of the bar near the server's order counter. She glanced once more at her watch.

"Her elegant mouth will get her in trouble one of these days," Art whispered again to Eddie.

"Do you think she's staying at the hotel?" Eddie whispered back.

Art shrugged his shoulders. "Naw, she's too snobbish to stay at this plain hotel." The two broke into a mutual laugh, coughing to disguise the sound.

"Say bartender, give those two another round of drinks before their throats become dry from laughter and I'll have another Jack and Coke with a twist of lemon. This time I want more of Jack and less of Coke."

"Why thank you Ma'am," said Art, his voice a mockery of southern hospitality.

"One mug of dark Beck's ale and one Gin Presbyterian," said Rogers. He handed the men their drinks.

"Thank you bartender," said Eddie. "Art, I don't see how you can drink that shit. Every time you order that drink, you make me want to say grace."

The woman grabbed another cigarette. Rogers was quick to lite it.

She took a long a good draw and looked at the two men. "Gentlemen, apparently, sometime during your child bearing ages, the most important time in the development of child personality, an important and vital nutriment was missing from your mothers' milk." Rogers nearly choked on the coke he was drinking. The two men stared at the woman in red. They did not speak. Silence became them. "Say bartender, this drink is still not right," she shouted. "Is there any drink that you are capable of mixing well and are known to be good at?"

Rogers smiled. "Mixing drinks is my livelihood. There are very few drinks that these hands cannot bring together." He proudly displayed his hands, the fingers moving in a rhythmic motion. Modest, he was not. "The drink all of my friends cherish is called a Slaughter Special. Some people have nicknamed it Headache Special. The drink gained its popularity from around the Vienna area. A wealthy investment banker introduced the drink to his guests at his beach house on a hot summer day. It's a great thirst buster, but if you are not used to it, the side effect is one hell of a headache. It can also bring on a very quick high and can put you in a very good mood."

Eddie was the first to speak again. "That's a hell of a drink; My

Bud Light can cure the most powerful thirst known to man without that kind of side effect." He raised his bottle and gulped the remainder of his beer.

"I'll take it," ordered the woman. "It better be good or you will have to find another tip jar."

A man appeared and put his arm around the woman. "Oh, it's about time. Where in the hell have you been?" She looked at Rogers and snapped her finger. "Bartender, give him a Chivas Regal and soda."

"I'm sorry I'm late," the man apologized and kissed her on the lips.

"You should be sorry; I've been waiting on you for thirty minutes. I'm going to the lady's room to freshen up." The woman squeezed his hand and smiled for the first time tonight.

"Chivas and soda, sir." Rogers placed the drink in front of his new customer. He gulped the drink down in two swallows.

"I'm going to be a naughty boy tonight. Let me have another one and make it a double."

The man looked at his watch. It was obvious, he was nervous. The woman returned ten minutes later carrying a black duffel bag.

"Bartender, let me have another Chivas and soda."

"No! Bartender, give me the tab," demanded the woman.

"Yes, damn you," snapped the man.

"If I told you once, I've told you a hundred times, you are too rough with me when you've had several of those drinks." The man's stubbornness infuriated the woman.

The man rolled his eyes at Rogers. "Look baby, I..."

"Don't look baby me. Get up and let's go," said the woman as she walked away. The man was silent. He got up and followed a step behind her.

"Oh, that poor man," said Art.

"Don't pity him," said Eddie, "he's the type that's probably into S&M and loves to be led around on a leash."

Everyone watched the couple walk to the club's entrance, when the woman stop and started walking back towards the bar.

"Here bartender, somebody left this bag in the lady's room. I took the liberty of opening the side pocket to see if some type of identification was in it. The only thing I found was a passport from South Africa. The woman in the picture on the passport claim appears to be the wife of a Zulu chieftain. Hell, this hotel is certainly going to the dogs, imagine allowing one of them use our bathroom." The woman stuck out her chest in a proud position and walked away.

Rogers grabbed his right wrist, opened the palm of his hand and rested the side of his face on it. He smiled an unblended hundred and fifty proof smile. "All along I thought my contact was one of the arms buyers and all along it was the woman in red. Man, are they good. Hell, they just may pull it off, and I will make a mint."

"Bartender, what's in the bag," asked Eddie.

Rogers looked into the duffel bag. His eyes widened. The payoff was there and something extra. One million dollars, in one thousand dollars bills."

"Oh nothing, just some old clothes."

CHAPTER TWENTY FOUR

Ask and You Shall Receive

South Vietnam – July 1964

General Gage fulfilled his promise to McClendon and was able to arrange an assignment in Vietnam. He arrived in Da Lat when it was intensely hot and humid. The war was still primarily a Vietnamese conflict. His strict orders and sole purpose was to help the South Vietnamese. McClendon was assigned to a Vietnamese captain, Nguyen Dang. The captain was in charge of South Vietnamese regulars fighting against the North Vietnam People's Army.

Jonathan was assigned to the 2nd Battalion, 17th Cavalry, and 101st Airborne. His orders were to offer only technical and military advice. The other U.S. military advisors were part of MAAG, and drew the unenviable task of building the South Vietnamese armed forces; a group of under–armed men and poorly advised leaders, into a military force capable of fighting the North VIETCONG, a well–equipped and well–armed enemy on his own terms. However, with fewer than 20,000 U.S. troops, most assigned to technical support and others restricted to advisory roles, the U.S. involvement in the war was still on a comparatively small scale.

In late July, the tide began to turn. The war continued to grow in intensity and more U.S. outposts became the targets of "Charlie," a nickname assigned to the North Vietnamese by U.S. soldiers. McClendon, in charge of two squads of U.S. soldiers, accompanied Dang and his platoon of Vietnamese regulars to a military camp near Ban Me Thuot. A few miles from their destination, they came under heavy mortar attack and machine gun fire. McClendon and his men dove for cover.

"Captain Dang! Captain!" shouted McClendon.

"Yes boss," answered Dang." He hid behind an old tree truck and lay outstretched in a muddy ditch. His hands were on top of the helmet and face buried in the mud. He rose only once to respond to McClendon.

"Captain Dang, spread your men to cover the right flank."

"Sir, we are pinned down by mortar fire, and Thieu was hit!" shouted Dang. He buried his head once again to escape the bombardment and the shells from the machine guns. Dang, although a captain, was picked to lead the regulars due to his family ties and political structure. This was his first exposure to combat duty. He was intelligent and the garrison commander, owing some favors to Dang's family, selected him when the North Vietnam killed the former captain in a surprise attack on the local village.

"Captain! Spread the men and cover the right flank. The VCs will kill all of us if we don't get in a defensive position. McClendon could see that Dang was hesitant "Get the lead out of your ass and scatter your men to the right. Move it, damn it!"

"Yes sir!" McClendon turned towards the direction of his squad.

"Sergeant!"

"Sir!" answered the Sergeant.

"Disperse your squad and defend the left perimeter!"

"You heard the man, let's go!" shouted the Sergeant to his men.

Mortar rounds exploded twenty–five feet in front of McClendon. He was covered completely with white dust, sand, and dirt. His body was no longer visible to the naked eye.

"Oh my God! The Major's been hit!" Cried Dang.

"Shut up Captain!" Responded McClendon. "Do as you were ordered." He spat sand and dirt from his mouth. "Corporal Stewart, where are you?"

"Behind you sir!"

"Good. Just stay there. You and your men cover our asses. Private Jackson, speak to me!"

"Over here sir, twenty yards to your left."

McClendon turned on his back and stared at Jackson, the

communications specialist. "Radio headquarters, under heavy mortar attack, coordinates, Alpha 25.5 north, Fox 12.5 west, need support power."

"Right–O sir, repeat, Alpha 25.5 north, Fox 12.5 west."

"Brace yourself men," shouted McClendon, "Charlie might try to use the mortar fire for cover to attack our position."

"Major McClendon," shouted the Sergeant. "Three hundred yards to the west sector. We've got company. Charlie's approaching!"

Dang froze. His eyes arched. Blood rushed to his head. "My God, there must be hundreds of them!"

"Captain Dang, shut up and hold your position." McClendon was afraid Dang's men would run if they saw their commander frightened. He had to take control of the situation. He looked into binoculars through a clouded mist and saw a line of VC stretching from one end of the rice paddies to another. To the left, he saw another hundred Viet Cong creeping through the tall grass.

"Sir, what are we going to do?" yelled Dang. "We're surrounded!"

"Dang! For the last time, shut up! Defend your position!"

"But sir, shouldn't we retreat while there's still time?" asked Dang.

"No! Hold your fire! Fix bayonets! The mortar attack will soon stop. The VC is getting too close for the attack to continue."

Gunshots rang through the trees, vibrating in the men's ears. The excited voices of the men could be heard yards away.

The Sergeant yelled at McClendon, "Major! They are setting up machine guns. We don't have enough fire power to withstand such an attack."

"I know what I'm doing. Hold your fire! I want every man to pull the cotter pin from your grenade NOW. On my command, you will throw the grenade as far as you can. You will not look at the enemy until after you have thrown the grenade. At that time, you will pick three targets and fire. There will be no random firing! You will cease firing immediately, and promptly throw a second grenade. Pick three targets and again open fire. Each man should have five grenades. Verify!"

"What? Don't look at the VC?" questioned Dang.

"That's the order, Captain Dang. Each man has five grenades, an M–16, and three magazines of ammo. That's more than the men had at some of the great battles fought in the past. Follow my orders precisely and you will live to fight another battle. Is that understood, Captain? Pass the order to your men."

"Yes Sir!"

The men pulled the pins from one of their grenades and lay the other four to the side.

McClendon, a reader of Kipling's poetry, recalled one of his favorite lines:

"If you can keep your head when all about you
Are losing theirs and blaming it on you;"

The mortar attacked ceased. Silence prevailed. McClendon's mind quickly returned to reality. The Vietcong activity commenced almost at once with machine gun and weapon fire coming from all perimeters. The VC were attacking.

"Here they come; One hundred and fifty yards. Hold your fire," ordered McClendon. "Position yourselves; One hundred yards. Get ready. Seventy–five yards. NOW! Let them have it!"

Seventy–two grenades found their mark, killing and wounding two hundred or more Vietcong troops.

"Pick your targets and FIRE!" shouted Jonathan. He and his men used their M–16's to drop the VCs one by one. "GRENADES!" The men promptly ceased fire and threw the second round of grenades, again finding and dropping the VC. "FIRE!" Jonathan's men performed in a precision manner, throwing grenades and firing at specific targets. Jonathan's plan was working. He knew that the Vietcong would be attacking in groups, which allowed his men to use the grenades to defeat each wave of the attack force.

After the fourth volley, some of the VC broke through and started a fierce charge towards them. "Die, American, Die!" shouted the Vietcong. They charged the camp like broken–field runners, moving in a zigzag direction to escape the precision firing. The first soldier hit was the Sergeant, followed by eight more of Dang's men.

"Hold your position! Hold your fire! Fire at random!" shouted McClendon.

The VC kept charging and a fierce battle started within the camp. McClendon ran to help defend the Sergeant's position and to protect the inner perimeter. He killed four VCs with his bayonet before issuing the order to regroup towards the center of the camp. The fighting continued for another twenty minutes before the Viet Cong retreated. Exhausted, McClendon summoned Dang and asked for a head count.

"Sir, thirty–eight accounted for; twenty–six able to fight and twelve seriously wounded. The rest are dead. The Sergeant bought it."

"Dang, listen. It's quiet. Find me a pair of binoculars."

"You're right, boss. It's too quiet." He handed the Major the binoculars from off the dead Sergeant's neck.

"I don't see a damn thing. They're gone."

"You mean we defeated them. Holy cow, we kicked their asses," sounded an exuberant Dang.

"No, Captain Dang. We merely won this battle."

The Major's successful defense was heard all the way back at Pentagon. General Gage wasted no time in recommending that a Silver Star be awarded to Major McClendon. The General was also doing some behind the scenes politicking to have the Major's name added to the Lt. Colonel promotable list. The victory earned Jonathan and his men several days of R and R in Saigon.

CHAPTER TWENTY FIVE

A Man's Sorrow

Johannesburg – 1968

Jan, thirty pounds overweight, rested in the Johannesburg hospital, recovering from liver problems associated with his excessive drinking. Right after Andrea's burial in 1964, he sat desolate in the rear seat of the funeral home's black car for thirty minutes. He watched the entire funeral proceeding from the car. Andrea was a very popular woman. Three hundred people attended, the vast majority were police officers. He did not want anyone to see him. Behind that tall frame, he was an emotional man. He cried like a baby, as if reaching out for his mother.

Jan's first instinct and desire during the return ride from the cemetery in Pietermaritzburg, Andrea's birthplace to Johannesburg, was to find Rogers.

He had traveled for three years prior to Russia and other places following a trail left by Rogers. A visit to both the British and Russian embassies produced evidence that Rogers was hired as a liaison officer. He worked as a British subject under the name of Rogers for the British embassy. At the Russian embassy, he was known as Yury.

Jan's obsession with Nigel's death, Roger's apparent affiliation, and the conspiracy surrounding the Circle, cost him his Detectives badge. Every clue he pursued ended nowhere. He became distant toward his friends and colleagues. They did not understand, nor believe him. He resorted to drinking. He was allowed to stay on the police force, mainly because of his excellent service record and respect for his father. However, the jobs he was assigned were minimal and ceremonial duties.

Dry–eyed, weak, and emptied of all energy, Jan was a defeated man. He was also alone. He became content with a routine job. He could never forget how Rogers had kicked his ass and the old man outsmarted him. His friends also ridiculed him.

Jan and the bottle had something in common. They both had been consumed. He let the cold water run in the basin, leaned against the sink, and looked into the mirror. His eyes were sunken, a dark discoloration covering both eyelids. He dressed and walked out of the hospital, disobeying the doctor's orders. He arrived shortly at his home, went straight to his library. The only thing he had left and cared about was his diary of news clippings.

The year – 1968

January 30 – Communist forces break a mutually agreed–upon Tet or Lunar New Year truce and unexpectedly launch a large offensive against 30 South Vietnamese provincial capitals.

March 16 – US soldiers sweep through the South Vietnamese hamlet of My Lai, gunning down at least 300 civilian men, women, and children.

March 20 – Jan Linden is admitted to the hospital for liver problems.

March 31 – President Lyndon Johnson announced that he would neither seek nor accept the nomination for another term as President. He also unilaterally ordered a bombing halt of North Vietnam except for the area right above the DMV.

April 4 – Rioting breaks out in major U.S. cities following the assassin bullet killing the Reverend Martin Luther King.

June 5 – Senator Robert F. Kennedy is shot and fatally wounded after celebrating victories in the California and South Dakota presidential primaries.

October 11 – NASA launches Apollo 7, its first manned test of the spacecraft designed to carry the first Americans to the moon.

November 5 – Richard Milhouse Nixon wins a narrow victory over Democratic candidate Hubert Humphrey for President of the United States.

CHAPTER TWENTY SIX

A Military Genius Meets the Leader

Washington D.C. – November 1968

"I can't believe this," said Djhon. "You suddenly reappear in my life outside my ROTC class to tell me you have someone for me to meet. And of all places, I am going to meet this person at a movie. Why in the world are we going to a movie? Who is this person?"

"Relax my son," answered the old man. "You and he will have a lot in common." Djhon was in his sophomore year at the University of Maryland and was a platoon leader in his ROTC class. Through encouragement from the old man and his dad, now a Brigadier general, he had decided to make a career in the military.

"I must go away for a long period of time. There is so much left to do, so much planning. This is why I must pair you with someone with the same ideas and goals as yours."

"What do you mean, pair me?" asked Djhon.

"I will explain at a later date."

"Sir, I never understood how you hold such a mysterious spell over me. It is as though I cannot refuse your requests. I know everything you have taught me is for a purpose, but what that purpose is, I don't know. Nor will you tell me."

"Patience. Djhon, you must learn to be patient. Wait until the time is right."

"Yes, I know. Yet I cannot pull away and tell you to leave me alone. Everything you have taught me, I have used in one way or another. There is a lot of good in you. Tell me, please, why are you spending so much of your time teaching me so many things?"

"In due time, Djhon, in due time. Ah, there he is. Michael! Over here!"

"Michael, who is Michael?"

The old man frowned. "Djhon, patience. Patience is another virtue we must work on. I want you to ask your dad to explain patience. Ask him how it saved his life and got him that star on his shoulders."

Michael approached. "Sir, it's nice to see you again. I did not understand the message you left. Meet you at a movie. I didn't think you were into movies."

"I'm not, Michael. You still have so much to learn about people. This is my son, Djhon. You and he have so much in common. I want you to get to know each other. You will need and depend upon each other in the future."

"In what way, sir?" Asked Michael. He reached out to shake Djhon's hand.

"In the next decade and a half, you both will achieve greatness. You, Djhon will become a famous general, highly decorated; and honored for your military strategy and maneuvers. You will achieve much greater success than your dad and at a much younger age. It has been planned.

Djhon looked at the old man and winked at Michael. "Forgive me, sir. A general in my thirties? Yeah, sure. What have you been smoking? Weed, marijuana? That's the latest thing now." The two young men chuckled.

The old man gave them a piercing stare. Their smiles quickly faded.

"You Michael, will become a leader and spokesman. You will be called upon to coordinate important events and will develop a reputation for understanding people. You will lead a nation."

"Sir, that's a little far–fetched," said Michael. "If I can predict the future, I certainly wouldn't be a leading spokesman. This is going a little too darn far. Sir, I have the utmost respect for you. You have educated me well over the years with your teachings, but for you to stand there and tell Djhon that he will become a great military leader, and a general at that, is bordering on the ludicrous and...."

Djhon interrupted, "Michael, I'm afraid you are incorrect. I have chosen the military life. I hope one day to reach the rank of general. I have read books and studied the battles of Alexander the Great, Napoleon, Rommel, and Patton. To achieve their greatness is indeed a dream of mine. The old man may be right!"

Exasperated, Michael spoke angrily. "For God's sake, Djhon, a general in fifteen years or so from now. These are not Napoleonian days. We are not conquering other nations and taking their territories."

The old man that they both knew and came to admire stood motionless; the smile slowly disappeared.

"Michael, fear of the unknown is common to all. The future is what one makes of it. Your future has been planned. Now, let us not debate what you don't yet understand. Here are your tickets. Go see the movie for it marks a new beginning. I want the both of you to get to know each other. You will not see me again until the time is near." The old man bid farewell to his pupils.

CHAPTER TWENTY SEVEN

Flush the System

Johannesburg – 1986

Jan had created a tremendous amount of irritation among the Police Commissioner, local politicians, and several members in Parliament. He refused to disclaim that a conspiracy existed between the African National Congress and certain Zulu tribes. The government officials acknowledged the ANC, anti–apartheid activities, none believed it was as organized as Linden proclaimed. It was rumored the department was too embarrassed by the publicity the war hero might receive if he was fired.

The Commissioner decided in 1981 to reassign Jan from Chief of Detectives to Captain in charge of Equipment Deployment. In his degradation, he drank heavily and considered early retirement in 1983 at the age of sixty–two. He had run out of leads and Rogers' trail was as cold as the Antarctic. However, he performed his assigned job and nothing more. The following year, he retired from the South African Police force and was living on his pension.

During the past twenty years, he had found an extreme fondness for both wine and beer. He had wine with his breakfast and lunch, and beer to wash down the evening meal. He had somehow managed to retain his captain's rank and retired with full benefits. He was happy; after all, his personal diary of news clippings had grown to ten cardboard binders. It was his life, his solitude. He intended to bequeath his entire historical collection to the museum. It would be of some value to someone other than himself. Reading history in the making was a pleasant way to enjoy his leisure. He believed true literacy was something more than just the ability to read and write.

He had become lonesome, but he felt the three things left in life for him were to find Rogers; expose the members of the conspiracy; and to enjoy his diary, which had become his life and soul.

His library during the past twenty years began to exhibit signs of wear and tear. The once light blue walls appeared gray. You could see the wear on the corners of the rug. Jan Linden's reddish brown hair and eyebrows were grayish. His face was weathered. The excessive drinking had deteriorated his physical well–being. He searched for the scissors to begin the cut and paste habit to which he had become addicted.

The year – 1986

January 28 – NASA's shuttle, the Challenger, exploded seventy–two seconds into its flight, killing all crew members aboard, including the first civilian crew member, a schoolteacher. The blame was linked to the shuttle booster–rocket system.

March 26 – South African police kill 23 people and arrest as many as 1000 blacks in Bophuthatswana at an illegal meeting over a squatter issue. The violence is considered the worst so far that year.

March 24 – U.S. warplanes attack two Libyan ships and a shoreline missile site after Libyan forces fired six anti–aircraft missiles at them. Quadhafi claims the planes had crossed the "line of death" in the Gulf of Sidra and urge fellow Arabs to conduct suicide attacks against U.S. targets worldwide.

April 28 – The world's worst nuclear disaster occurs at the Chernobyl nuclear plant near Kiev in the Soviet Union causing 13 deaths and wounding several hundred. Ninety–two thousand people are evacuated from a 19–mile danger zone around the stricken reactor.

May 16 – A military aircraft disaster during routine training maneuvers at Fort Ord, California, kills 32 army personnel. Four–star General Jonathan McClendon, commander of the European forces, was among three people in the VIP audience killed instantly. General McClendon was on hand to witness the demonstration of an advanced F–16 fighter plane.

June 23 – Millions of blacks strike in South Africa, marking the tenth anniversary of the 1976, Soweto uprising.

October 21 – General Motors says it will pull out of South Africa, mainly due to growing U.S. opposition to apartheid. The automaker, one of South Africa's biggest employers, intends to sell its operations there to a group including local General Motors' managers.

October 22 – A South African Pullout was announced by IBM: the second major U.S. firm to withdraw in two days. The surprise move deals a major blow to Pretoria and to other U.S. companies hoping to remain in the country.

Jan had been lolling around the house all day when he received a telegram from an old detective colleague from the United States. The telegram was delivered to his old police station and brought to his house by an officer assigned to work his area of town.

> *Captain Jan Linden, Johannesburg Police. New evidence has surfaced concerning the deaths of Andrea Krueger and Dr. Russell Browne. Concerning Roger; he is under surveillance. He works for an investment firm in Montreal, Quebec, Canada.*
> *Signed:*
> *Captain Samuel LaRue*
> *Chief of Detectives*

Three words in the telegram inspired Linden's confidence. Jan mixed several strong glasses of baking soda, salt and water alternated with vinegar solution. He ate no solid foods during the next five days. His body shook with the hives. He drank on chicken broth for nourishment and the baking soda, vinegar and salt–water solution to clean out his body. He also down three to four garlic tablets each day.

Each morning he would sit on the floor of the shower for several hours feeling the beat of cold water. He prepared himself for the return trip to Washington, D.C. and the final confrontation with Rogers.

CHAPTER TWENTY EIGHT

The Achilles Heel

Montreal, Quebec – September 20, 1986

Jan was surprised, having heard so many tales of Canada's executive flight, to find how the English quarters of Montreal were still intact. The English–speaking citizens may have control of the economic life of the province, but they have never been able to dominate the tone of the city. Fifteen to twenty years ago, the inner suburb of Westmount was at that time exclusively English speaking. Yet, Jan heard French on every one of its steep streets he walked and from behind the high pickets fences voices in its natural dialect echoed in some its old grand houses.

Jan was lost. His attraction for the city diverted his attention from the directions on the map. He turned up on boulevard St–Laurent and soon found himself in the Italian quarter. He parked the car on rue Mozart, a few paces to the Marche' du Nord, that resembled a display of prize fruit and vegetables. He picked up a huge sooty, black plum, the size of a tennis ball, rubbed it against his coat and took a large bit, spilling some of it juices on his shirt.

He decided to walk around the area; he always enjoyed fresh cool air. Thirty minutes later, he was back to where he had parked the car. He was unaware that Montreal police had a diligent tow–away and fine system for cars doubled–parked or stopped in a no–stopping zone during business hours.

He waved down a taxi. "Est–ce que vous Centre de Commerce Mondial de Montre'al." (Take me to Montreal World Trade Center)

"Oui, Monsieur," answered the taxi driver.

Jan stepped out of the taxi and stood before a tall building. He wondered on which floor the office was located. A couple of phone calls to LaRue confirmed that Cirelli & Clements was on paper a small investment house dealing in gold and diamond futures from South Africa. He went into the lobby of the building looking for a pay phone.

"Cirelli & Cements, may I help you?" answered the receptionist.

"I'd like to speak with Christopher Cirelli."

"One moment, please."

"Mr. Cirelli's office, Charlotte Burke speaking."

"Mr. Cirelli, please. This is Mr. Brody calling."

"I'm afraid I don't recognize the name. Does Mr. Cirelli know you?"

Jan looked at the time on his watch. It was 9:15 a.m.

"No, I'm..."

"I'm sorry, Mr. Cirelli is busy."

"I'm from South Africa. Your office in Johannesburg had handled some investments for me several years ago. I'm now living in a suburb just a few miles east of Washington D.C., and would like your firm to make several speculative translations for me."

"I'm sorry; Cirelli & Clements are not accepting any new clients. We'll be happy to recommend the firms of..."

"No new clients? That's odd, since when do investment firms refuse new clients?"

The secretary swabbed her mouth with a paper napkin. "Sir, our customer base has always been small, which is the reason the firm has been very profitable. If you will call the firm of Simon Marsh, I am sure they will fit your needs. Thank you for calling."

"Damn, strike one and out." Jan thought. He tried to figure out how to find out more about Christopher Clements. He smelled the aroma of strong, freshly brewed coffee and followed the scent to the coffee shop. He was sitting at a table near the cash register for over thirty minutes reviewing his notes, when he overheard a familiar voice.

"Coffee, please. Black." It was Cirelli's secretary. She turned, looking for a place to sit, when he promptly stood up.

"Hello Charlotte! If I knew the voice on the other end was so attractive, I would have insisted on meeting Mr. Cirelli's secretary. Please, have a seat," smiled Jan. He pulled out the chair from the table.

Charlotte smiled. She too recognized his voice. "Your voice does sound familiar, oh, Mr. Brody."

Jan grabbed her hand, held it in his palm, and gently caressed the back of her hand with his other hand. "Please call me Jan, Charlotte."

She liked what she saw. Properly cleaned and shaven and well dressed, he was still a handsome man. She glared at him and then giggled. "Mr. Brody, flirting with me will not help you. Cirelli & Clements are not accepting any new clients. It's been over five years since we had a new client."

"Who's flirting? I've already taken your advice and made an appointment with Simon Marsh for tomorrow afternoon."

Charlotte gracefully sat down and the two carried on a conversation exchanging various tidbits of information about Johannesburg and the Nation's capital. Charlotte was always quite the talkative type, always laughing. She blamed her personality on her red hair. She was attractive with large blue eyes, but a little heavy on the mascara and makeup. Jan just sat there, looking into her eyes and being very attentive.

"Oh my God, Mr. Cirelli is going to kill me. I've been here for twenty–five minutes."

"I hope not."

"Oh don't worry about that. They are not so smart. I know their little secret. And the beauty of it is they don't know that I know."

"What little secret?"

"Now, Now. Curiosity killed the cat," said Charlotte, waving her finger.

"Yes, but satisfaction brought it back."

Charlotte gave out a loud laugh. "Oh you're cute. In fact, you are better than cute. You're down right handsome and too good to be true."

"Thank you, it goes both ways. I want to see more of you. What time do you go to lunch?"

"I take a late lunch, you'll probably be starved by then."

"Probably. I like your lips. Did anyone ever tell you have beautiful tempting lips?"

Charlotte was flattered. "There's more to these lips than meets the eye. Make it around one o'clock."

"Great, then I will come pick you up at 1:00 p.m. to fetch you."

"No! Mr. Cirelli does not want visitors in the office, only clients. I will meet you outside the door." She quickly excused herself. When she got to the elevator, she turned and waved at Linden.

The two ate lunch at Craw Daddy's. Charlotte recommended the place because she knew the crowd started dwindling around 1:00 p.m. and she loved seafood.

Jan continued to be attentive to Charlotte. He touched her hand from time to time as they talked. Charlotte found herself being "snowed" by the attention from a highly eligible bachelor. She admired and preferred older, mature men. At the age of fifty–two, she had not had a serious date in the last five years. She was very intelligent and had tremendous business savvy. She had always felt comfortable and safe with older men.

Charlotte had agreed to meet Linden for dinner at 8:00 p.m. She gave him a map of directions to her home, left by her late husband. Barely getting out of the office in time, she rushed home to dress. She was beaming at the idea of going out on a date. It was a positive stroke to her ego for a man to make a pass. She was pleasantly nervous about the dinner. She didn't know how to dress.

Jan had refused to tell her where he was taking her, saying merely that there was a five–star restaurant and a twelve–star view.

He picked the perfect restaurant. Pooling the last of his remaining funds, he gambled on this single lead to the Circle. He ordered a Chateaubriand for two, accompanied by a bottle of Merlot.

Charlotte was impressed. Everything so far was going the way he had planned. Linden made sure he made no overtures towards Cirelli & Clements. The time was not right to start asking questions. After dinner, they talked until closing time. Charlotte was having such a good time she invited him inside her home for a drink.

Jan excused himself, went outside, opened the trunk of the car and reached for a bottle of one of his own favorite South African wines, Kanonkop.

After two more drinks, Charlotte was now tipsy. She felt terribly clear–headed, but somehow everything seemed to be more amusing than usual.

His persistent attempts to get information struck her as funny, and she began to giggle. "Do you like working at Cirelli & Clements."

"At times yes, at times no."

"Why?"

"Oh, those bastards made so much money last year and Mr. Cirelli gave me a lousy five percent raise. Hell, his reasons were times were tough and the inflation rate was four percent, so I should consider myself lucky."

"No, no, Jan, you just don't understand. It's not insider information that gives C & C the edge, it's..." she collapsed into giggles again, "it's outsider information." She rested her head on the back of the sofa.

Jan seemed puzzled. "I don't get it."

"Of course you don't. Neither does anybody else. That's why they're making money, and you're here trying to find out why." Charlotte pulled him closer, and whispered throatily into his ear, "CIRelli and CLEments, don't you get it?"

"No, I don't."

"Oh, you're no fun. Kiss me and I will tell you more. "She smiled at him, her lips were a light soft red, nothing demanding, just tempting.

Jan obeyed her command. He needed answers and his body was for sale. Their lips parts. Charlotte sucked his index finger. "Now, one more time. CI–Re–li and CLE–ments belong to a secret group.

"C–I–R – C–L–E?" said Jan, perplexed.

"CIR – CLE – CIRCLE, CIRCLE, you dummy. It's a circle, like a yo–yo, like a ball, like a merry–go–round. What goes around comes around. What goes up must come down. The money comes from the stinking Communists, and Cirelli & Clements launder it through the biggest capitalist machine of all times; the stock market!"

Jan was half convinced that he had overdone the booze, and the secretary was off into cloud–cuckoo land. On the other hand, this was probably his only chance to find out what she knew. "Since when do the Communists invest in the market?" he probed.

"Since 1948, that's when!" Charlotte responded triumphantly, as if this were proof that she knew what she was talking about.

"Why, and what do they do with all the money?"

"Sssh... It's a secret! The Communists don't know they are in the market. They think the money's for guns and guerrillas. They think they are supporting the African National Congress. I don't know where the money goes. Some goes back into the market and the rest goes to the old man."

"OK, OK, it's a secret. If it's so secret, how do you know about it?"

"I do know. They think it's a secret but secretaries know everything. The money used to come from Rogers, but now it comes from Wingate. And I know the old man's name, too, but I think it's a pseudo. I think it's not his real name. Who ever heard of an African chieftain named Williams?"

Jan's mouth dropped. He could not believe his ears. All these years, he searched for the answers. He had his ass kicked; ridiculed by his superiors – laughed at by his colleagues – became an alcoholic, and lost someone he loved. Moreover, the answers to all of his questions come from a babbling secretary. "Leopold Williams," he whispered.

"What did you say? Asked Charlotte.

He did not answer. He now knew what he had set out to discover. His thoughts were rampart.

"Leaders of eight of the largest tribes in South Africa formed an organization called the Circle. A plan was put together to send their sons to the United States to be placed in homes of some of the most influential blacks. Each family possessed a single strength of character and quality, which the child would draw from. The old

man was sent as the messenger. He possessed the power to hold the Circle together. Now the old man will pass this power to the future leaders. But why? Wait a minute. Once all eight members unite, together they would hold the power to bring South Africa to its knees. But what is the power? Surely, eight men, regardless of how well educated, cannot defeat a country."

"You who! Wait up. Honey, where's your mind. I believe the wine is doing a number on you, or is it me. Anyway, I asked you a question."

Jan now knew what to do. "Charlotte, you talk too much. Let's go to bed. I have something to quiet you down."

"Mmm, maybe so, maybe not," smiled Charlotte. She grabbed him from the rear and led him to the bedroom. For the first time since Andrea's death, Jan had a fully erect penis. His energetic mind saw the light. "Why do you have that silly smile on your face," asked Charlotte.

"Baby, it's been years since my investments have paid off. The last few days, I have had more leads pan out. Things are beginning to look up."

He was so possessed with the turn of events that he hardly noticed Charlotte making her own moves. In a matter of a minute, his shirt fell over his belt and his pants were down around his thighs. His rejuvenated penis released and the once talkative Charlotte did not monopolize the conversation, the sounds came from Jan.

CHAPTER TWENTY NINE

The Torch is Passed

September 22, 1986

During the next eighteen years, Leopold Williams had witnessed many things: the birth of apartheid, Prime Minister Henrik F. Verwoerd of South Africa getting stabbed to death in parliament, the assassination of Dr. Martin Luther King, the first men to land on the moon, President Nixon's eight day visit to China, the Chernobyl nuclear accident, Djhon's first tour of duty in Cambodia, the eventual end of the Vietnam war, and the explosion of the space shuttle Challenger. But of all that he had witnessed, he was most pleased with Djhon's rapid rise through the military ranks of the Army.

He was also pleased that Dr. Riley had received nominations to the boards of directors of General Motors, IBM, and Exxon; and had attained tenure at Harvard University. Michael awarded the Medal of Freedom by the President of the United States, for exceptionally meritorious contributions to national security, world peace and significant public service to humankind. In addition, his theorems in proof of the Jacobson Theory had earned him the International Fowler Award.

Jonathan achieved his goal and became a four–star general. He and Phyllis tried to have kids, but Jonathan discovered after an examination that he had a low sperm count.

Phyllis waited outside the doctor's office when Jonathan appeared somewhat dejected and told her the news.

"How low?" she asked

"Below normal," he whispered.

"Jon, for heaven's sakes, honey, how low did the doctor say?"

"Oh, about twenty–five million."

On May 16, 1986, Jonathan died in a military aircraft during routine training maneuvers, at Fort Ord, California. An F–16 fighter pilot suddenly did a nosedive and crashed adjacent to the crowd gathered to watch the show, killing thirty–two military personnel.

Phyllis took Jonathan's death quite hard; she went into a depressive state. Nine months later without saying a word to Djhon and others, she packed and joined the Feed the Hungry Crusade in South Africa. She was last known to be teaching school in and around the mining towns of Capetown and Durban.

Djhon, like his father, became a rising military officer on the fast tract. The old man's prophecy became true and he was about to become one of the youngest generals in modern times.

———————————————————————————————————

Pentagon, Washington, D.C.

"Congratulations on getting your first star, General McClendon. I'm sorry my wife and I could not attend the ceremony," said General Shaw, one of the oldest generals to obtain the rank of Brigadier general. The two bumped into each other in the Pentagon corridor.

"Thank you, General Shaw.

"Young man, times has certainly changed, to become the youngest Brigadier general in modern times at the age of 37 is quite an accomplishment."

"Yes sir, you're right. It's a good thing that times have changed."

"McClendon, at your age I was just a major. I did not get my first star until the age of 59. However, not many of us old timers had the backing of a general as powerful as General Gage, much less a father who is a legend in the Army."

Djhon hesitated before replying; he respected the General's candid remarks. "Sir, thanks for the compliments. Since your greetings are lukewarm, General, I will let my record and long list of accomplishments speak for themselves. I learned many things from my dad, not the least of which was to stand on my own two feet. Now, if you would excuse me, I have a job to do." He turned away and proceeded down the long corridor to his office.

"Morning, General," snapped the young lieutenant.

"Good morning, Lieutenant."

"Sir, congratulations, I'm pleased and honored to be assigned to your staff. Please, let me get the door."

"Thank you, Lieutenant." Djhon stopped in front of his office, smiled, turned his head and looked once again at his new star before the lieutenant opened the door.

Ah... tend... hut!" shouted the young lieutenant.

"Now this is some sight, the whole darn office, standing at attention, shoes shining, brass brightly polished, and look at the secretaries. Captain, this is too much. What did you do, threaten to demote the officers and fire the secretaries if everyone did not jump to attention when I walked in?" Djhon smiled. He privately loved every minute of the attention he was receiving.

"No sir, we're just giving you well–earned due respect," said the Captain.

"Well, at ease, and you know saluting is not required in the Pentagon. Let's continue to work smoothly together as we have done in the past."

"Sir, you have a message from a Leopold Williams. He called twice, once at 07:30 and again at 07:50," said Staff Sergeant Judy Wilkerson. .

"Yes, I know Mr. Williams, please get him for me."

"General McClendon, we just received a telex from Pac–Com for authorization."

"Captain, let me answer this call first." Djhon walked to his office and flipped his hat on the chair.

"Sir, I have Mr. Williams on the phone."

"Thank you, Judy," said the general, closing the door to his office behind him.

"How are doing, sir? It's nice to talk to you again. I've never figured out how you are able to find me regardless of where I'm stationed."

The old man's voice was weak. "Djhon, listen carefully. The time is near. The time has come. We must act. Your father is depending on you."

"Sir, are you all right, you don't sound well? What does this has to do with my father?"

"No, I am not well. The years have finally taken its toll on me. I must see you. This will be my final request."

There was concern in Djhon's voice. "Sir, don't talk that way. You are much older than anyone I know. You have taken care of your body..."

The old man interrupted. "I need to see you tonight. I'm in Montreal, Quebec."

"Canada, you're in Canada. What are doing in Quebec?"

"I would have traveled there, but I'm too weak." The old man gave a small short laugh. "After all these years, it was me that came to see you, now my son, you must come to me. It's only a three–hour trip by plane. I traveled it many times. Continental Airlines has four daily flights from National Montreal."

"Sir, after all that you have done for me, coming to see you is not the problem."

The old man raised his voice. "Then, there is no problem greater than this. I want to see you tonight, 5:30 p.m., at the Green Street Hotel." The conversation ended with a dial tone.

Djhon took a deep breath. He had not expected this. He hung up the phone. His respect for the old man was unquestionable. He told Judy to quickly make flight plans.

The old man's wisdom had aided Djhon in the past, but he always talked in riddles. Djhon stood up from the desk and began preparations for at least his first half–day on the job as General Djhon McClendon.

Montreal – 5:25 p.m.

"Bon soir, Monsieur. s'il vous plaît faire Place aux dames," "Good evening, sir, please make way for the ladies," said a tour guide, escorting a small group of old women.

Djhon pardoned himself. He turned towards someone shouting his name. He turned and was surprised to see Michael. "What are you doing here?" He waited for a response.

"Whoa!" came immediately from Michael. "I could ask you the same question. This is not an area of town you would normally visit."

"An area of town, hell, this is another country." Djhon opened his mouth to ask another question.

"The old man. He said to come immediately. He needed help. I had this envelope and message taped to my apartment door."

Djhon was curious. "It's peculiar and interesting that the both of us were summoned to come to this particular hotel. Let me see the message."

"Here, but I'm not sure I understand, especially the part about my true father."

Djhon read aloud the words on the note.

"Your true father sent me to be your guardian and when the time was right to reveal your destiny. Meet me at the Green Street Hotel, Room 618, tonight at 5:30 p.m. It's signed, Leopold Williams, Umbiki – the messenger, your true father. I do not believe it. Michael, I didn't know you were also adopted."

"Yes, my parents finally dropped the bombshell, the day after my high school graduation."

"That's nothing. I too, am adopted. Dad and Phyllis finally got married and informed me on the day of their wedding. I must have walked around in a daze all day. What does this have to do with the old man, do you think we're related."

"No, I don't think so. I remember the old man appearing in my life from time to time and he always had something of wisdom to say. It never made sense at the time, but he always said 'the facts can be deceiving.'"

"Well Michael, we're not going to find out standing here. Let's see what the old man has to say."

The two walked towards the elevator, pressed the button and waited for it to descend from the second floor. When it arrived on the main floor, they both were surprised to see a very old man seated on a stool. The old man smiled, turned the crank to the right. The two stared at the old man in complete silence, then at each other and back toward the elevator attendant. It had been six to eight years since they had seen the old man.

"What's the matter boys, surprised to see someone my age running an elevator?"

"Ah, no sir, I, ah, we thought for a moment you were someone we met before," responded Michael."

"Well, sonny, I find that hard to believe. I will be eighty–one next month and there are not too many of us around that live that long. But if you should find your friend, tell the old rascal that I would be glad to test his wits in a game of checkers.

Michael stopped talking. He was silent, studying the old man's clothes. Djhon shook his head as if to clear away the memory. The old man clothes were similar. He also wore a dashiki. He turned and looked at Michael. "No, our friend is much older."

Sixth floor; watch your step! Odd numbers to the left and even numbers to the right."

The two continued to look at each other in amazement. They stopped and spoke almost at the same time.

"How? How did..."

Djhon shrugged his shoulders. They walked to the right towards Room 618. Upon reaching the door, they paused and took a deep breath. The two grown men felt like young boys again. They sighed and prepared themselves to meet the old man who had meant so much to them as children.

Michael knocked on the door.

"Come in," said the old man in a low whisper. Michael was the first to enter. "Come my children; come closer so you can hear me better." He lay in bed and did not rise.

Michael rushed to his side. He could not believe his eyes. He knew the old man had years upon him, but he looked elderly and frail. "Sir, are you all right."

Djhon approached. Tears rolled down his cheek. He could see the old man was dying.

"Come closer .The time has come for me. I have a story to tell you and it will answer all of your questions."

"Sir, we want to know why you brought us here," asked Djhon.

"Patience, Djhon. Patience is a virtue you must master. A Zulu warrior and chieftain must learn the art of waiting. He could waste many lives by striking too soon. Let me tell my story. I'm an old man dying from many ills and I don't have much time left."

"I'm sorry sir, please enlighten us," said Michael.

"Thank you, Michael. You are the chosen one."

"Chosen one! What do you mean the chosen one?" shouted Djhon.

"Don't upset yourself," said the old man as reassuringly as he could. "Everything is fine now."

"I'm sorry sir, please continue," said Djhon.

"Michael, my son, it's left up to you from this day forward to teach Djhon, our military leader, patience. Sit down! Be quiet! I will begin." The elderly man's vacant eyes stared at the ceiling as he spoke in a half–whisper.

"I'm known in our country as Lamizana. My people also call me 'Umbiki',the messenger. Djhon, the man you call your father was a powerful general in the United States Army. You have followed your own goals to become a power in your own right. Your true father is also a brave and powerful warrior. And your true family has carried on a military tradition for many, many years. Your family is from the Zulu tribe. You my son, are a Zulu warrior.

"In 1878, Djhon's great–grandfather, Ladula, led an impi of 4000 Zulus against a British battalion stationed in Natal, outside of Durban. His warriors moved silently and furtively to the rear of the

column. Ladula did not know the British had camouflaged a Gatling gun. The leading warriors had already reached the main defense post before Ladula spotted the men uncovering the Gatling gun. The British expected an attack and had extra sentries posted. They had spotted the advancing Zulus. For what seemed like an hour but lasted only minutes, the camp was filled with smoke, the deafening sound of rifles and the constant barrage of gunfire. In that short period, Ladula lost 1500 Zulu warriors. The weapons of the British were superior, their technology light years ahead of the Zulus. A small force could easily defeat thousands of warriors. Ladula withdrew to fight another battle. He was able to defeat the British and Boer forces using trickery, cunning, skills, and his knowledge of the country. He won seven more battles, killing 3000 white soldiers over a three–year period before their superior weaponry defeated him at the battle of –Ndondakusuka. Ladula was captured, sentenced and hung before a crowd of several hundred Zulus surrounded by armed troops. The British army was now 20,000 strong, with sufficient transport for the columns to start marching deeper into Zulu land. His brother, Moshwestobe, your great–uncle, found himself in command of a Zulu army of over 10,000 men, facing complex odds. He pulled the Zulus together, divided them info five groups armed with assegais and stones with a plan to attack the advancing British troops' food and water supply. Moshwestobe and his warriors stayed out of sight and purposely waited until the advancing party was days deep into Zulu land. He ordered his 2000 warriors from the rear to poison the water holes, while the Zulus from north and south attacked with arrows and assegais, concentrating on killing their cattle, oxen, and ruining the barrels of water. Before the British had realized the nature of the attack, 1500 cattle and oxen were slaughtered and three–fourths of their water supply damaged. The British, with less than 50 cattle to feed 20,000 troops, had not yet engaged in a real battle. Moshwestobe and his warriors retreated and for the next two days, small groups of ten Zulus, hidden from view, fired arrows into the advancing party, wounding and killing several men on each attack. Moshwestobe *knew as each day progressed that the British were traveling deeper and deeper into Zulu land. Without proper food, water and supplies, time was on his side. He was willing to sacrifice warriors by sending the small groups to be a constant thorn to them. The British did not know the territory; therefore they would become more apprehensive of each other and disease prone. This gave Moshwestobe, more time to recruit more warriors. There were at least another 40,000 armed men in Zulu land divided in many different regiments. Word was sent to Tshwayo, chieftain of ten regiments, consisting of 15,000 Zulus of the advancing British troops and the pending battle. The small attacking force killed and wounded some 800 men over the two–day period while the Zulu losses were less than 100. The British commanders placed the men on rations and tried to calm them down, for they were firing at anything that moved. By the end of the third day the regiments of Moshwestobe, Tshwayo, and Usibu had joined forces numbering some 40,000 warriors. On the morning of the fourth day, Zulus were all united on top of the plateau in a long massive line, chanting a deep chorus song and war cry. They beat their assegais rhythmically against the oval cowhide shield, giving cover to the entire body. They chanted the war cry moving closer to the British lines trying to determine the British firepower. Hundreds of Zulus fell as they crept closer. Suddenly the warriors crept backwards until not a single Zulu was injured from the volley of gunfire. The three Chieftains standing on top of the plateau sacrificed hundreds of men to determine the range of the enemy's firepower and the time period it took to load the single shot rifles. Moshwestobe raised his assegai and ordered the Zulus to advance to the 'line of death.' The warriors chanted and crept slower to the point ordered using the shields to completely cover their faces and bodies. Suddenly, all chanting and war beats stopped. Moshwestobe once again raised his assegai and pointed to the regiments to the Zulus in front of him. Tshwayo also raised his assegai and pointed to the warriors to the south, while Usibu raised his and pointed to the men to the north. This was the battle that everyone had wanted. The hatred was so* strong on both sides, that this was the only way to end it. With a movement of the arms, the Zulus attacked, again, and again. The British had 5,000,000 rounds of ammunition, firing in sequence by formation. The battle lasted for two days. When it was over, the British had killed 15,000 Zulus and they themselves had lost 3,000 men. The Zulus were a defeated tribe and the Zulu power was gone.

"Thus began the regime of the South African government over the black population. The people of South Africa have continued to suffer at the hands of the government. We are treated as third class citizens. Apartheid is designed to keep all our peoples separate and confused. We must rise once again, but this time as a united people. This time it will not be the Zulus the government will be fighting. This time it will be all the tribes of South Africa. It's time to act."

Djhon forgot his personal feelings. He became interested in the military problems involved. "Sir, with all due respect, do you honestly believe the blacks of South Africa can realistically overthrow the government?"

"Djhon, I must again ask you to be patient. Let me finish, for there is a plan."

"I want no part of any conspiracy to overthrow the South African government or any other government," said Michael.

"Help me up, Michael."

"Djhon, grab a hold of his other arm."

"Ah, thank you. One must not lie still too long, for death is fast approaching. Help me to my bag over there. This, my sons, is a picture of your true fathers.

The two men were in awe of the pictures.

"As you can see, there are eight Chieftains in the picture. The one standing is Abozuthu. He is your father, Djhon. He is a Zulu chieftain. The one seated at the extreme left is your father, Thambo, Michael. He is a Xhosa chieftain and his people are known for their intellect. They are thinkers, lawyers and doctors."

"Sir, you talk as though they are still alive," asked Michael.

Djhon grew angry. "Then why did they give up their sons and

what about our mothers."

"Your mothers are well and alive. It took great sacrifice on their part to give up their first–born. They did it so that your brothers, sisters, and their brothers and sisters can one day hold their heads high and fight this apartheid."

"And our fathers," said Michael.

Your fathers gave up their first–born sons to go to a country more advanced than ours. They wanted their child to learn great things from prominent people; to study the economy; to study its science and to study its banking and money system. Most of all it was important for them to study and understand its military system and understand its foreign policy and international affairs. In addition to learning and mastering its technology through the use of computers, studying and becoming a part of its political system would also be beneficial. Once this was accomplished and the time was right, all eight would be brought home to lead our people to victory."

"Wait a minute," demanded Djhon. "We were their first born."

"I don't believe this," said Michael. He too was angry, but it did not show. He kept his composure. "Do you mean there are eight of us that were placed in homes of people possessing the skills in these areas?"

"Yes, Michael, that's exactly what I mean."

Djhon was caustic in his remarks. "Even if you and our biological fathers were successful in carefully choosing eight of the then future leaders in the United States and having them adopt us, the eight of us cannot possibly go back to South Africa to start any type of movement to overthrow the government."

"Djhon, I did not say all eight were adopted."

"If they did not adopt all of us, then how did you..." Djhon was interrupted.

"In some cases, the parents believed that the sons are their natural children. We merely swapped babies."

"You sir!" shouted Djhon, "you and your people took innocent babies away from their natural parents and swapped them with other babies!"

"Calm down Djhon. You're letting your emotions cloud your judgment."

"Calm down! After listening to this, you're telling me to calm done."

Michael put his hand on Djhon's shoulders. "Yes, I am. Now relax. I want to hear more. How else are we going to find our true parents? Wouldn't you like to sit across from your father and ask him, why?"

"Professionally, yes. I would like to meet this great Zulu warrior."

"Sir, tell me about my father," asked Michael.

"I'm sorry to say he is in a South African prison. There is a movement going on to get him out. The government is feeling a great deal of pressure to release those held captives for false crimes."

"Why is he in prison? Was the government aware of the plot?"

The old man continued, "Yes and no. He is charged with citing a riot and speaking out against the South African government. The white authorities fear his release and others like him. They treat our people as children. They don't believe we could organize a plan to successfully defeat them. However, there is one man. He suspects. He is getting closer to the truth as each day draws nearer. His name is Jan Linden. He was a captain in the South African Police. This man has spent thirty–four years trying to convince the South African Police and the government that a conspiracy exists. He knows where the money is coming from. He knows some of the members of the Circle. He does not know of you or the plan."

"The Circle. Who or what is the Circle?" asked Djhon.

"The men in the picture are known as a council of eight. The Circle is the name of our movement."

"That's odd. Since my father and seven others have plotted to overthrow the government, why was he drawing attention to himself?" asked Michael.

"They are not planning to overthrow the South African government. There is another way, for Thambo has a plan. Part of the overall plan was to create a diversion. We knew it would take thirty to forty years to be in position for the plan to work. We did not want our people to become passive and accept the practices and rules of the South African government. If no one is stirring up trouble, people have a tendency to accept a way of life. We knew it would have to be the young people to bring about a change. We wanted the young people to realize that there is a better way of life. Thambo chose to speak out and to become a thorn in their side. By keeping him locked up, the whites have made him immortal, a messiah and a leader of hope."

"How long has my father been locked up," asked Michael?

"Twenty–two years," said the old man.

"Nelson Mandela? Michael, your father is Nelson Mandela," beamed Djhon.

The old man frowned. "Michael please forgive Djhon, it takes considerable forbearance to overlook his faults. In some ways, he is exactly like Thambo. Mandela is not your father. The South African authorities often incarcerate political offenders in mental institutions. Your father has been in the institution for twenty–two years."

"For speaking out against the government," shouted Michael.

"Yes, your father has done well. The Afrikaners are afraid of what he stands for and what he can do."

"Sir, what about my father, how is he?"

"Abozuthu, Djhon, is at this moment laying the foundations for your return."

"What foundations and what about the other six? By the way, who and where are the other six?"

"One question at a time, Djhon," smiled the old man. "Until today, no one knew of each other. I have arranged the pairing and each paired person knows one another, but does not know each other is adopted or from South Africa. None of those who are paired know of any other twosome."

"Then how will we meet or get together?" asked Djhon.

"Michael, in the corner on top of the night stand is a small binder. Those are my notes. They will lead you to the other six members. Guard them with your life."

"This man, the police captain," questioned Michael. "If he knows so much, why haven't the South African Police or even the government arrested the members of the Circle?"

"He has not presented proof. All of his information and suspicions are what they call circumstantial. Although his government recognizes that rebel activities exist, they wholeheartedly believe that the blacks are not capable of organizing in force, forming an army or having the military expertise or common sense to rule a government. They also know that we as a group of people have certain tribal customs and continue to fight each other. There are many old scars to overcome. Some tribes have histories of trying to dominate each other. We have fought each other too long. The time has come. It's time to act."

"Sir, I'm a general in the U.S. Army. I fought in South Vietnam and was decorated with the Medal of Honor. I also participated in a secret mission behind the Russian lines to obtain valuable intelligence data, for which I received the Distinguished Service Cross and Distinguished Service Medal. I am not afraid of a battle. But how in the hell do you expect me to lead a group of native tribesmen with no military training against a well–armed, well– trained and well–organized South African Army? It cannot be done! And I am not sure I want to go back to South Africa. In the U.S., I am well respected. I enjoy the Army life and above all, I'm free to move about and go anywhere I damn well please!"

"Djhon, you have certain loyalties to your father, your family, and your people. You have been entrusted with gifts, traits, and skills to bring back home to help your people." The old man's voice hardened. "We have people here in the United States supporting our cause. We made you a General. We helped open those doors. We made sure that you took advantage of every opportunity, and WE can bust you back down to a second lieutenant faster than the time it took you to rise to general."

Djhon was stunned into silence, but the strategist in him recognized that the old man spoke the truth. "Sir, with all...."

Michael interrupted, "Sir, I agree with part of what Djhon is saying. How do you and our fathers expect us to lead a successful revolt? This will not be the first time several tribes revolted against South African government policy and lost. I too have problems leading a conspiracy."

"Patience, my sons, patience. A revolt, a conspiracy, those are just words. There is another way to have a meeting of the minds. You will know the plan in due time. You, my dear Djhon, may not have to strike a single blow. You will wait for the strategic moment, and then strike. Once I've explained the plan Thambo has outlined, and you both still disagree, I will release you from any commitment."

The old man talked to Djhon and Michael for the next forty–five minutes. His last words were instructions: Djhon was to walk out the back door of the hotel, carrying with him the old man's bag, which held eight carved necklaces. Michael was to leave a few minutes later, carrying only the diary, which the old man had left.

Wearied by the long conversation and content of the message that had been passed on to the two new leaders, the messenger quietly slipped into a deep sleep. He lingered on long after he could function normally.

#

Three Old Men

Montreal, Canada – 1986 – 7:00 p.m.

Jan Linden sat stone–faced in the back seat of the red and yellow Co–Op taxicab as the driver maneuvered his way through the downtown rush hour traffic of Montreal.

"Vous imbecile!" shouted the young curly–haired cab driver as he gave the finger to another cabbie who cut sharply in front of him. He cast a brief look through the rear– view mirror and stared at Linden's six–foot–two body frame and the look on his passenger face, displayed an air of confidence. What the cabbie could not see in the man's face was that his mind and his decisions were the victim of a self–imposed malignant cancer, eating away at his thoughts for the past thirty–eight years. With each passing day, Jan Linden became more convinced that a terrorist group from the African National Congress was responsible for blowing up the barracks that had killed his father in 1972.

The rebels had adopted a Program of Action calling for 'freedom from white domination and the attainment of political independence.' Their secret code words were sacrifice, service, and suffering.

By now Jan Linden should be dead. The past three days, there had been two attempts on his life. Perhaps it was a payback for the men he had killed in his quest to find his prey.

It was nearly dark and he wanted to make sure no one was following him. Time was of the essence, but he had to stop. He motioned for the cabbie to pull over a few blocks short of his destination. He opened the door, paused, and inhaled a deep breath.

"Merci." The cabbie smiled and thanked Jan for the tip. Jan nodded. He buttoned the top two buttons on his gray wool coat. He started to walk at a brisk pace.

"Man, it's cold, really cold," he whispered. "The sidewalks are filled with dirty and murky frozen ice." Jan had not grown accustomed to the cold temperatures. He was uneasy walking without solid footing and traction. He stopped after walking a block and started rubbing his left leg.

"Oh brother, it's stinging like hell." Jan's left foot was cold. It felt nearly frozen from his poor circulation. A full minute later, he was able to continue.

Jan's unexpected visit to Montreal resulted from a phone call he had received from one of his sources. The plane mix–up and confusion had caused him to leave his briefcase that contained vital documents in the terminal. The events had turned his schedule topsy–turvy.

"Whew! I am not a young man anymore. Man, do I need to slow down." When nervous, Jan had a peculiar habit of talking to himself and letting his thought run rampant.

Jan stopped. He looked around and smiled. Despite the ugly snow, there was a certain fragrance in the air. This was his first impression of Montreal. He was surprised at the city's lack of urban decay. He was also in awe of the vast civic development of underground arcades, and its

all–weather access to modern facilities of every kind. He continued on to the next block.

He came to another abrupt stop. Jan admired the colorful sidewalk cafe, especially a planted tree centered in the eatery area. It reminded him of a favorite restaurant that he and Andrea last visited just before she was killed. The veins on Jan's forehead enlarged and his smile slowly turned to anger. Her unexpected death had also added fuel to his growing cancer.

Jan placed his right hand on the shoulder holster and felt the gun. He swore vengeance for the murder of the only woman that truly loved him with all his faults: First, my father, and then my fiancé. Their day will come.

A waiter with a white cloth folded over his wrist approached him.

"À Montréal à ce moment d'année, le café sent comme les champignons frais," (In Montreal at this time of year, the coffee smells like fresh mushrooms) said the waiter as he placed two fingers on his lips and gestured a kiss.

"Oui. La saison d'automne est également suffisance avec de belles couleurs." (Yes. The fall season is also sufficient with beautiful colors) Jan nodded and smiled. He turned and walked away from the waiter.

Another hundred yards later, Jan found himself standing in front of the Place Ville Marie Hotel. He looked up and let his eyes follow the contour of the building. Thirty–eight, no, that building must have at least forty–two floors. Impressive, but the person I seek is not in that hotel.

Jan knew where he was going; his source had given him directions to the old Landmark hotel. He passed an alley and found his mark, a limestone building.

Jan, an active man for his age, jumped down the three short steps facing the hotel's narrow entrance and onto the lobby floor to catch the elevator. He rounded the corner with his long legs stretching out in an even rhythm. A sharp turn brought about an abrupt halt that caused him to favor his right hip – the side with the pin. His tired eyes did not see the bronze Indian statue with its hands folded or the janitor with a light trash sweeper until he nearly ran into him.

"Sir, watch where you're going," snapped the janitor.

"Oh, I'm sorry." Jan then stared at several small indentations on the statue's forehead. The two shared something. They were exactly the same height and approximately the same shape and build. Their eyes also shared the same elevated plain and it appeared the two were staring at each other.

Two feet to the right of the statue's head was a small rectangle mirror. He turned, looked down the corridor, and then glanced at the mirror. His bloodshot eyes camouflaged their natural blue color. Despite five days without a good night sleep, he was alert and his mind was keenly aware of everything within its sight. His journeys had taken him to four continents in search of another person, an elderly man on the six floor.

Jan paced the floor and waited for the elevator. It was stuck on the sixth floor. He became impatient; his face could not hide his disgust.

"I don't like this." Jan said quietly. He tried to maintain his composure. He adjusted the baggy pants around his waist. His suspenders lay on the nightstand back at the lodge in Washington, D.C.

Jan noticed a young woman drinking a diet coke and sitting on the lobby couch. She smiled at him. Jan arched his eyebrows. She reminded him of someone he once loved. Her beauty and smile filled him with awe.

He also noticed that the attractive young woman was watching him. They made eye contact. Jan had a habit of staring into people's eyes. He felt it gave him an advantage. Coupled with his size, this tactic worked well for him in his line of work. Jan did not break eye contact with the woman. She slowly opened her legs, slightly enough to get Jan's attention.

'White panties, white bra; I like what I see.' He smiled and envied the young man reading a book next to her.

The woman broke eye contact, and then stared once again at Jan. Their eyes met for a second time, and she gave him an approving smile.

"Another day, another time, but not today," he mouthed to her with his lips without uttering a sound. For a brief moment, Jan was elated that he still had what it takes to get a woman. He took three paces forward and looked at the rustic dial. He watched it moved slowly–but–steadily from floor to floor. The corroded hinges creaked when the gate to the elevator opened. It stopped three inches short from the marble floor.

"Watch your step. Floor please," said an older man, sitting inside on a metallic stool.

That raspy voice and tired foreign accent sounds familiar. 'I *heard it before.'* Jan thought to himself, but he is not old enough. Jan gave him a hard stare. He had a small head with cream–colored kinky hair. The dark blue V–neck dashiki he was wearing, partially revealed his frail dark chest and curly white hair. He swiveled on the stool and rested his back against the elevator's graffiti–covered wall. The hand he rested on the elevator's hand crank had deep wrinkles. He was whispering a tune from a western he loved to watch on the television.

"Sonny, do you recognize the melody?"

"No!" Jan was not in the mood for conversation.

"It was the best western on TV," said the older man.

"It was called Tombstone Territory."

"We don't watch American westerns," snapped Jan.

The man's eyes suddenly focused on something lodged in the corner by his shoe. He ignored Jan, bent down, and picked up the opaque object. He spat lightly and rubbed it on his dashiki. He looked up at Jan and smiled, revealing the few stained teeth he had remaining. "Well looky here, a 1948 wheat–line penny." He marveled at his new found discovery. He and the antiquated elevator shared something – they were both the same age.

The hotel, part of the city's history, was once manned by coat–tailed and tuxedoed servants who wore polished black shoes on the ivory marble floor. The surface of the man's black shoes and the elevator floor were weathered with cracks.

He stared at Linden and waited for him to enter the elevator. "Floor please, watch your step. Well sonny, what are you waiting for?"

Jan swallowed hard before walking onto the elevator. The sight of the man in the dashiki gave him a nervous feeling. He stared at the operator. He noticed a thin translucent coating that covered the older man's enlarged blood vessels extending from the cornea. *'He cannot be the one. He is not old enough.'*

The man smiled again at Jan. "What's the matter, Sonny, surprised to see someone my age running an elevator?"

"Ah, nothing my dear fellow, I mean, sir. I thought for a moment you were the man I, ah, came to see." Jan spoke with a mixed accent of Dutch, British, and English dialect. Even at his age, Jan did not forget his upbringing; his father had taught him to respect his elders.

He leaned forward and pushed the gate forward with the weight of his body, turning the crank to start the elevator. He looked at Linden and grinned.

"Well Sonny, I find that hard to believe. I will be eighty–one next month. My vision may be failing, but I have not seen you around these parts. If you should find your man, tell the old rascal I'll be glad to test his wits in a game of checkers."

"Sir, the man I seek will not be playing a game of checkers, unless it's behind my prison walls." His facial expression displayed a look of disgust.

The elevator stopped suddenly, bobbed, and weaved. The unsteady motion caused Jan to grab the handrail. He opened the elevator door and shouted.

"Sixth floor!" Watch your step! Odd numbers to the left! Even numbers to your right!"

Jan walked off the elevator and turned to his right. It suddenly occurred to him that he did not give the older man the floor number. He stared at the man as he closed the elevator door and watched the dial slowly descend down to the first floor. He glanced down the empty narrow hallway. He heard nothing, not a sound or a whisper, nor noises coming from the rooms or the sound of a radio or television. He stopped, feeling his heartbeat quicken, turned and looked back at the elevator. He saw no one. He looked to his right and once again to the left. He pulled a silver–plated Luger from his left shoulder holster and walked slowly down the hall. His informant said the man he sought was in room 618. Jan gripped the gun and slowly raised it until his eyes and the tip of the barrel were in line.

Jan stopped once more to rest his back against the wall. He rubbed his temple with the nozzle of the gun and stared down the corridor and back towards the elevator. He was now positive the older man running the elevator was not his prey. He saw the man he wanted only once, and even then, he could only guess at his true age but he knew the man he hunted was an elderly man once reputed to be remarkably youthful in appearance for someone his age.

The elderly man he sought and wanted had unknowingly brought him grief and ridicule from his government and friends. He did not know his true name, only that he was known by some of his people as Lamizana; others called him Umbiki, the messenger. It had been thirty–eight years since Nigel's death.

Jan recalled how he had tracked the elderly man following a trail from South Africa to Russia, Britain, the United States, and now Canada. Each time he came close to a source, either the person died a horrible death or the evidence somehow was destroyed. He felt his sources were frightened and feared for their lives.

Jan blinked several times; his bloodshot eyes ached for sleep. When he closed his eyes for more than ten seconds, his head would suddenly snap backwards. He felt that one slip into subconscious and he would fall into a darkened abyss.

Beads of sweat covered his brow. He was not afraid of the elderly man; it was his followers and the way they murdered Nigel. He believed the elderly man's apocalyptic views would doom the people of South Africa.

"Now is the time to confront destiny," he whispered to himself. "I can feel it."

Jan continued to walk slowly along the hallway. He wrinkled his nose. Damn, the hallway carpet smells like someone pissed on it. *This is not my day. Some of the rooms have no numbers.*

The tension in his body grew with each step, especially in his groins. His leg muscles began to tighten, producing a sharp piercing pain. He stumbled before regaining his balance. It was difficult to walk because his right foot had fallen asleep.

'Oh, shit. I need to pee.'

He tried to control the pressure in his bladder. Suddenly and without warning, he felt a warm flow of water on his high inner thigh. He paused and looked down at the crotch and noticed a long thin wet spot down his right pant leg.

"Damn Jan, get a hold of yourself," he muttered. He raised his head and rolled his eyes at the ceiling. Jan felt embarrassed, when tense and excited, he always had trouble controlling his bladder – a previous operation he had was to cure the problem.

He leaned on the wall and waited for the blood to circulate in his foot. He closed his eyes, and within an instant of a second, his entire body jumped as if stung with a cattle prod. He quickly snapped his head. Jan's eyes enlarged and he looked dazed, like a soldier suffering from battle fatigue. He had almost slipped into a subconscious state.

'Relax you fool. Just relax.'

Jan decided to rest a minute. He recalled the years he had spent searching for the truth. Years of sweat torment, and frustration were about to unravel. He could now prove the conspiracy actually existed. His mind moved in rapid flashbacks, South Africa – a birthday celebration – Andrea –Johannesburg – Transkei –an assegai blade – Nigel's head.

"No! No!" He shouted and looked around. Did anyone hear me?

'Hell yes, you idiot, you are blowing it.'

Jan's heartbeat accelerated. He took more short steps, stopped and looked down the hallway. A window near the fire escape was open. He felt the cool autumn air blowing in the window. He rested his head against the wall, scrawled with religious and obscene ravings. Across from him, scribbled on the wall in red paint are the words, 'Umbiki! Ngadla!'

"Eat this." He whispered and gestured with his middle finger. Damned. I lost track of the room numbers.

He paused and looked up at the ceiling and smiled.

'Yes, Andrea, I know, quit talking to myself.'

He looked at the room across from him. Room 620. Shit, I'm standing next to it. He stooped down on the left side of the door marked 618 and listened for sounds coming from the room. He heard nothing. He cocked the Luger and slowly reached for the doorknob. He was surprised to find the door unlocked. He opened it a few inches and saw a hall mirror, a small bed, and a dim lamp.

Someone is lying on the bed. It looks like the elderly man. Before taking another step forward, Jan paused.

I must be a fool; the world just waits for you with all the glories and hidden traps. His heart pounded with each step he took.

"Where are his comrades?" A small drop of sweat rested on the tip of his nose. He rose slowly and paused to catch his breath; he knew the moment had finally come. The chase had ended.

For a brief moment, Jan was reluctant for it to end because the elderly man was a formidable foe. He took a deep breath, kicked the door open, and rushed into the room with both hands on his Luger.

"Freeze! Don't move! Mr. Leopold Williams or whatever your name is. Mr., you have led me on one hell of a journey. You're the man in the riddle; you have the power, and now you will lead me to the other eight."

The room had a smell of death about it. He suspected something was wrong. His eyes quickly searched the room. The dark–skin elderly man lay peacefully with a smile on his face and his hands folded across the chest that resembled the sign of a victory. His body revealed the wrinkles and sags of age. Jan had arrived too late. He screamed when he saw the elderly man's dead body.

"Damn you! Damn you! How dare you die on me! Thirty–eight years I have hunted you, I have grown to know you, respect you. I've longed for this moment when I could stare into your eyes and talk to you face to face." He dropped the gun and buried his face in his hands. A long second passed and he looked up and walked to the bed. He stared at the elderly man's frail body.

He cried and fell to his knees. "Damn you. How could you be dead? No way! Not after all this time. You have led me in a circle. I have so many questions I wanted to ask you! How dare you think you could possibly succeed?"

Jan pulled a handkerchief from his pocket and blew his nose hard. "The riddle. Who are the eight witnesses and what is the Power? I cannot believe you are dead. Hell, you cannot die on me! Not after all these years."

Jan pounded on the man's chest. The tears he shed for the elderly man represented a major part of his life. He too had suffered. He sat on the floor facing the dead body. His gun lay on the floor beside the bed. He sat crouched with arms wrap around his knees and buried his head.

Jan Linden was an Afrikaner, a retired captain in the South African elite police force. A proud man obsessed that a conspiracy threatened his beloved country. No one believed him, not his superiors, or the woman he loved.

One hour later, he lifted his head and stared at the elderly man. "Williams! It took me twenty bloody years to put that damn riddle together and I still don't know what it all means." That night was the nights of all nights. It was the beginning and somehow the end of everything that really mattered in his life. Jan rested his head on the edge of the bed. Although it was a cool night, sweat covered his forehead.

The moment Jan wanted had finally come. The time for hunting and stalking his prey had finally ended. Jan did not wish it to end. The old man was a formidable foe. Taking a deep breath, Jan pushed the door open, and with both hands on his Luger, walked briskly into the room, turned towards the old man in a semi–crouched position.

"I've grown to know you, respect you, I've longed for this moment when I could stare you down face to face. So many questions I wanted to ask you. How did you think you could possibly succeed? I understand Nigel and Tomar's deaths, but how did Rogers fit in? And Dr. Browne, why did he have to die? Who killed Andrea? Why? What is the Power? Damn you, old man! You cannot die on me. Not after all these years," said Jan, pounding on the old man's chest and crying profusely.

Jan cried for several minutes and then sat on the floor next to the man. His gun lay on the floor beside the bed. He sat crouched with arms wrapped around his knees and head down for what seemed like an hour. Then, he lifted his head.

"Old man, who are you? You know it took me twenty years to put that riddle together. But I still don't know what it all means. I don't understand completely why or what is the significance of a boy dancing around a wag–n'–bietjie tree. Unless he is celebrating something. But why is it a boy? It said you would rise and give power to eight witnesses. Are they your followers? What power did you give them?"

Jan picked up the phone and called the Montreal police authorities to report the old man's death.

Fifteen elapsed. Jan still sitting on the floor became startled when he heard a familiar voice. He quickly pulled himself together.

LaRue reached about to shake his hand. "I haven't seen you in eighteen years and once again you are at another death scene."

"What are you doing in Montreal?" Jan responded.

"It should be obvious. When I sent you the telegram, I really did not expect you to come. Why did you?"

Jan tried to smile. "You love your job, just as I do, and besides, old warriors never die. By the way, I should ask what are you doing in Canada?"

"It was in my telegram. Rogers works for Cirelli & Clements. You may have forgotten, but we still have an unsolved murder case on our hands. I am here on temporary assignment working with Canada finest. We hope to gain enough evidence on Rogers to extradite him."

"Well good luck, that Rogers is a cunning rascal."

"What do we have here, besides a dead old man?" asked LaRue.

"He's the one. There lies the clue to Dr. Russell Browne's death. Unfortunately it died with him. I found these leaves wrapped in a pouch, laying on the nightstand. I want an autopsy performed..."

LaRue interrupted. "Don't tell me, I will find that he died from the same type of poison which killed Dr. Browne."

"Yes, I believe the old man knew he was slowly dying and wanted to end it now. Let me know what the autopsy reveals. I'm staying at the Holiday Inn Downtown."

Jan again shook the detective's hand. "Thanks for sending me the telegram. You don't know how it bought my life back together."

"Forget it; we detectives must always help each other fight crime."

Jan somehow he suspected that the old man may have told the truth about Andrea's death. Her death had been an accident caused by others determined to stop his quest for the identity of those involved in the conspiracy. It suddenly occurred to him that greed has no color. There was profit to be made by those willing to finance a cause. Jan had lost his career to the pursuit of the Circle, and he had lost Andrea in its web of conspiracy, but the old man had not lied to him.

CHAPTER THIRTY ONE

Four Nines Fine Gold.

The following morning – Washington D.C.

"You're right Michael; the old man has paired each of us together to lead a specific attack. I wonder if Bubba and Christopher know he's dead," said Djhon.

"I don't know, perhaps they do now. The old man did not work alone. AboZuthu's spies, as he called them, may have informed them. In any regard, it's time to make contact and launch the first attack. Christopher is in New York City and Bubba's here in D.C. lobbying the House of Representatives to strengthen the sanctions on textile and farm products to South Africa. He is setting the stage for Congress to override President Reagan's veto on imposing economic sanctions on South Africa. If so, other nations will follow. How do you suggest we make contact?"

"By phone," said Djhon.

"Why by phone and not face to face? Aren't you curious or even anxious to meet them?"

"The time will come. I am concerned about this Linden fellow. Any person fool enough to stay on a trail for over 30 years is dangerous. The old man surely discussed the password, 'the time to act is near' to be used at the time we are to come together. Let's make contact and call Bubba and Christopher, and tell them, 'It's time to act!'"

Christopher Cirelli had regularly scheduled lunch dates on Fridays with Frank De Salvo, of Nicolas Brothers De Salvo was known as a reliable source of information on the stock and futures market. He also started well–placed rumors to benefit himself financially.

Christopher was aware of this and from time to time, dropped tidbits of information to him, when it also benefited his firm.

"Did you hear that Jake Reynolds checked into the hospital? Exhaustion, they said," said De Salvo, picking at his salad.

Christopher, now with a poker face said, "Yeah, I hope that's all it was. I hear that a lot of his money is being unloaded into oil stocks. He is selling his gold reserves from South Africa. The investors have to put it somewhere. You'd be a fool to keep it in gold when they're sending up trial balloons about demonetization."

"That's a strong word, demonetization," said De Salvo, "It has a tendency to even make the strongest of men pee in their pants."

"Salmone, Smith & Brothers is also watching the Platinum–Group Metals. They are concerned about South Africa and the effects of the sanctions."

"Bullshit! If the President's veto is defeated, the economic sanctions will take months if not years to have an effect."

Christopher glanced around the room. "It's not the sanctions, they'll worry about," he whispered. "It's this Mandela thing and the potential uprising." Salmone, Smith & Brothers is going to play it safe. In the very near future, they predict an unstable market in futures. They're going to issue the word to their stock brokers to only advise their large investors to temporarily switch commodities."

De Salvo excused himself a few minutes later to go to the bathroom. Christopher watched, amused, when he saw De Salvo headed to the phone instead of the men's room. The surreptitious phone call would cause gold to drop $40 an ounce before lunch was over. Several well–placed rumors from key brokerage houses started the slide.

The innocent Jake Reynolds, who had checked into the hospital to have a chin tuck, had to check back out to combat the chaos in his office. It seemed the rumor had gotten out that gold was on its way to the bottom, and his $30 million invested in futures stood to be wiped out. He wasted no time in calling up old sources to determine the source of the rumor, but they insisted on treating him like a pariah. Solicitous and careful, they seemed to think he was past it. Reynolds became extremely depressed, confirming indirectly the rumor of his suicide attempt.

The word "demonetization" was whispered in hushed tones over telephone lines from New York to Zurich. Like a rumor of a social disease, the effect was far out of proportion to the symptoms. Rumors of the possibility of a gold auction spread across the Wall Street wires.

THE WALLSTREET JOURNAL
@1986 Dow Jones & Company, Inc
Wednesday, September 24, 1986
Gold Auction – Rumors are being circulated among Wall Street gurus that the federal government is considering a gold action. Attempts by this newspaper to verify the source of the rumors have proved futile.

WASHINGTON POST
@1986 Washington Post
Wednesday, September 24
The government unloaded large amounts of gold. Sources
claim the gold auction, the first since 1971, will provide the Federal Government with hundreds of billions in cash flow. The White House is refusing to comment, and the Treasury Office is denying the rumors.

LONDON DAILY TELEGRAPH
@1986 London Daily Companies
Thursday – September 25, 1986
United States – The world's largest holder of gold bullion is contemplating auctioning part of its gold holdings. According to sources, the money will be

used to reduce a large part of its national debt. The British financial community has expressed outrage at the dumping of such a large amount of gold on the market. The move is viewed as a further weakening of the pound.

HOUSTON CHRONICLE
Thursday, September 25, 1986
Investors caught off guard, Gold in doubt
. . Although there has not been an auction of gold by the U.S. Treasury in years, the last one created a huge increase in the price of an ounce of gold. The U.S. government, thinking that the auction would make the price of gold drop, found that it quickly soared to over $800 an ounce, creating a frantic buying and selling crisis, but quickly closed at 328.75 an ounce.

An auction now would have the reverse effect, since gold has stayed over $400 for several years. The price has been artificially inflated by the limited supply of gold to the world market.

THE STAR
Thursday, September 25, 1986
Johannesburg – The rumors of a U.S. auction were floated in financial circles in Amsterdam, Berlin, Paris, Rio, and Moscow. The U.S., with over 450,000 gold bars at Fort Knox, represents a huge proportion of the world's supply of gold. Rumors were circulating that the U.S. is considering selling over thirty–five million ounces of gold to help pay off one trillion in national debt. Parliament views the U.S. actions as a serious blow to its economy, which will sharply reduce the market price of gold.

THE WALLSTREET JOURNAL
@1986 Dow Jones & Company, Inc
Friday, September 26, 1986
What's News ————————
Gold drops to $200 an ounce. The volatile nature of gold prices has. The gold market began its slide on Tuesday at noon, and by the weekend, had dropped $200 an ounce. Stunned observers were reminded that the price of gold, like any other commodity, was highly responsive to rumor and speculation. Rumor has it that South Africa's cumbersome gold mining techniques were having great difficulty in mining gold with a fineness of .9999 or as the experts calls it "four nines fine gold," or even a fineness of .995 or better which is generally accepted by banks and retailers. Faced with crashing gold prices, foreign investors suddenly embraced divestiture. They wanted to be as far as possible from the financial crisis, which would be inevitable for the country. South Africa, with a yearly production of 700,000 kilograms, represents 50% of the world's production each year. South Africa's balance of trades depended for years on gold bullion to make up the deficit. The South African Reserve Bank purchases and disposes the entire gold output of the country. Gold represents a huge percentage of the country's foreign trade. The European trading partners of the nine commercial banks began to cut off the burgeoning lines of credit.

NEW YORK TIMES
Monday, September 29, 1986
FOUR NINES FINE GOLD
Johannesburg. The Pretoria government denies the vicious Rumors. "Our gold is four nines fine gold," says the Foreign Minister.

MONTREAL GAZETTE
Monday, September 29, 1986
FOUR NINES – IS IT FINE GOLD?
Krugerrand plummets. Local government officials and investors are concerned about the rumors on the quality of South Africa's gold reserves. Canadian's Prime Minister stated that he has talked personally with high officials within the Pretoria government as well to South Africa's Prime Minister, Botha, and was given one word in response to the rumors, 'Ridicules'

THE WALLSTREET JOURNAL
@1986 Dow Jones & Company, Inc
Tuesday, September 30, 1986
Whose gold is pure?
Gold falls below $200.00 an ounce since the depression. South Africa in deep financial trouble. Hundreds of thousands of South Africans, whites, coloreds, mulattos, and blacks are without jobs with no visible means of supports. Riots prevail throughout major cities.

The Circle's attack had begun.

CHAPTER THIRTY TWO

Phase Two – Trouble Lies Ahead

Washington, D. C.

Djhon sat back in the chair thinking that after thirty–seven years, his destiny was about to unfold. He wondered if his dad, if still alive, would continue to be proud of him. His dad taught him how to be a military leader, and the old man taught him wisdom, ingenuity, and cunning, all traits his true father possessed. The more he thought about the old man, the more he felt a sense of loss. The old man's death had left only three members of the Circle who would have lived to see their dreams come true.

His training led him to seize the moment. Although he had argued the plan's futility with the old man, he realized that the members of the Circle had indeed planned well for the future. He welcomed the challenge and the power of execution. Djhon recognized that success depended on him.

"How clever the old man was!" his thoughts wandered. "He had made sure that no more than two of the eight children knew of each other. The old man had watched over each child to make sure his heritage was carefully nourished. At particular points in their development, he reappeared with a message and a thought. Each time he gave us growing young boys a riddle. He gave us a gift of knowledge that we did not understand at the time. When he was away, he had spies watching over us. He gave orders to kill anyone who came close to harming us or the cause. I guess I met his expectations and he selected me to be the military leader and Michael to lead us all in a united effort designed to bring about a change in the South African government. The plan will work if all forces and each member specifically carried out his assigned responsibility."

Djhon again reviewed the plan, looking for inconsistencies and weaknesses that could destroy their strategy. He wondered had they underestimated the South African police, or more importantly, the South African civilians? Would a people who had been taught since birth that they were superior to other races, specifically superior to the natives of their own country, ever give up? Would they ever be able to live together with the blacks, the coloreds, and the Indians, or would the battle continue until there were no more whites or blacks alive?

He knew that those who worked to change South Africa from within could never win. They picked up the old man's diary and began to read.

..... *The overwhelming fact was that the battle against apartheid had raged on since the 1920's, although the whites were outnumbered by over ten to one. Even now, with political awareness finally coming to the young people in South Africa, the end result could never be victory. To protest having to live in proscribed substandard housing, the blacks refused to pay rent. The response from the whites was quick and violent. There were evictions, followed by riots, followed by shootings. A dozen blacks had died, or at least that was the official count. More would certainly to follow.*

To protest the fact that their education was to be taught in Afrikaans, the blacks boycotted the schools. Their motto was, "equality now, education later." But later could never come for a people who had a whole generation of illiterates coming of age. Education for the non–whites had been substandard for years. Now it might be non–existent.

The members of the Circle had been right to send the children to America. A successful coup could only come from the outside world. But world opinion alone would not cause the South Africans to cave in.

As strategic leader of the younger Circle, Djhon was

the only one who had access to all the facets of the strategic operation.

The attacks would come from many areas directed to the heart of South Africa. They were to be carefully coordinated and timed. The South African Defense Force, the country's instrument of military power, must be rendered powerless. Djhon's plan called for countermeasures to be taken at a time when the SADF would most probably react to the emergency by mobilizing all personnel in the reserves.

The SADF was one of the best–trained military forces in the world. Their regular fighting force of 150,000 could be supplemented by 200,000–trained reservists from the Civilian Force within a matter of days.

Djhon picked up the phone and dialed Michael's number.

Michael was so engrossed in reviewing the plans that he did not hear the phone ringing at first. They had divided the old man's notes that pertained specifically to their strengths. Michael was so fascinated by the old man's writings that he kept on reading while he prepared a sandwich of peanut butter and margarine and ignored the jar of grape jelly he really intended to put on the bread.

...This journal is written in English and not my native tongue. It's one of many languages I know. You will be more familiar with it than our African dialects. The whites have tried to educate us in Afrikaans, but we have always believed that this is the language of slavery. We are forced to speak Afrikaans in the cities, but we have always studied English in secret, for this is the language in which we will speak to the world. Your fathers began to plan for your future when we first realized that the Circle would not be complete until after our own deaths. We first met as a group in 1948.

Michael, you and Djhon were each present at that

meeting, although you were tiny infants at the time. You were watched over by the tribes' trusted caretakers, Nyerere and Rhosida. Djhon's stepfather stumbled onto our village while vacationing. He had a military assignment in Zaire. Unfortunately, his wife had a miscarriage. You became the first to be adopted into your new family. Michael's adoption occurred the next month. His parents were already on a waiting list in Washington, D. C., to adopt a child; we merely hastened the arrangement while your father was doing research in Rhodesia.

I have addressed this journal to you two, because you will be the first to know the full plan. I am completing this diary now, in 1986, because I have realized that I will not live much longer. Many people have thought that I would be dead by now, but my people have always lived long lives. I will survive long enough to let you know about the Circle.

Michael's father, Thambo, formed the Circle, along with me and Djhon's father, Abozuthu, in 1948. Thambo knew that we must unite with the other tribes if we were to bring to an end to Apartheid, the pass regulations, and to accomplish equality in South Africa. We brought together the strengths of each tribe to make up the Circle. Abozuthu's tribe, the Zulu, were known for its military strategy. Thambo's tribes, the Xhosa, were the planners. The Sotho were cultivators and farmers. The Tswana were great developers of law and respect of justice in the tribal system. The Swazi were great spiritual believers and musicians. Ndebele established a territory with complex political institutions. The Venda people were astute entrepreneurs. Tsonga's tribe, the Shangaan, were known as expert traders.

I was known to the members of the Circle as 'Umbiki,' the 'Messenger.' I, with Abozuthu's spies, was to follow the children to America, find them homes, and most importantly carry the power. As each boy grew, he was to be reminded that he had a purpose in life. I am also of the Sotho tribe. I was chosen for this job because my travels have taken me to areas few had traveled I gained the respect of many powerful people in other countries and had been working to organize world opinion against apartheid since before the war. Now, my work would go on, but it would be done in silence. We asked our friends to support us in deeds rather than in words.

I traveled to and from America six times that first year. Six more children were taken from their homes in Africa, and put in new homes in America. I used my contacts in America, and met with new ones to arrange for these children to be placed into the mainstream of American society. All must be accomplished in secrecy, for if word of the plan got out, its mission would be aborted.

Robert Frederick Walker was the American name given to the child of Chieftain Gowon. Through a source in the Midwest, we assisted in placing a three–month old infant in the home of Fred and Angela Walker. Unable to have children, the couple had applied to adopt and placed on several waiting lists, but found that there were no healthy infants available for adoption. They had contacted the Tri–County Welfare Office in Wakoma County, Oklahoma. There, they were surprised to learn that a healthy baby boy was awaiting their application. The adoption took place immediately. Fred Walker was a farmer. He had a small but prosperous farm in Wakoma County. Our people helped to insure that the farm stayed prosperous, even during the bad years. Like his father, Gowon, Robert Walker was a born leader. He was raised by Fred and Angela to respect the land, to work hard, and to love his country.

"Robert Frederick Walker was given the nickname Bubba. He was not extra smart, or extra tall, and he was

never very large. Nothing came easy for him, but he seemed to relish the challenges. He worked at everything from his first steps to his first touchdown with great gusto, and those around him caught up in his struggles and soon helped him to succeed. He was a born leader. He understood struggle from deep down. He tried out for every sport. The coaches finally got tired of saying no, and let him play.

Bubba's greatest love was football. Even on the high school playing field, though, he was not the sort of solo star who does it all. Rather, he depended on the blocking of his teammates to support him. Somehow, his desire for the team to win increased their own skill and desire. They pushed, they pulled, and they scrambled their way to the state playoffs. The scouts marveled at the teamwork from what was obviously a team of average athletes.

Bubba made friends everywhere he went. In high school, he made fast friends with Christopher Anderson. Anderson was not athletic; he was, however, the smartest kid in high school algebra. He tutored Bubba in return for football passes. His college scholarship took him to Wharton, not Oklahoma State, but the boys shared several things.

It was January of 1965 when I made a visit to Pryor, Oklahoma to see the boys. I found Bubba in an empty locker room after he had a particularly bad practice session that discouraged even a buoyant young man. He was dog–tired. He had heard nothing from the many grant and scholarship boards to which he had applied, and the team was 7 wins, and 3 losses for the season. The weather had settled into a biting cold drizzle, and threatening snow. Bubba's shoulders slumped.

I sat in the shadow of the lockers, waiting for him to arrive. Bubba looked up and saw me. He shook himself and grinned, "It's been three years since I've seen you, Mr.

Williams. I missed you."

I told him. "I haven't been far away, Bubba. I saw you play against the Fairview Tigers last month. It was quite a battle."

The boy's face lit up. He was right! He had known, somehow, that I was always there watching. The occasional anonymous gift on his birthday, the books, which were left in his private and secret tree house where only his best friends were allowed, and the riddles I left for him told him that his life was to be special, mysterious, and terribly, terribly important.

The first riddle had come when he was twelve. It was in Zulu, although he did not know it then. His parents had passed it off as a student's secret code, and he had finally been convinced to put the note away, for a later time. It was not until the team traveled to Oklahoma City, years later, for a game that he pulled the much–folded piece of paper from its hiding place in the tree house. He begged the coach to let him visit the university on the pretext of visiting the financial aid office. He visited the foreign studies department instead. However, the translation, when he received it in the mail several days later, was still a puzzle to him.

University of Oklahoma City
2216 Turners Blvd
Oklahoma City, Oklahoma 12788
 November 16, 1965

Dear Mr. Walker,

Listed below is the translation of the note you left at our foreign studies department.

Watch out! Great things occur as time passes. The boy goes and dances around a wag'–n–bietjie tree. A sick old man shall rise and bestow power to eight witnesses and they shall shout, "I have eaten!"

The note is of Xhosa/Zulu dialect. We hope the translation aids you in your endeavors.

Sincerely,

Frederick Carter, Ph.D.

Dean, Foreign Studies

On that visit in 1965, Bubba was so intrigued that he walked out of the locker room without his books. He turned back to retrieve them. When he passed the library on his way back, he saw me seated at a study table in the library with his best friend Chris. He overheard me telling Chris, "The sheep can kill the elephant. Study the system well, for in any political or economic system are weaknesses which can be turned against itself. Remember that your true father was a trader and a great chief. He knew the weaknesses of all the tribes, as well as their treasures."

Bubba silently crept away. Christopher said nothing and Bubba never mentioned the incident. Gradually the other events of their lives took precedence. It was the year 1967 when I saw Bubba again, the day of his high school graduation, when he handed me the University's attempt to translate the riddle and asked me its true meaning. Bubba also wanted to know my relationship to both himself and Christopher. I replied "The strong tree has many branches."

Bubba Walker is now the de facto spokesperson for the Worldwide Farm Coalition. The group had grown out of the American farmers' disaffection with U.S. farm policy in the seventies and eighties. For the first time in history, world communications allowed even the poorest farmer to know the facts about his situation, and that he was not alone. Television spread the word through the Midwest and on across the country and overseas. Farmers, who had always gone it alone in their grim fight against the weather and the forces of nature, found that they were fighting a bigger foe: bureaucracy and the Federal Government. It seemed that Bubba had reached manhood at a time when these staunch individualists were finally ready to work together to get something done in Washington. Under his leadership, they passed unheard–of restrictions on foreign imports to protect the breadbasket of America.

My student carefully laid the groundwork. Bubba and the others had contacted all the opinion leaders, personally, as long as three years before. Never was there any suggestion of immediate action, just the planting of an idea: That apartheid in South Africa was an affront to the little people, the farmers, and another symbol of the big business that was anathema to them. Feeling their political power for the first time since the forties, the farmers were ready to flex their muscle in the worldwide arena.

Bubba's old friend Christopher Anderson had been working on his part of the plan for the last ten years. Under my direction in high school, his natural talents for trade took off in the arena of the stock market. He had learned well the lessons and riddles which I had brought him over the years: Lessons of patience, perspective, and economics. He learned about his Tsonga–Shangaan ancestors, who traded with the Portuguese five hundred years ago.

He was flabbergasted. "Djhon won't believe this." Michael whispered. "This is unreal. The old man does indeed have a plan." His thoughts were interrupted by the telephone.

"Michael, for Pete's sakes where have you been? I've been trying to reach you for the past hour."

"Nowhere, I've been here in the apartment. Djhon, you have to read the old man's diary. It can be accomplished. Bubba and Christopher have already started Phase Three."

"Where are Bubba and Christopher?"

Michael was excited. "I don't know, but they have certainly carried out their part. They also have the power. We must find them. The time is growing nearer!"

"You're right. To cause a panic and doubt in South Africa's greatest weapon, its currency can certainly bring a powerful country to its knees in a hurry. Can you imagine the repercussions if the Soviet Union became bankrupt, much less South Africa."

"I know what we must do. We must get together to discuss strategy. Do you remember the old vacant building on Cleburne Street we looked at the other day? Meet me there at 6 p.m."

"Djhon, why don't you just come over here? Why meet in that crummy old building?"

"Michael, do you realize what we are contemplating? We could be tried for treason. Man, we could be executed or hanged. Have you forgotten about the South African police captain? This Linden fellow. The old man said that he was always one–step behind. The old man has eluded him for over 30 years. The old man is dead. We don't have all of his wisdom. We must be extra careful."

"I'm sorry, Djhon. You are entirely correct. We must practice prudence. The old man was wise in selecting you to be our military leader. I just was caught up in the cause when reading his diary. I'll see you at 6 p.m." He hung up the phone, picked up the diary and continued reading.

Bubba's true father died in 1957. He was tried by the government in 1952, on charges of organizing a terrorist society. Because the authorities had confused our members with the Mau Mau, they never had enough evidence to convict him. However, they held him on lesser charges of conspiracy to revolt, and he died on Robben Island in 1957, a political prisoner.

Christopher was the son of Chieftain Mugabe Sekou, of the Tsonga–Shangaan. He was a merchant before the whites took away his home and his business. He was sent to the so–called homeland territory of Bophuthatswana, a land he had never seen, and he died there in 1968.

John Cirelli arranged to adopt Christopher privately, through one of our people in New York. Christopher's adoptive father was the partner in the small, successful investment company of Cirelli & Clements. The firm gained a reputation for solid, if unconventional, positions. An uncanny ability to predict world events led to substantial profits in both long and short positions on multinational stocks.

Cirelli & Clements favored the sugar and tobacco markets in early 1961, just months prior to the Bay of Pigs. They predicted the Arab oil situation in 1973 and sold their energy–based portfolio months before, realizing excellent profits. During the early 1980's they invested millions in Conoco, Marathon Oil, Cities Services, Gulf Oil, Belridge Oil, at bargain prices months prior to the companies being acquired by Dupont, U.S. Steel, Occidental Petroleum, Chevron, and Shell Oil respectively. Cirelli & Clements were able to maneuver a moderate capital base into a sizable position in the next few years. Their investors were few. They accepted no new clients, although many tried to buy a piece of their very profitable pie.

He visited Christopher to teach him of his ancestors, the Tsonga–Shangaan, who were trading with the Portuguese five hundred years ago, and with the Arabs for centuries before that. The Tsonga bartered hoes from their Venda neighbors in return for cloth and amber from the coast of Africa; copper from the Sothos; ivory, rhino horn, gold, and furs. They traveled on foot and by canoe from the Nlomati and Limpopo Rivers. Christopher had studied the ancient trade routes, based on the seasons and climate as well as rivers and coastlines.

From his adoptive father, Christopher had learned economics. By the time he was twelve, he had mastered the fundamentals of supply and demand, the business cycle, the Keynesians, the monetarists, and the Phillips curve. Later, his father introduced him to the study of financial statements. He studied Benjamin Graham's criteria for judging the value of a bargain stock; the psychology of the market according to Stanley Kroll and Robert Wilson; and the inspired market moves of Warren Buffett and John Templeton. He plotted the rise and fall of the Fortune 500 on his dad's personal computer.

He taught Christopher how the world economic situation affects the American corporations. He studied the European economic Community, the Japanese, the Chinese, and the Russian bear's influence on the dollar, the mark, and the rand.

The South African economy was an enigma. Christopher's bar graphs leapt off the chart between l960 and l975, as foreign investment soared from R13 billion to over R40 billion. As the internal problems of the South Africans multiplied, so did their dual dependence on foreign investment and imported goods. Although South Africa was a yearly winner in the balance of trade, that balance was heavily weighted by gold bullion. As Christopher attempted to make a model to predict the effects of divestiture, he realized that none of the conventional predictions would apply. The South Africans were not to be swayed by world opinion. The American and European corporations, which had invested heavily there, had a huge investment in the status quo: Apartheid.

It was not until l985 that Christopher was acknowledged as the genius of Cirelli & Clements. The rumor on the street (never substantiated) was that the anonymous investors who provided his capital were fronts for insiders at the great multinational corporations; that Cirelli & Clements were dealing in insider information of the blue chip variety.

Michael read on as the old man told of the religious and political powers of the Circle.

Chief Kwame Kasauubu, leader of the Swazis, was a great spiritual leader. He believed by talking to his God, he could make it rain. Kwame also believed that there was only one God and that all religions were worshiping the same God. He believed that humankind, from the beginning, had misinterpreted the words to form his own bible.

His son was placed in the home of Reverend Nathan Robinson. He was considered by most blacks in the United States to be an outspoken force for civil rights, but most importantly a true believer in the word of God. The child was christened Nathaniel. I first visited Nathaniel in the year 1955, when his adopted father as leading a boycott against a city segregation ordinance. He was seven at the time. I asked him if he understood what his dad was doing and why. His answer reassured me; he was learning well and he was beginning to believe. The next time was in 1960 when I carefully placed the riddle in the Reverend's Bible, and once again in 1963 when Reverend Robinson was in Alabama leading a demonstration against segregation. It was not until after his adopted father died in 1970 that I started Nathaniel's involvement and recognition as a religious speaker and campaigner for human rights. During the last ten years, he has carefully worked out my plan of speaking out against South Africa's apartheid policies. He has led successful boycotts of companies' products for their treatment of blacks, and their involvement with holdings in South Africa.

The son of the Ndebele chieftain, Mikhane Ashwante, was Allen Dugmore. James Lee Foston, an active behind–the–scenes man in the Georgia Democratic Party, adopted him. Allen studied political science and graduated from

Howard University with a Masters degree. Allen also enrolled as a law student but dropped out in his freshman year. Allen used his education and knowledge of politics to apply his limited legal background in non–traditional ways. He became a negotiator. I taught Allen that the Ndebele tribe was known for its mastery of intricate political structure, and Allen learned my lessons well. He learned in the tough arena of local politics.

Allen gained notoriety as assistant to the Mayor of Atlanta. During the 1960s and 1970s, when Atlanta had over–built and suffered devastation in the recession, Allen Foston negotiated settlements with the police, firefighters and teachers unions, resulting in benefit concessions. The unions would have bankrupted the strapped city treasury without his aggressive and innovative stance. He gained the respect of the city and state political organizations. During the crime wave that threatened to panic Atlanta in the late 1970s, Allen pulled the gangs and law enforcement together with the churches to prevent violence.

He later became a powerful force in dealing with the corporations for social change. He negotiated divestiture agreements with institutional investors at a time when the business community said it could never happen. I guided him to concentrate his efforts on the opinion leaders. The institutions follow the fads of the marketplace to a great extent, and when one goes, the rest of the sheep follow. The institutions are more susceptible to lawsuits than the individual investor is. Allen has been pursuing the institutions with threats of lawsuits and legislation. One by one, they see the future coming and are selling off their South African holdings. At the same time, the rumors about the gold market begin to make them worry about their money.

Allen had also encouraged the U.S. firms with foreign investments to pull their resources out of South Africa.

An international business company was advised very privately that a significant class action suit would stop them from introducing a new 32–bit communications device on the market. The independent computer firms have friends at the commissioner's level in the Federal Trade Commission who will issue a Restraint of Trade Order unless the company pulls out of South Africa.

G. E. Electric learned that certain unscrupulous competitive tactics have been monitored and will be released to the media if its plants are not shut down or sold to black shareholders. G.W. Electric protested that it was a leader in opposing apartheid. It cited an incident where G.E. employees were encouraged to protest whites–only beaches, by the company indicating that it would support the employees if they were arrested. G.W. was informed that we are now playing hardball, and the stakes are much higher than a piece of sandy beach.

Michael laid the diary down. He washed his face and stared into the mirror. He gave himself the thumbs up sign. It was now clear to him why the old man had chosen him to be the Circle's leader and spokesman. There was so much to be done in such a short period of time. Before his death, the old man had set the wheels turning. In a matter of days, the events in South Africa would turn a full circle.

"Two more of us to go, Michael," said Djhon. "Who are they?"

"I don't know. I've been too busy with my part of the plan."

"You don't know. Don't you think before we precede with this scheme, we ought to know who all the players are?"

Michael shook his head in disgust. "This is not a scheme. The old man and our fathers have carefully and with precise timing put together a plan that will free our people. Where is your faith, your guts?"

"That's not fair. Believing as I do that man is not perfect. Faith can get you killed. I want to see the plan succeed, but I also want to be alive to tell my kids about my role in it."

Michael looks at him. "Let me read you the last section of his diary."

CHAPTER THIRTY THREE

Never Say Die

Montreal, Quebec

For the past several days, Jan remained in Montreal. He camped himself across the street from the Cirelli & Clements office building and monitored the traffic in and out of the 1000 de la Gauchetie're, Montreal's tallest building. The unmarked van was fitted with a one–way viewing window, courtesy of the local Montreal police, friends of Detective LaRue.

The previous day, LaRue was ordered back to Washington, D.C. He had already spent two weeks in the province and his surveillance efforts to find Rogers were futile.

Linden no longer answered to higher police authorities. He continued to see Charlotte, satisfying her desires in hopes that she would reveal when Rogers was coming. He had also been consulting with his contacts in the U.S. as well as South Africa, trying to uncover additional evidence to support Charlotte's claim that Cirelli & Clements was actually the cover name for the Circle. He was not overly concerned over the move towards sanctions against his country by the United States government.

There had been legislation introduced by members of Congress for the past several years to issue sanctions if the Pretoria government did not end apartheid. Certain members of the Parliament felt South Africa could retaliate by restricting sales of platinum to the U.S. traders. Some members were under the opinion that, since platinum represented only a fraction of South Africa's export earnings; they could get the world's attention by cutting back on platinum exports. Jan was very concerned, however, over the attacks on the purity and fineness of South Africa's gold production.

He did feel that he and his government shared the same common belief. The major threat to the South African government did not involve movements of national liberation, fueled by legitimate African nationalists or even the African National Congress. It was the Russians who wanted South Africa because of the strategic importance of the military bases it could offer and the country's mineral–rich resources.

ANC's financial support came from many sources, including the United Nations, the Organization of African Unity, the World Council of Churches, the Swedish government, the governments of Denmark, Norway, the Netherlands, and Canada, but mostly from the U.S.S.R. When the ANC was outlawed by South Africa in 1960, it had become a well–organized and internationally supported movement. Through the Organization of African Unity, the ANC received its arms from the Soviet Union.

"If I can somehow prove that Cirelli & Clements received its money from the Russians and how it was filtered down to the Circle, my government would react quickly to prosecute the members," he whispered. But the South African government had no jurisdiction in the United States, especially now, since there was talk among members of Congress and President's support for gradual reform of apartheid had eroded.

One week later – 10:30 p.m.

"Shoo! Shoo!" Jan sneezed into the palm of his hand in an attempt to muffle the sound.

"Are you all right?" asked LaRue. He handed Jan his handkerchief to clean his hands.

"Yes, I'll be okay. I just sneezed myself into a damn splitting headache."

"Yeah, you should see yourself. Those blue eyes of yours are so red."

Detective LaRue was back in Montreal. One of his friends in the police department had picked up a hot tip on Rogers. The stakeout was just east of 76 Rue Roy, in the fish market district.

Jan and LaRue were in an old beat–up car a block away but in sight of the fish warehouse. In the opposite direction, were two Canadian police officers in a van with lettering painted on the door that read Warshaw's Supermarket.

"The informant said to my friend the fishery was a distribution point for money laundering," said LaRue. "Rogers is supposed to be here to pay off his contacts."

Jan blew his nose once again. "It wouldn't surprise me that they don't use the dead fish to conceal the counterfeit bills."

"Yeah, I wonder where the counterfeit plates and the printing press are located. The transfer of funds was rumored to occur in the wee hours of the morning."

"Close the window and stop that draft," said LaRue. "I don't want you getting sick on me."

"I hope your source is right on the date and place. I don't take kindly to freezing my butt off for a bad tip."

The night was long and starless, only the light from the full moon permeated the street. The longer they waited, the colder it became.

At 3:50 a.m., an explosion shattered the plate glass windows of the fishery market building. The blast ripped the metal frame from its hinges and slamming its contents into the streets.

"What in the hell! Damn, what was that?" shouted LaRue. He pulled his revolver from his shoulder holster. "Jan, this may be a diversion. Take the car around the rear and block the alley." His quick exit from the car left Jan amazed at how quickly a man his age could move. LaRue ran towards the fishery.

Jan sensed something was wrong. His will to survive was instinctive. "LaRue! Wait!" He obviously did not hear him. "LaRue, it's a trap!"

The two Montreal police detectives also ran towards the fishery.

Suddenly there was another flash of light. A gunshot was followed by two more.

Jan saw LaRue drop in the street, mid–stride. The two other detectives were also hit. He tried to see where the blast of gunfire came from. It was too quick. The gunshots were instant. The deaths were quick. Silence filled the night.

He waited approximately three minutes, using the back of the old car for cover. He heard nothing. Jan ran to LaRue. He felt for a pulse. LaRue was dead. A single shot into the heart.

He then ran to the other detectives. They too were dead; a single shot to the head killed the large frame officer. A single blast to the chest, downed the second man.

Jan ran back to the car. He looked for the walkie–talkie. "Damn it, LaRue has it." He was without radio contact and there was no other communication device in the car they drove. The streets were dark, except for one lone streetlamp. He jumped behind the car door when he heard another gunshot. It shattered the streetlamp. His back rested against the passenger side fender, his Lunger was cocked.

He waited. Darkness was everywhere. Again, it grew silent as a morgue. He felt the assassin moved like a cat on silent feet.

One minute passed.

He heard nothing, but the beat of his heart.

Two longed minutes had passed.

"Damn you Linden, you've got to do something. You just can't wait here until sunrise," he muttered.

Jan heard the puttering sound of a car's engine. He looked over the edge of the car's hood. He saw another car fifty yards down the street.

"Rogers, it must be Rogers," Jan said, "Only he can be this good." He looked up and saw the headlights flicker on and off. He stared at the car wondering who was behind the wheel and could it really be Rogers.

The car suddenly accelerated, then came to an abrupt stop. The tires shrieked against the pavement as the driver held the car in check. Once more, he flicker the headlights and the tires squealed forward and stopped by the streetlamp.

Jan could not see the driver, but a man with dark glasses and a big smile raced the engine until the smell of black exhaust emission filled the air. He had one foot on the gas pedal and another on the brakes. The red car rocked forward when the driver applied pressure to both pedals. It was evident he had played this game before.

Jan had had enough. He raised his gun and stood to face the stranger. He walked to the center of the street.

The stranger accelerated the engine and raced towards him. Jan fired once, twice, three and four times at the car's driver. Each shot missed its target. Jan jumped out of the car's path and landed hard on his right shoulder. The back of his hand hit the pavement hard causing him to lose control of the gun. It bounced down the pavement.

Jan turned around and shouted. "Oh my God!" The car hit LaRue's body with such force that his belt buckle was caught by a piece of metal attached to the muffler. Jan fell to his knees and choked as if a large hand had grabbed him by the throat. He searched for his gun. He felt helpless.

The driver stopped at the other end of the street unaware that LaRue's body was underneath. Suddenly the car spun in a circum-rotating manner to face his prey: Jan. The tires ground against the pavement when the driver again rocked the car. The smell of burnt rubber filled the air. The car's swaying motion released the lifeless body it once held in its grasp. The driver flickered the headlights again.

Jan noticed the air was still. There was no breeze, only the smell of exhaust emitted from the hunter's car. The car's engine noise reduced to a quiet patter.

One second passed, then another.

Jan and the stranger stared at each other. The driver could clearly see him, but Jan could not see him. The bright headlights blinded him; he saw only the silhouette of a car. His feet felt heavy. He tried to lift them; they moved only a few inches.

The car's engine noise increased. A loud roar from the car erupted. The car backfired. The driver rocked the car several times, and then accelerated toward him.

Jan ran. He jumped over a fence and ran for thirty full minutes, down 76 Rue Roy, then left on Rue St–Denis, all the way to av. du Mont–Royal and right on Rue Clark before he stopped, gasping for air. He was drenched from the showers of sweat that saturated his clothes.

It took Jan nearly two hours before he would return to the crime scene. The question he kept asking himself was, "Why did LaRue have to die? It was he who pitifully ran like a panicked heifer.

Jan was back in his hotel room; he slept hard, with his Lunger by his pillow. It was past seven o'clock in the morning when he heard a hard and rapid knock on room door. He had ordered a continental breakfast and a newspaper from room service to be delivered at 7:15 a.m. He looked at the clock and noticed it was exactly 7:15.

He signed the room tab, sat down, took a sip of coffee and glanced at the newspaper. The *New York Times* feature headline, *"Purity of South African Gold Challenged,"* drew a wrinkle across his forehead. When he opened the paper to continue the article, an envelope fell to the floor, inside was message typed on a piece of paper.

I believe we share interest in a mutual cause. If you are concern in helping your country and want to learn the identities of members of the Circle, meet me at 7:00p.m. at the hockey arena. Come alone. Don't forget your ticket.

Jan looked at the ticket and saw it was for tonight. The ticket seat assignment was Mezzanine level, Row 25, seat 17D. The Montreal Canadians were hosting an exhibition game against the Toronto Maple Leafs. He looked once again at the clock and wondered to himself if the message he was reading was not an invitation to his own murder.

"Surely," he thought, "the old man before he died must have warned the others about me, especially since I had followed his trail for the past thirty–four years."

Jan remembered his first encounter with the old man. He had

not had him killed earlier because he never had concrete evidence against the Circle.

Jan felt he was always one–step behind. The old man's sudden death might have caused his superiors to suspect there was some truth to his claims. Still, he could not pass up this opportunity. He must go. As a kind of insurance, he would gather all his notes, including the most recent, and give them to the front desk to be mailed to the South African Embassy, if he were not back by tomorrow morning.

He arrived at the hockey arena one hour ahead of schedule. It was earlier in the hockey season and the game was not a sellout. He drove his rented car and parked a couple of hundred yards away from the entrance. He purchased a ticket on the other side opposite Row 25, seat 17D. He also brought his binocular.

Thirty minutes later, people started to arrive and occupy their seats. Linden, dressed in a blue uniform jacket, stood most of the time on the ramp leading up the mezzanine. He had earlier observed one of the porters throw an extra uniform jacket in a linen closet. He looked through the binoculars, scans the seating area of the mysterious ticket, and observed nothing peculiar in anyone's actions. His surveillance of the area presented nothing out of the ordinary: just kids, families, tourists, and more tourists. The arena was nice but cool, a perfect night for game of hockey. It was 7:20 p.m. before anyone sat in what appeared to be seat 17E. Jan felt assailable. He did not know what his contact looked like. If he sat in 17D, he felt like an idiot waiting for someone to either contact him or kill him. He looked again at the man in 17E. He looked like an ordinary person, shouting and yelling at the players on the ice rank.

A small boy approached him. "Mr. Linden. Jan Linden."

Startled. He looked the boy. "Yes, boy. Don't tell me. You have a message for me."

"Yes sir, I do. A man paid me ten dollars to deliver this."

"What man?"

The boy turned in the opposite direction and pointed. "He's gone. The man said this envelope will tell you where to find him," said the boy before he took off running.

Linden felt slightly relieved. He now knew the man did not want him dead. All he would have had to do was to pay any street assassins; a thousand dollars and they would gladly have cut his throat. Better yet, if the Circle now wanted him eliminated, a well–placed sniper could have blown his brains out. He looked through the binoculars again at seat 17D. The same man was in 17E and he seemed to be enjoying himself. However, there was an attractive woman in 17C. She looked in his direction. She was smiling. He lowered the binoculars and opened the envelope.

> *Are you having fun? Go back to your car and drive to the Montreal's train depot. Take the stairs to the snack shop, order a ham and cheese sandwich and a can coke, not fountain, a can of coke. Sit near the rear, facing the train yard. Don't eat or drink.*

It was nearly eight o'clock before he arrived at the train depot. He did as he was told, ordered the food and noticed a couple leaving a table in the back of the snack bar.

He patiently waits to be contacted. He did not eat the ham and cheese sandwich nor drank the coke. He felt like a puppet. A boy dressed in soiled clothing slowly walked towards him.

"Excuse me sir," asked the boy. "Are you Mr. Linden?"

"Yes I am, young man. Do you have something for me?"

The shy boy gave a meek reply. "No sir, but there's a cab waiting for you at the entrance directly to your left. Sir, the cab number is 618. Please hurry, the cab will only wait three minutes." The boy quickly grabbed the sandwich and coke and ran.

Jan walked briskly down the stairs and towards the entrance. As the boy had said, cab 618 was there waiting. He looked around for a second, and then got into the back seat of the cab.

"Monsieur, where to?" asked the cab driver.

"You tell me. Who sent you?" responded Jan.

"Look Monsieur, the dispatcher radioed me to pick up a fare on the east side of Grand Central with instructions to wait several minutes and if the fare did not show up in that time, then go to the Place Ville Marie Hotel, because the fare may be there," the driver said in a brassy tone.

"Then let's go!" Jan ordered.

He was amazed at how the man was driving. He was cutting in front of cars, speeding up whenever he was next to a lane that merged into his and not letting the other driver in, riding the horn constantly and occasionally shooting the finger at his victims. The cab driver turned down a side street and stopped for a red light.

The cab driver's head lurched forward, the side of his face smacked against the steering wheel. A small black dart had struck the side of the cabbie's neck.

Before Jan had a chance to react, three men jumped into the cab from the red Mercedes parked next to it. Two entered the back doors and third men jumped in the front seat. One of the men in the back pointed a gun covered with a newspaper at Jan. The man in the front seat pushed the cabbie from the steering wheel and started driving, while the third man in the back merely smiled at him.

"Detective Jan Linden. You've been a very busy man over the past few days," said a well–dressed man in a dark blue wool suit, a tailored white shirt with gold cuff links and the initials, DLR.

"I'm afraid I don't have the privilege, Mr. D.L.R.," said Linden.

"You are quite observant, Detective Linden."

"If you know my name, then surely, you ought to know that I am no longer a police detective. I'm retired."

The stranger seemed surprised. "Retired, Mmm, maybe I should fire my source."

Jan laughed. "Or better yet, find yourself a better snitch."

"Touché. If you are indeed retired, what brings you here to our beautiful city?"

"Vacation."

The stranger made an attempt at a reassuring smile. He grew weary of the exchange. "Don't take me for a fool, Mr. Linden. My name is Daniel L. Roark. Dr. Douglas L. Roark gave the name to me.

My real and nature father was a Venda chieftain named Tshivase Shakororo."

Linden eyes widened. "You're from South Africa."

"Just a minute," said Roark, "Bobbie, find a place to dump the cabbie's body."

"Is he dead?" asked Linden.

"No, but he will be out for several hours. Roark leaned forwarded and pulled the dart out of the cabbie's neck. "A nice little weapon. My ancestors used it from time to time." He then placed the dart's pointed edge against Jan's neck.

"Careful with that," Jan tried not to move.

"The old man told me to only kill your enemies, or those that threatened us."

Jan's voiced cracked. He was afraid Roark's hand would slip from the car's motion. "Is that why you killed Detective LaRue?"

Roark laughed. "Who in the hell is LaRue?"

"Last night, someone killed him and two Canadian police officers."

"Sorry, it was not me."

"Then who?"

"Why don't you ask the people responsible?"

"Are you going to kill me?"

Roark took a long breath. He watched Jan sweat. "You, my dear detective, are not my enemy."

Jan angrily pushed Roark's hand away from his neck. "If the old man wanted me dead, he would have placed my head on top of an assegai blade and had someone placed the spear in the center of police headquarters for all to see."

The Mercedes turned into a side street and stopped midway in the alley. The driver turned around and pointed a gun at Linden. The other man pulled the cabbie out to place his body beside a dumpster. The driver waited for the other man, and then quickly exited the alley.

"Your note said we had something in common. I don't believe we do. I already know the identities of four members of the Circle. Now five with you. I also know the meaning of the Circle and how it's funded."

"Mr. Linden, unless you wish to end up like the cabbie, don't ever again take me for a fool. If you know so much, then why did you come? Don't bother to answer. You don't know shit."

"Mr. Roark. I know more than you think I know."

"Bull shit! Tell me what are the identities of the four you mentioned. Go ahead! Tell me! Who is now the leader?"

Jan did not answer. He looked away for a moment. "I, I mean..."

"The problem with you, Mr. Linden, is that you have always suspected but you never had the evidence. I mean real concrete evidence to hang your hat on. Your credibility is shot. You are viewed by the South African government as a self–acclaimed crusader. Your government has said the same thing as I. 'Show us proof!'

Silence filled the taxi. Roark continued. "Well Mr. Linden, I'm waiting."

Jan stared at him.

"Good! Now that we understand each other, I will give you the proof needed to finally convince your government that a conspiracy is about to unfold."

"Why, Mr. Roark, are you being so bloody helpful, when the so–called proof may hang you or get you killed, if they found out?"

Roark laughed. He glanced out the window for a few seconds. "Jan, may I call you Jan, I feel I know you. The old man told us so much about you. I am surprised he just did not have you killed."

Jan came jumped to the old man's defense. "He had principles."

"Yes. Yes, you are right. Your death, he felt was not necessary. When he first told me of my destiny, I was behind the whole thing. Oh, how he trained me! My adopted father sent me to the best medical school in the country, but the old man taught me about how to care for people, the ability to be creative, the power to heal and cures unheard of by the common man. I cured people destined to die. I invented cures for man that doctors are using all over the world. I am well–respected throughout the world and am considered a leading authority on cancer research as well as other strange viruses or diseases my peers cannot control. I am also working on the cure for a new disease that will take this country by surprise. Its call AIDS. Other doctors have sent their patients to me after the drugs administered or operations to halt the disease have failed. I'm the witch doctor." Roark laughed repeatedly.

Jan's face darkens with frustration. "Don't get too carried away with yourself. You are not God."

Roark rolled down the window and pitched the dart outside. "No, but I'm a damn good witch doctor. Ah, shit. Witch doctor, my ass!"

"Okay," Jan said, "enough is enough."

"Mr. Linden, there's one thing about America. It has a tendency to spoil you. You get fat and lazy after you climb that mountaintop. I like this life. I am wealthy. I have a damn good practice. Hell, the old man did not ask me how I wanted to live my life. I enjoy what I am doing and I don't want to care for a country of sick, starving people. Money and success spoiled me. I don't want to go back to South Africa!"

"Then don't!" shouted Jan. "Why in God's name should I believe you? This whole thing could be part of the Circle plan to lead me astray."

Roark leaned forwarded. "Tell me Jan, do you remember the last time you had your butt kicked?"

"What in the hell does that have to do with this? You can't intimidate me with threats!"

"No, you misunderstand me. I meant the question literally; do you remember the last time your butt was kicked real good by someone? I mean to the point you felt totally defenseless and your life was in the hands of that person." Roark watched for a reaction.

Linden felt subdued. His somber voice reflected his mood. "Only once, years ago," he said. "It was something in the past."

Roark beamed. "Yes, you were at the mercy of your assailant and if it wasn't for his lover, you would be dead today. The year was 1948 when Rogers said he did a real good old fashion number on you. Oh, how he bragged."

Jan lurched forward and grabbed Roark by the throat.

"Rogers! Where is he?" demanded Jan.

The second man quickly hit him with the butt of the gun on the side of his head, just hard enough for him to let go of Roark.

Roark gave Jan a long side longed stare. "Don't, Mr. Linden! I repeat don't ever again touch me like that, or I will forget the old man's teaching and kill your ass. This sir, is not South Africa." Roark straightened his coat and tie.

"Uh, oh," muttered Jan as he rubbed the back of his head. "What about Rogers." Jan's head ached. He lowered his head. He had a wet feeling on his fingers. He looked and saw blood.

"He's dead. The old man sent him to my clinic. The old man did not care much for Rogers; however, he did find him useful. He was the connection or go–between for Cirelli & Clements. Rogers had contracted AIDS from his lover. Since the origin of the disease was believed to have occurred from certain areas of Africa, the old man had arranged for various grants and research data to come my way."

"Oh, too bad for the bloody bastard. It couldn't have happen to a better person."

"The old man had a way for making sure you succeeded in your specialty. Rogers came to me too late. The treatment had no affect due to the stage of the disease. When a person is dying, it seems as if they want to be forgiven for all of their sins. Rogers talked about his lifestyle, his Russian involvement with Africa, his love of and taste for the finer things in life, and of course, how he came so close to killing this South African police officer. Rogers died three years ago. His lover Wingate is now the go–between."

"Just a second," replied Jan. "Detective LaRue had him under surveillance. He can't be dead."

Roark laughed. "Oh you police officers. You are all the same. The name Rogers was known through many circles of the organization. Wingate just assumed his identity. He also knew too much of Rogers' activities when challenged.

"Wingate, where can I find him?"

"He's your least concern at this moment. Time is running out on you and your country. The Circle has begun their attack."

"What do you mean my country? It's your country as well! And what do you mean time is running out? For God's sake, Roark, what will happen? Exactly how much time do we have?"

"I don't know the full plan. That's Djhon's area. All I know is it will happen in several weeks. Phase two has been launched.

"Phase two? What's phase two?"

"Jan! Where have you been? Don't you read the papers?"

"Oh please, give me a break. The gold rumors. Ha. That's a bunch of bullshit."

"Don't underestimate the Circle. They are powerful. They have friends in and out of the United States Government that will benefit greatly if South Africa folds. Land, my dear fellow. It's also about land."

"The gold and platinum reserves," whispered Jan.

"Besides, I don't want to go back to South Africa. I don't have the foggiest idea what it's like. I have been in America all my life. I have grown to love this country."

"Damn it, then don't go, we were there first anyway."

"Jan, Jan, Jan. You don't really understand, do you? You Afrikaners are all alike. You don't realize that the old man had the power. He passed it to Michael. I have no choice. I have to go back. That is why we have something in common. I need you and you need me."

"Power, power! All I have heard is power. What is this power? It has driven me to the point of exhaustion! It's in the riddle, isn't it?"

"Yes, it is," answered Roark. "Michael has ordered us back to South Africa. We will be meeting in the same remote village where it all began: The birthplace of the Circle. I'm told the two of the original members are still alive and will be meeting with us: Thambo and Abozuthu."

"Who are they?"

"Thambo conceived the idea, and set forth the plans. Abozuthu sent out the spies to protect us and the old man gave us wisdom and knowledge. If I don't return to South Africa, I will be killed. I know the date, time and place. We will be in South Africa, where you have jurisdiction to arrest the Circle members."

"If the Circle organization is powerful enough to have Nigel killed, as well as Tomar and Dr. Browne, then they can get to you, regardless of where you are."

"No one needs to know the source of your information. The South African government will have to execute and hang them. Throwing them in prison will not stop the Circle. From what I understand, the elders are still in control. The young blacks are revolting, but they can be controlled, it's only a handful of them. The elders still believe in the power. Once you get control of the power, your government will continue their dominance of the blacks," smiled Roark.

"I'm not sure what you want from all of this," said Jan.

"My life. That is all Mr. Linden, my life. I don't believe and never have believed the plan would have a fat chance in hell of succeeding. I don't envision spending the rest of my life in some South African jail, or worst yet hanged for conspiring to overthrow the government."

"What makes you think the South African government will believe me? After all, some of my superiors feel I should be committed to a mental hospital for trying to plant ideas in the black's minds!"

"Tell them the outlawed ANC leaders will be there also," answered Roark.

"So there is a conspiracy to overthrow the government. I was beginning to believe that the old man had a different plan in mind. When and where is the meeting?"

"Soon, very soon. You go back to South Africa on the next available flight and arrange things. I will be contacting you when the time is near. Bobbie, stop the car. Jan, in a few weeks you will become a national hero."

The driver pulled alongside the curb as the man in the front seat got out and opened the rear door. He motioned for Linden to get out.

"Wait a minute, how will you be contacting me?"

Roark looked out the window and smiled back at him. The car sped away.

CHAPTER THIRTY FOUR

And the Plight Goes On

Washington D. C.

Michael and Djhon met with Nathaniel to advise him it was time to act and gather his forces. Nathaniel's plan was already in process. He was going to lead a march of 30,000 people outside the Capitol. They will be of many nationalities and dominations, all fighting for human rights. Well–known movie stars, young adults of the most wealthy, and poor and homeless people gathered. The march was legal. Nathaniel had received the proper permits. The march would begin early the next morning in an effort to sway the Senate to follow the Congress's lead in overriding the President's veto.

The next day, Nathaniel held a secret meeting with institutions holding heavy investments in platinum and diamonds. Later that evening, he had dinner with several key officers in GE Electric. They discussed human rights violations in South Africa.

- -

"All you have to do now, Michael, is advise everyone to sit back and wait. I have completed Phase II of the plan," said Djhon. "It will take two to three weeks before I have launched enough pressure on the South African government to put a major dent in its defense."

"Excellent! In accordance with the old man's timetable, a meeting of the Circle members has been arranged. We are going back where it all began. I will issue travel instructions to the rest of the members to meet in South Africa in ten days. We must travel separately and become part of the African culture. Here is your package. Follow the instructions carefully. You will be contacted by someone who will say, *'It will take more than two to make a complete circle.'* That person will be your guide. Until then, be careful," said Michael. The two embraced and departed the room separately.

New York News
Thursday, October 2, 1986

Senate overrides Presidents' veto
Washington – The Senate overturned the President's veto by a vote of 78–21, setting the way for enactment of strong sanctions against the Pretorian government.

Houston Post
Friday, October 1986

Congress overrides President on South Africa
Washington – The Senate overturned the President's veto of tough sanctions against South Africa, enacting the measures into law and handing the president a foreign policy setback Thursday.

LONDON DAILY MIRROR
Saturday, October 4, 1986

The British government follows U.S. lead – Sanctions. The British Prime Minister in an effort to block a move by parliament issued tough new sanctions against the Pretoria government. The move was highly supported by the European Economic Community. The Common Market countries had earlier tried to persuade the Prime Minister to issue stronger sanctions against South Africa.

YOMIURI SHIMBUN
Monday, October 6, 1986
In a rare move towards world solidarity, Japan, one of South Africa's largest exporters – its Prime Minister follows the United States lead in issuing sanctions against the Pretorian government.

Washington Post
Tuesday, October 7, 1986
G. E. – introduces synthetic diamonds – General Electric called a press conference to announce emergence of a true synthetic diamond. General Electric, after years of research, has perfected the manufacture of synthetic diamonds and will begin shipments immediately. This is a major breakthrough in replacing the highly expensive diamond use in the industrial sector.

NEW YORK HERALD
Wednesday, October 8, 1986
U.S. investors sell foreign securities
Investors, afraid of losing their shirts due to the recent turn of events, are selling their foreign securities in South Africa. Beers Mining fell 5 5/16 to a low of 2 19/32. Gold Fields dropped 4 3/16 to a bid of 3. Driefontn traded at an all–time low of 4 3/16 and Vaalreef declined of 7 3/16 sent out a panic selling.

ATLANTA SUN–TIMES
Wednesday, October 8, 1986
Coca–Cola Co. said it plans to sell all of its assets in the troubled South African country. Coca–Cola has a relatively large market share in South

Africa's soft drink industry. The company has been receiving threats of a national boycott from the Christian Fellowship Conference; a large group with membership in excess of 10 million whose purpose is human rights.

JOHANNESBURG NEWS
Thursday – October 9, 1986
Gold's price falls again – Gold takes another beating. Pretoria is inviting foreign and local investors to observe the mining process in person in an effort to bring confidence and quell the unfounded rumors regarding the purity of the country's gold reserves and mining procedures. In a related matter, the platinum market, has taken a downward spiral during the U.S. sanctions. The degree of confidence and reassurance to foreign investors has eroded. Platinum opened today at $507.445 in U.S. dollars but closed under $500 for the first time in fifteen months at $298.50.

CINCINNATI POST
Friday, October 10, 1986
Proctor & Gamble Company agrees to sell the South African operating unit of its Richardson–Vicks Inc. Increasing pressure is mounting daily on U.S. firms to end business relations with the South Africa government.

JOHANNESBURG NEWS
Friday – October 10, 1986
Zulus calls for summit
Pampierstad, South Africa. – Zulus want their own sovereign state and are having calls for a summit and work stoppage. Adding to South

African woes, the Zulus for the first time in modern history have call on the other tribes to attend a conference. Their aim is to have the same constitutional powers and status enjoyed by most monarchs throughout the world. In a separate matter, the American government has banned South African Airways from landing in the United States. The Regan's administration has however delayed enforcing the economic restrictions.

Johannesburg

Michael had arranged for each member of the Circle to arrive separately in South Africa under forged passports.

Christopher used his firm's Johannesburg offices as an excuse to visit that city, accompanied by Allen Dugmore.

Nathaniel and Dr. Daniel Roark were booked into a touring group representing various religious as well as humanitarian groups. Although they were considered to be anti–apartheid, the South African Government considered them harmless, in fact, rather tame, and the group was rumored to support the mild reforms recently enacted under Prime Minister Pik Botha.

Bubba Walker and Michael would enter Pretoria from the North, along with a group of laborers coming in from Zimbabwe. Djhon used his military connections to pick up a standby passage on an airliner bound that would refuel in Capetown. Being in South Africa for the first time, none of them really knew what apartheid was all about. They had been taught about discrimination, the hard way, in the United States, where the expectations for black schoolchildren were still lower than those for their WASP brothers had had. They had learned even more about race relations in the marketplace, as they climbed the ladders of military and corporate power. But neither the hypocrisy nor the realities of power had prepared them for this.

Christopher and Allen, traveling as businessmen, received second glances and a thorough inspection of their luggage by customs officials. It was when they disembarked, however, that the second glances turned to hostility. The customs lines in the airport were divided into "Whites Only" and "Non–Whites." Nervously, Christopher nudged Allen toward the "Non–Whites" line. The normal routine questions were asked of the strangers to South Africa. Christopher entered one line, Allen another.

The custom official gave Michael a long stare. "Purpose of your visit." They glanced through his passport and papers.

"Company business."

"Is it an American company?"

"Yes, it is."

"How long will you be staying?"

"Two maybe three weeks."

"The nature of your business?"

"Investments."

The custom official finally looked up. "Did you say investments? What type of investments?"

"Our Johannesburg offices handle futures investments."

"Wait one minute." The custom official went over to his supervisor. The men looked at him. The supervisor picked up the phone and started speaking to someone.

Christopher remained calm. He glanced momentarily at Allen. He also was detained.

The custom official returned with two other officials. "Sir, come with me."

"Where? Why? Where are we going?"

One of the other custom official grabbed Christopher's arm. "Don't ask any questions. Just do as you are told."

Christopher was lead to a room in the back. The room was cold. He was alone for twenty–minutes before a man wearing a suit entered.

"Mr. Cirelli, I'm Detective Rudolph. Where will you be housing while in South Africa?"

Before he could answer, another man entered. He too wore a business suit. Christopher's connections took over. His Johannesburg investment office had arranged for them to stay with a partner there, rather than in the approved housing for non–white tourists in South Africa. The local partner was a well–known white business leader.

Detective Rudolph and the business partner talked for a few minutes in the corner. The two men shook hands.

The local business partner walked towards Christopher. "Mr. Cirelli, it's a pleasure finally meeting you. I am Alec Booyse. You are free to go. Hurry, my car is illegally parked."

When Christopher reached the custom area again, he saw Allen was still being detained. It took hours for his proper papers to be completed, to satisfy the pass laws that these non–whites were visitors, and entitled to be in the city. Extensive documentation was demanded, and supplied by Allen, regarding his position, business reasons for being in the country, and plans to travel while there.

The Johannesburg partner, who had worked in New York until two years previously, knew that this one encounter was the purpose of his original posting in South Africa. He had worked to establish the firm's rapport with the city officials, making no waves, the model corporate citizen. Now the work would pay off.

He also arranged for Allen to be picked up in a chauffeur–driven limousine. He was taken to the company flat, where he changed quickly from suits and ties to the drab clothing of day workers.

The partner and Christopher left the apartment by the back door, in the company of another black man who had been recruited by the company to be its contact with the ANC underground. At 5:00 p.m., they joined company with the thousands of blacks and coloreds who were making their way toward the black townships where they live, since the pass laws don't allow them to live in the cities where they work. By sundown, they must be outside the city limits, in the black ghetto township streets of Soweto.

Djhon selected a flight, which would arrive in Johannesburg Sunday night. His plan called for the Circle to take action within the next twenty days. As he disembarked in South Africa, he found himself in a whole new world. Suddenly, the young man who was a part of the American military establishment became a member of a sub–group of society. The customs authorities left no doubt as to his status.

He was not detained; the military government had him cleared through customs. As he stood outside the custom building, Djhon couldn't help noticing the headlines from the local Johannesburg newspaper,

"SOUTH AFRICA FIGHTS BACK AGAINST
SANCTIONS."

"Oh shit," Djhon thought as he tried to make his way to the newspaper stand unnoticed. The article went on to print a statement from South Africa's largest manufacturer's group, the Federated Chamber of Industries, indicating the industry would do what it had to do to survive sanctions and to operate in a society under siege.

No longer accompanied by a military escort, and out of uniform, he felt completely exposed to the attitude of apartheid. He tried to convert his military bearing to a bowed, shuffling stance as he made his way to the old rooming house, which would serve as the base for the conspiracy, which would rock the country. Conversations were rapid among local people as well as the travelers discussing the recent turn of events in the country.

"Have you heard that Prime Minister Botha is removing the Law and Order Minister from his post?" said a fellow, lighting his cigar and filling the area with tobacco smoke.

"What the bloody hell for?" asked his companion. "What's Pik Botha up to now?"

"The papers said he was receiving too much criticism from the way he been handling the racial unrest during the past two years," said the man.

"Pik is only using him as a scapegoat," replied his companion. "The man he really wants for the job is Huffmeister. Owen Huffmeister. He has the Prime Minister's ear."

"Then he bloody well better get on with the job before this country gets itself into a civil war. You know the South African

Reserve Bank reported yesterday that the value of our gold reserves has decreased forty percent in the past several weeks."

"Perfect!" Djhon thought to himself. "Just as the old man said it would happen."

Djhon felt as though he was being followed. He paused and slowly looked around. Nothing but faces, lots of black faces and children gazing through the fence that separates the white Afrikaners from the rest of the community. He started walking again following the instructions given to him to find the boarding house. He paused once again, glancing to his right, nothing but faces.

"Am I that obvious?" he thought to himself, looking across the road. He continued walking, this time a little slower. His military instincts told him he was being followed or being watched. Djhon stopped, looked around. "Wait a minute! I have seen that face. Customs! He's the one following me." Djhon tried to figure out what to do next and not to give notice that he had spotted his pursuer.

He reached into his pocket, pulled out a piece of paper, and proceeded to look as though he was reading. Wary of the unknown, he carefully glanced in the direction of his stalker. "He's gone! Damn it Djhon. You're slipping," he cursed himself. Djhon turned and crossed the road, stopping occasionally and reading the sign numbers, playing a lost person's role.

"It takes more than two to make a complete circle, Mr. McClendon," said the stranger. He suddenly appeared as if out of nowhere.

"Jesus!" said a startled Djhon.

"We must hurry, there's little time left. What detained you? The others are waiting. I am Tobe, your guide." The stranger grabbed Djhon by the arm, led him to a waiting car, which quickly sped away.

"It was a zoo in customs," said Djhon. "There was so much chaos. I didn't realize the old man's plan would have this much of an effect, especially so soon."

"The old man?" stared a puzzled Tobe.

"Yes, Leopold. Leopold Williams."

"Oh, you mean Umbiki. He was also known as Lamizana.

Chieftain Lamizana Moshoeshoe. The Traveler. It was not his plan. It was Thambo who conceived the plan and it was Abozuthu who sent out the warriors and spies to protect the old Chieftain and the children. Abozuthu is your true father."

"You said was, as in past tense. Then you know about the old man's death.

"Yes. We all grieved."

"You are partially correct about the plan, and the point is not worth debating, but if it were not for the old man's lessons and counsel the plan would not have succeeded. I would like to meet my father, but it's too dangerous for him to have visitors. I'm sure the authorities have him under close observation."

"You can still see him. He has been released for over three months. However, Abozuthu is under house arrest. They released him in an effort to calm the riots. The day of his release was also planned, and timed to occur during Phase II. The government is afraid for him to be seen on the streets or participating in demonstrations. They thought that by placing him under house arrest, his visitors could be monitored. The police think we are stupid enough to try to camouflage or smuggle a member in to see him. You my friend will see your father."

"How? If he's so closely monitored?"

"You should ask me!" shouted Tobe. "You, the son of Abozuthu, Chieftain of the once mighty Zulus. We were told that the son of Thambo was sent to the United States to learn modern warfare, military strategy, and the wisdom to lead us towards restoring our self–respect. Abozuthu is a sick old man, but even he has figured out a way to escape."

"You are right, Tobe. In any military situation, there is a weak link, and if I had studied the enemy fronts as my father had, then I too would have devised an escape plan. Where are we going?"

"Where it all began: A little village, unknown to this very day in Transkei. It's a day's travel from here due to the fact we're taking extra precautions."

"I still don't know how we are going to succeed. It cannot be a military victory. Do you know the final outcome?"

"No, the elders said there were only three who knew. Thambo, Abozuthu, and Lamizana," answered Tobe.

"Now, there are only two," responded Djhon.

"The only thing I know is that something major is going to happen. It took over thirty years for all the blacks to finally believe in the same cause. We are united for a first time and it will take more than the government closing over forty schools near the Cape to stop the movement now. Ha! They say the schools were closed because of the boycotts and will stay closed until the young ones demonstrate a willingness to attend classes."

"It's happening all over again," said Djhon. "First the strikes, then the demonstrations and now the riots."

"No, it will not exactly come about that way. Here, it's a long ride, read the American newspaper. Michael brought it with him."

Djhon's attention was quickly captured by the headline.

LOS ANGELES TIMES
Thursday, October 9, 1986
U.S. becoming a force for change in South Africa.
JOHANNESBURG, South Africa – the United States is quietly becoming a major force for political, economic and social change in South Africa, working with black activists to establish majority rule here. The United States is now educating hundreds of blacks, at both South African and American universities in the belief that they will become this country's leaders within the next decade. It's helping to pay the legal fees of political activists, some charged with treason and subversion, and is underwriting a program to assist children and others who have been detained without charge. And, in its boldest moves yet, the U.S. Embassy in Pretoria is allocating $2.3 million to black groups to help them organize their

> *communities, train grass– roots leaders and develop self–help programs. These actions recall similar efforts during the U.S. Civil rights and anti–poverty campaigns of the 1960's.*

"Stop the car! We must stop!" shouted Tobe.

"What's the matter?"

"The evening edition of the newspaper is out. It has happened!" answered Tobe.

"What has happened? For Pete's sake man, what in the hell has happened?"

"Pull closer so he can see the Citizen," said Tobe to the driver.

"Black Workers Strike." This caught Djhon's attention. "What does this mean?"

"It means that the Federation of South African Trade Unions, the Congress of South African Trade Unions, the National Union of Mine Workers, and the General and Allied Workers Union have just begun Phase III of Thambo's plan. A country–wide boycott. We must hurry before the police arrive and a curfew is ordered and the roads are blocked," said Tobe.

The following day

> *JOHANNESBURG NEWS*
> *Saturday, October 11, 1986*
> *Barclays Bank will leave South Africa.*
> *Johannesburg – Barclays, Britain's second largest bank, announced it will leave South Africa due to its racial segregation laws. The loss of the Barclays Bank spells potential future disaster because British companies are South Africa's largest foreign investors.*

A special emergency, Saturday session of the Parliament was called by Prime Minister Botha to discuss calling for a state of emergency and a way to end the deterioration of the country's economy.

"Order! Order!" demanded the Parliamentary Secretary. "Bang! Bang! Bang!" could be heard by everyone when the gavel made contacted with the podium. "Order! We cannot get down to business with every member of Parliament shouting at the same time. Order." He pounded the gavel several more time. "Order," she shouted. "The Prime Minister has sent the new Law and Order Minister, Mr. Huffmeister, here to speak. He's here to reassure us by telling us how he plans to control this uneasy situation." Chaos filled the assembly. The members argued among each other as to the proper and feasible way to handle the crisis.

"Order. I must have order." She now had most of their attention. "Now if my colleagues would momentarily refrain themselves and let the gentleman speak. The chair recognizes the distinguished gentleman Mr. Huffmeister."

"Speak! Speak!" shouted several members.

An angry Parliament member shouted, "When you're in an economic war such as this country has had waged against us, you don't crawl, you don't grovel against the United States and its Allies."

"You're bloody damn right. You fight back!" shouted another angry member of Parliament

"Precisely! Yeah! What in hell are we waiting for?" shouted even more raged members.

"Order!" Thump! Thump! Thump! could be heard by the gavel. She pounded it even harder.

"Send in the military and shoot every one of those black bastards that does not obey the order to return to work!" shouted another.

"We cannot give way to Apartheid! We cannot give them equal representation!" the outburst continued.

"To hell with representation. It's the union leaders we should jail," cried another.

"Let's fire a few shots across the bow. If we give our black neighbors and the outside world a little taste of what can happen when our backs are pushed to the walls, this outbreak will die down."

"Order! Order!" The Secretary shouted. "It's not the blacks we need to be worry about. If we don't rectify this gold crisis, there will be no South Africa. Order! I say again there will be no South Africa if the gold crisis is not resolved."

Huffmeister, growing weary of the outbursts, reached inside his coat, pulled out a revolver, and fired three shots towards the ceiling of the crowded chambers. Silence was immediate. The assembly grew even quieter. The assembly members stared at the podium.

The Parliamentary Secretary calmly looked at him.

"Now that I have your attention, the secretary recognized the distinguished gentlemen from Cape Town, Our Law and Order Minister.

"Gentlemen," he began, pausing and slowly looking across the room to see if he had everyone's attention. "The Foreign Minister asked me to speak to you about the grave situation at hand. I am sorry for the display of gunfire, but it was mild compared to your outbursts. Now, if you would bear with me, I will give you a summary of this government's plan of action in dealing with what is now confronting this country. First of all, we must examine what is actually happening. This strike is like none the country has faced before. In the past, the country succeeded in handling such strikes because it was either this union or that union, or this group of blacks or that group of workers. Before, not every member in the union supported the strike. We are now faced with a unified action by all the unions. Secondly, this group is well–organized. Third, The Sanlam Properties Group, one of the country's largest developers of food shopping centers has indicated that for the past three weeks, the supermarkets and food stores have experienced a heavy trade in business. The stores have sold more food to the blacks than in the last six months combined."

Someone shouted from the floor, "Where in creation are they getting the money? They are on strike."

"Yeah! The factories and the mines are shut down," shouted a burly fellow.

"They couldn't possibly save that much money from what we pay them," laughed another parliament member.

"It's the ANC and those blasted Russians," yelled another.

"We should have crossed the border years ago and hanged them all," came from a man boldly rising with a clenched fist.

"Yeah! Yeah!" agreed a score of members.

"Order! Order! Unless you care to witness another display of fireworks I will have order," demanded the Parliament Secretary.

Huffmeister held out both arms and motioned for the members to be seated. "To violently suppress the unions, as the government has done in the past would, I'm afraid, incur a measure of wrath this country has never experienced. This government can either go backwards in time or act in a repressive manner, or it can dismantle apartheid."

"End apartheid. Never!" bellowed the burly fellow.

"No. No. No. Apartheid must remain in effect. It would make reforms more difficult!" shouted another.

"Yeah, Yeah," said the parliament members as they disagreed among themselves.

"Madam Secretary, Madam Secretary," said the burly fellow.

"The chair recognized the distinguished gentleman from Durban."

"Distinguished colleagues. Please wait a moment before you drown me with your outbursts," shouted the burly fellow. "It seems to me that South Africa has two problems. The blacks unified work stoppage and the perceived gold crisis."

"Yea! Yea!" responded the members."

The burly fellow walked to the center aisle, being a large fellow, perspiration oozed from his pores. "Then it seems to me that we dispose of the easy problem first. Let us give the Zulus their homeland territory and recognize their independence. How can they harm us? They have no army, no weapons. Hell they still use spears."

"You coward!" yelled someone.

"My dearest fellow, cowardice is far from the truth...."

Huffmeister interrupted. "We could have a civil war that could last for years. Our source indicates that a military leader and a modern army, trained and equipped with strategic weapons, are in place and ready to act if a peaceful solution cannot be reached. Our sources..."

"Sources! The hell with your sources. For all you know they may be in cahoots with the rebels from the ANC," shouted the representative from Port Elizabeth."

"Quite right," responded Huffmeister." However, if the distinguished gentleman from Port Elizabeth will indulge me; The government owned agents have confirmed that our sources are indeed correct in their evaluation that a leader has been picked to form a new government, separate from the current regime if a peaceful solution cannot be reached. This new society calls themselves the Circle.

"The Circle. Did you say they called themselves the Circle?" laughed the gentleman from Kimberley. "What are they doing, dancing?" The other members also laughed."

"It's possible," Huffmeister acknowledged. "But, let us not forget that they were once powerful tribal leaders. The Zulus and the Sothos still are. There are certain traditions not lost that are passed on from family to family. It starts with the first born; the blood is always the utmost with their families."

"Hogwash. What has the Law and Order Minister been eating lately, collards greens," shouted the gentleman from Pretoria.

"Listen to me," shouted Huffmeister. The Circle consists of the eight leaders of the major tribes in South Africa. The Prime Minister has ordered me to meet with the new leaders before this government reacts to the contrary. We will at least establish some type of dialogue before we engage this country in a civil war, regardless of who may win the eventual outcome."

Owen Huffmeister argued his position for another twenty minutes. It was obvious the parliament was deeply divided. He soon excused himself. Unknown to the members and others, he had arranged a secret meeting with his sources and members of the Circle. He met his informers five miles north of town at a deserted mine shack. He was blindfolded and later would be transported to Transkei.

Deep with the homeland and territory of Transkei in an unknown village in a circle, stood eight chieftains, each representing a tribal group. In the background were two old men sitting on a neatly knitted and decorative blanket matching the pattern of the dashikis they were wearing.

The first to speak was Michael, a Xhosa chieftain, and the new leader.

"Djhon, are you ready?"

"Yes, Michael, we are. The ANC members have also joined our forces and the renegade members that did not wish to convert and go along with us have been disposed of. We will only use force if warranted. Hopefully, we can arrive at some sort of peaceful solution."

"Owen, what do you think?"

"I believe the Prime Minister, along with many key members of Parliament, is willing to end apartheid. There are many of the whites who wish to end this thing. Their primary fear is retaliation by the blacks and loss of power. The plan for a working government with both sides sharing the wealth and power is something I think I can sell as Law and Order Minister," answered Owen, chieftain of the Tswana and son of Macomma Lethu.

Michael addressed Huffmeister, "Thambo and Macomma were very good friends. He told me that when your father married a mulatto woman, there were many who scorned him. When your mother died in childbirth, your father saw it as an opportunity to help our people. You have lived as a white man. You acted as one of them. The old man taught you well. Go and present our plan."

Michael turns to Daniel Roark. "Djhon informs me you gave the police lieutenant, Jan Linden, valuable information about the Circle. Unfortunately, for you, Mr. Linden went straight to the Law and Order Minister. Owen found him useful, and no harm came to any member of the Circle. Therefore, no harm will come to you. Thambo has decided that you are free to go against the wishes of Abozuthu and Djhon. Go, before our minds are changed. You are lucky that your head was not staked on an assegai blade."

Roark stared at the other chieftains and then at Michael. "Why then, do you let me live, knowing that I have dishonored you? I feel like a traitor to all of the things, the old man believed in." Tears filled up in his eyes and he started trembling. He feared Djhon.

Michael walked towards him. He put his arms around him and whispered. "It's because of the old man and his teaching. He taught you well. You could have become the great witch doctor. You would have brought great medicine to all of the tribes. The old man loved you. Michael's voice then turned cold and harsh. "Now go, before it's too late." Michael patiently waited until Roark was led away by two of Djhon's men.

"Fellow chieftains, tomorrow marks a new beginning for our country. The time has now come. We, along with the Afrikaners can work together and form a new government. If not, we will destroy each other. If we work together, the international community will come to South Africa's rescue and help us rebuild this country."

Six years later – March 1992

South African white voters gave their current leader, Prime Minister F.W. De Klerk, the authority to negotiate for an end to white minority rule.

Nelson Mandela, now a freed man and President of the African National Congress, saw the vote as a step toward black rule.

Friday, February 17, 1995

President Nelson Mandela opened the second of South Africa's first democratic Parliament with a tough warning to the racists and to militant blacks who had misread "freedom" to mean "license." In his state of the nation message only after nine months in power, Mandela, at the age of 76, called for discipline from the victims of apartheid and cooperation from its perpetrators. His words were clear.

"Let it therefore be clear to all that the battle against the forces of anarchy and chaos are unified. Let no one say that they have not been warned. All of us, must rid ourselves of the wrong notion that the government has a big bag full of money... mass action of any kind will not create resources that the government does not have. Some of those who have initiated and participated in such activities have misread freedom to mean license. Some have wrongly concluded that an elected government of the people is a government that is open to compulsion through anarchy.

"Those who are responsible for these crimes of racism must be brought to book without delay. We need no educators with regard to the matter of rooting out corruption, which will be dealt with firmly and unequivocally."

Jan stood and listened to Mandela's speech. Michael approached him.

"Mr. Linden."

"Yes, what can I do for you," he whispered.

"Mayibuye Afrika!" "Let Africa come back!"

CPSIA information can be obtained at www.ICGtesting.com
Printed in the USA
LVOW122153240313

325799LV00001B/4/P